About the Author

Peter Tallon has been a professional geologist who, after a period of surveying and prospecting in Kenya and Egypt, joined the construction materials industry, rising to managing director of a multi-million-pound company. Married, with two children and four grandchildren, he has lived in Suffolk for the last forty-two years where the beautiful coast and countryside form the background to three of his previous books. *Michael Shapmire* is his fifth book and is also based in Suffolk.

Michael Shapmire

Peter Tallon

Michael Shapmire

Olympia Publishers
London

www.olympiapublishers.com
OLYMPIA PAPERBACK EDITION

Copyright © Peter Tallon 2023

A CIP catalogue record for this title is
available from the British Library.

ISBN: 978-1-80074-612-1

This is a work of fiction.
Names, characters, places and incidents originate from the writer's
imagination. Any resemblance to actual persons, living or dead, is
purely coincidental.

First Published in 2023

Olympia Publishers
Tallis House
2 Tallis Street
London
EC4Y 0AB

Printed in Great Britain

Dedication

To my mother and father, who made me, and Stonyhurst College, which was the making of me.

Acknowledgements

Thanks to Neil Amos for drawing the map of the imaginary Hobbswood area for me, Hetty's Little Copy Shop in Halesworth which prepared the final manuscript for me and the staff and wardens who patrol and preserve Dunwich Heath for the benefit of us all.

Author's Note

Anyone who knows the Suffolk coast will soon deduce that I have placed the fictional village of Hobbswood somewhere between the Minsmere Nature Reserve and Dunwich Heath. It was necessary to do some tinkering with the local geography and landscape in order to isolate Hobbswood more effectively, but I hope I have captured the sense of wildness and mystery of the area as it was in 1995. Dunwich Heath is still a wonderful piece of Suffolk countryside, especially when the heather is in flower in August. It's well worth a visit.

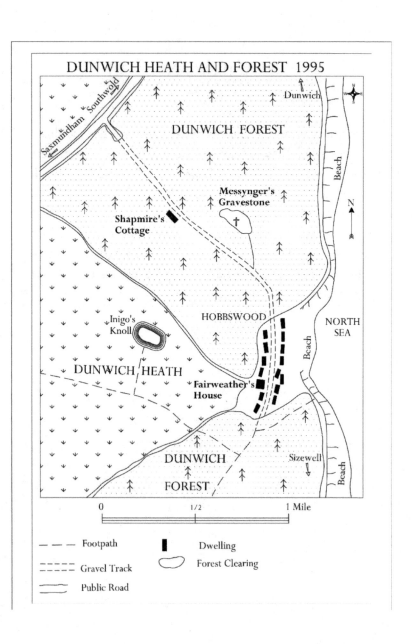

DUNWICH HEATH AND FOREST 1995

Chapter One

Inigo Boscabel stood at the Leiston-Saxmundham crossroads; he was also standing at a crossroads in his life. Beside him, waiting patiently while his master examined the East Suffolk Ordnance Survey map, sat Wellington, the two-hundred-and-twenty-pound English mastiff, who was as big as Inigo and certainly much heavier. The large dog was uneasy, for he could sense the disquiet in his master, and more importantly, the routine to which he had become accustomed during his five years of life had been broken.

Three times each year, Inigo would come home to his parents' London flat near Regents Park, which was Wellington's home, for a break from his work at the Jesuit seminary, where he was studying for the priesthood. These were the times Wellington lived for. The walks, the laughter, and the games, usually ending when he inadvertently trod on Inigo's foot, were such an exciting change from the quiet, peaceful existence which accompanied most of his days. But now Inigo had remained at home and the happy atmosphere, which was always created by his visits, was gone. There were compensations though. Inigo had spent his school years at a Jesuit college in East Lancashire, which was surrounded by fells, where he had learned to sooth his soul during difficult times by taking long walks through the rugged countryside.

Although there were no fells along the Suffolk coastline, the open East Anglian landscape and huge skies had qualities of their own that could recharge any man's depleted batteries. For

Wellington, this was a walk of unprecedented interest. He had been nervous during the train ride from Liverpool Street station and could not help himself from watering the station master's leg when they changed trains for the rural East Suffolk line at Ipswich. When they arrived at Woodbridge, they set out on the coastal path and walked most of the day, where the mastiff encountered a host of strange, exciting new scents; foxes, rabbits and even pheasants, so much more interesting than the stale London parks.

Inigo folded his map and said quietly to himself, "I think we've strayed from the footpath, but if we keep going northeast, we should make Walberswick by tonight. Might mean cutting across country though. Hope the farmers won't mind."

He had not brought a tent because there was supposed to be no shortage of bed and breakfast accommodation along their route, and there should be plenty of vacancies. The school summer holidays were not due to start for at least a month.

Man and dog set off again, taking a shortcut through fields of ripening wheat towards Dunwich, which was their tea time target. From there, it was only a few more miles to Walberswick.

It was now early evening and glorious June was surpassing itself. The midsummer sky was almost cloudless, larks sang as they hovered above the fields of wheat and flowering potatoes, and a small herd of red deer, grazing along the edge of a pine plantation, looked up and trotted away, startled by this intrusion into their private domain. The gorse, which heralded the beginning of the untamed heathland so characteristic of this part of the Suffolk coast, was no longer in flower, but as the two travellers left the cultivated fields behind them and entered the rough pasture south of Dunwich Heath, patches of campion added splashes of pink and white to the flat, green landscape. Yet the peace and bounty of his surroundings only served to accentuate the anguish in Inigo's soul as he strode purposefully onwards, towards Walberswick.

Ten wasted years! Ten years of concentrated study and scholarship, the great sacrament of ordination only twenty-four months away, but what was there to show for all that effort now? It took twelve years for the average scholastic to qualify to become a Jesuit priest, the most intellectual and fearsome of all the priestly orders, and the scholastics were anything but average, having survived a selection process that had already weeded out the 'average'.

Inigo did not really understand how he had lost his vocation; there was no blinding flash of reason, no young woman who had overcome his devotion to his God. It seemed to be a simple question of faith. Six weeks earlier, he had felt the first stirrings of that deadly enemy of faith, doubt. Perhaps it had been his first reading of Darwin's *On the Origin of Species*, or maybe it was the possibility of there being no place in the modern world for such a militant organisation as the Jesuits. He would never know, but slowly, insidiously, doubt had worked its way into his consciousness, eroding his confidence. By refusing to face it head on until it was too late, he had allowed it to destroy not only his vocation but his faith as well.

The rector at the seminary had been sympathetic and disappointed, for Inigo had been one of his best students. He had seen the signs in others before and understood the depth of the crisis.

"Take some time off, Inigo," he had said, but neither of them expected to see each other again.

And now what? thought Inigo angrily. *How can I formulate another career with my qualifications? Degrees in philosophy and Middle Eastern ancient history, fluency in Latin and Aramaic, both dead languages, what use were they now in 1995?*

His old school in Lancashire had two primary objectives for its pupils, the armed forces or the priesthood, and in the case of the latter, preferably the Society of Jesus, better known as the Jesuits. These were not dissimilar careers and Inigo had selected the priesthood, much to the disappointment of his father. Being an only child, Inigo was the last bearer of the Boscabel name, a family which claimed ancestry back to the Conqueror. He had gone straight to the seminary from school, never having tasted life in the real world, and now he fretted he might have become institutionalised, like a lifer in Wormwood Scrubs.

Inigo's sombre musings were abruptly halted as Wellington took off into some thick undergrowth, which bordered a dense birch and pine forest on his right. He had been so deep in thought that the gradual increase in woodland, which now chequered the countryside, had escaped his notice. He could not see the mastiff but could mark his progress by the numerous irate pheasants and partridges that fluttered, squawking, into the air as they were rooted out by the huge, black muzzle.

"Wellington! Wellington!" he shouted, petrified that his ill-behaved companion might come up against the wrong end of an angry farmer's shotgun, but Wellington had suffered an attack of that well-known canine ailment, selective deafness.

There was no alternative but to follow the trail of devastation, so taking a deep breath, Inigo plunged into the forest. The sudden darkness in the shadow of the green canopy forced him to stop for a moment while his eyes adjusted to the gloom. A heavy blanket of silence replaced the cheerful birdsong of the open heathland, and as he strode forward, trying to avoid the brambles that seemed to be doing their best to trip him up, he noticed that even the sound of his footsteps was absorbed by the cushion of pine needles lying thick on the forest floor. He reached a firebreak and realised that the forest was, in fact, a plantation, perhaps forty years old or more, in which the trees had been planted with the symmetrical regularity of a parade of Grenadier Guards.

The thick undergrowth, which provided ideal hideaways for roosting birds, suggested that the plantation had been neglected in recent years, but the disturbance being created by Wellington was likely to attract the attention of all the game keepers for miles around.

Ten minutes passed, yet Inigo seemed no nearer his fleet-pawed companion. He paused for breath and wiped blood from his arms where they had been ripped by brambles. He suddenly realised he had no idea how far he had come or where the route back to the heathland lay. To make matters worse, Wellington's trail had gone cold. Either the mastiff had caught a pheasant and was quietly munching through the carcass, or he was resting.

"Wellington! Come here, you awkward bugger!"

Hardly appropriate language for a student of the cloth, thought Inigo, but no one could hear him, and he was beginning to worry that something serious might have happened to his friend. A rustle to his left, on the other side of a clump of bracken, drew his attention. *Thank God,* he thought as he forced his way through the leafy fronds, but before he reached the other side, the world seemed to spin as he trod on thin air and fell headlong into a deep, narrow cutting, used for the line of an abandoned narrow-gauge railway that had been constructed to supply large guns mounted on the shoreline cliffs during the First World War. He fell badly and struck his head on a large flint at the bottom of the cutting. Then everything went black.

II

Inigo awoke to a pounding headache. Wellington was sitting beside him, looking like the incarnation of canine innocence, an image somewhat flawed by the clutch of coloured feathers clinging to his muzzle. Although it was still daylight, Inigo was unsure how long he had been unconscious because his watch had stopped, and the tall pine trees hid the position of the sun. From the congealed state of the blood on his forehead, he guessed two, perhaps three hours. He tapped his watch, which began to work again, apparently none the worse for its knock. He sat up and removed his ruck sack to reassure himself that the cloying dampness on his back was not blood. Fortunately, the only mishap was a broken thermos flask; sticky black coffee had worked its way through the canvass of the sack to his shirt, soaking his map of East Suffolk and his spare clothing, but all-in-all, he had escaped the twenty foot drop lightly. Or so he thought until he tried to stand up.

A sharp, stabbing pain in his left ankle quickly returned him to the sitting position. He had wrenched it badly, and on closer inspection, Inigo could see that his injuries were not so superficial after all. His ankle was already swollen. He dared not remove his boot to take a closer look in case he was unable to get it on again. Now his top priority was to find a phone. The sides of the cutting were too steep for a man in his condition to climb out, so he would have to follow the cutting until it opened out. But to his left it was filled with rampant brambles within a few yards of where he was sitting.

"We'll go right," he said decisively.

Wellington sniffed the air as if in agreement, while Inigo carefully got to his feet, putting all his weight on his right foot. After a few painful hops, he found a broken pine branch which, with a little trimming from his penknife, would serve as an adequate staff, and together they slowly followed the cutting. Judging from the position of the shadows, Inigo guessed they were heading more or less in an easterly direction, and being so near the solstice, they probably had at least another hour of daylight to find help. But it took almost an hour to cover little more than a hundred yards, much to Wellington's undisguised frustration. The thorn and bramble bushes ripped at Inigo's skin. He was only wearing a light, sleeveless shirt, and the pain in his ankle was getting worse. He knew he would soon have to stop and resigned himself to spending the night under the stars, but he could not risk lighting a fire because the woodland was tinder dry. There had not been a drop of rain for weeks. In any event, the coffee had ruined his matches, but the June night was warm. Sleeping in the open air would not be too bad.

"Just a little further, Wellington, and we'll call it a day."

But the mastiff, oblivious to his part in the mishap, was more concerned that dinner was overdue and trotted round the next bend in search of something to scavenge. His master, following slowly behind, found persistence rewarded because suddenly the cutting opened out into a valley about half a mile wide, and hallelujah, there were a dozen or so cottages in it. The woodland retreated to the upper slopes of the valley but returned again on the far side of the hamlet, so unless you had a purpose to visit it, you would never know of its existence.

Inigo offered up a quick 'thank you' to God, scholastic

habits die hard, and hobbled towards the nearest house, a neat, single-storeyed flint cottage. He looked at the westering sun and estimated the time to be about eight thirty p.m. In the front garden of the cottage, which was full of rose bushes, a large man in his mid-fifties was pulling weeds out of a small footpath between the rose beds. He was so intent on his work, he did not hear Inigo approaching.

"Excuse me," said Inigo, "I've had a bit of an accident."

The gardener spun 'round, startled by a stranger coming from an unexpected direction so late in the day.

He stuck his spade in the soil and said offhandedly, "Hurt your foot then?"

Brilliant, thought Inigo, but reprimanded himself for being impatient.

"I got lost in the woods and had a fall. I may have broken my ankle."

"That's what happens when you leave the footpath."

Inigo felt his hackles rising but still controlled himself.

"Do you have a telephone I could use?"

"No."

"Is there anyone here who has?"

"No phones are kept here. We have no need of such modern appliances."

The gardener turned to resume his weeding but Inigo, who had never been noted for his patience, finally snapped.

"What do you suggest, then? Shall I chop my leg off!"

Unperturbed by the outburst, the gardener replied, "No need for that sort of old squit. Why don't you see the doctor?"

"You have a doctor here?"

"Just said so, didn't I. He lives at the large house yonder, the one with the motor vehicle parked outside."

"Thank you for your help." Inigo could not keep the sarcasm out of his voice, but it was lost on the gardener.

Let no one accuse the English countryman of being too friendly, he thought to himself. But still, finding a doctor in such a remote location was a stroke of luck, and he slowly hobbled his way to the two-storeyed red brick building, with Dutch style gable ends, in the centre of the hamlet where the car was parked.

The front garden was bordered by a low, ranch-style fence, which Wellington sedately stepped over, and like all the other gardens in the village, it was immaculately kept. Inigo, now in serious pain, limped up to the black front door and rapped the large brass knocker. He stood for a while, waiting for a response, and was about to knock again when the door opened to reveal a plump, grey-haired woman who would never see fifty again, wearing a flower-patterned dress that was rather too small for her. The sleeves were rolled up, revealing large red elbows and arms sprinkled with flour. It seemed Inigo had disturbed her baking. She looked at him coldly, waiting for him to speak.

"I believe a doctor lives here?"

"Yes, but surgery is finished, and I doubt he'll see you now."

Inigo took a deep breath, trying to restrain his frustration, but before he could answer, a strong, cultured voice called from somewhere at the back of the house.

"Who is it, Ivy?"

"A man wants to see you, but he's not from the village. I was just about to send him away."

A moment later, the doctor himself came to the door.

"My dear fellow, you appear to be in trouble."

"I've had a fall. I think I may have broken my ankle."

"Come into my study and I'll take a look. Ivy, bring some

21

hot water and look after this huge dog."

"He's not been fed yet," said Inigo. "There are some tins of dog meat in my ruck sack, if you wouldn't mind?"

He took off the ruck sack and added, "Two tins should be sufficient."

As Wellington happily followed Ivy into the kitchen, attracted by the delicious baking smells, the doctor said, "You must forgive us. We seldom see strangers here, but we mean no harm; it's just our way. Sit down in the armchair while I remove your boot and sock."

The doctor looked to be about forty-five. Tall, and what most people would call elegant, the silver streaks in his raven black hair lent an air of distinction to a man who had, to judge from the books lining his study walls, diverse cultural interests. Inigo found himself wondering why this sophisticated medic would choose to live in an obscure Suffolk hamlet.

"My name is Lucas Fairweather," said the doctor. "You may call me Lucas."

"Thank you. I am Inigo Boscabel. Does this village have a name?"

"Hobbswood. It dates back to the Middle Ages, or even earlier."

Ivy bustled into the study with a bowl of hot water.

"Will you be needing anything else, Doctor, or can I get on with my cooking now?"

Lucas replied, "That will be all, Ivy. I'll try not to disturb you again."

After she left the room, he smiled. "Ivy is a good-hearted and protective woman; no man could have a better housekeeper. Now, hold still while I examine your ankle."

Inigo winced as the doctor washed his grubby, swollen ankle

and moved it gently from side to side.

"It looks like a severe sprain rather than a break," said Lucas. "So I shall be able to treat you here."

For the first time, he looked Inigo directly in the face. His eyes were of the palest grey, a most unusual and disconcerting colour.

"Inigo; now that's an unusual name."

"It's a shortened form of Ignatius. I was named after the founder of the Jesuit Order, Ignatius Loyola."

"A Spanish mercenary, I believe," responded Lucas, with a twinkle in his grey eyes.

"True," acknowledged Inigo. "I'm surprised you know that. Are you a Catholic?"

"No, just a student of history. Does it not seem a paradox to you that a great religious order should have been founded by a warrior, and a mercenary at that?"

"Perhaps, but not if you know the Jesuits. Loyola instilled his new Order with the military discipline of the best army in Europe at the time, and with a thirst for knowledge inside and outside the Bible, qualities that the Catholic Church was desperately lacking in the sixteenth century. The Jesuits went on to form the spearhead of the Counter Reformation."

Lucas nodded. "Really?"

But somehow Inigo felt that his knowledgeable listener was already well acquainted with Jesuit history.

Inigo sat back and tried to relax while Lucas attended to his ankle, letting his eyes wander round the study. The table, chairs, and desk were all carved in heavy, dark wood in the Jacobean style, contemporary with the house itself. The soft furnishings, too, were of that heavy, embroidered, seventeenth century provenance, while those parts of the walls that were not covered by books were oak panelled, except for the large, brick-lined, inglenook fireplace, which would no doubt warm the entire house in winter time.

"So, why Ignatius?" enquired Lucas as he began strapping the injured ankle. "Do you have a religious background?"

"Not really. My father is a retired soldier, but the family has always been Roman Catholic, so I was sent to a Jesuit school. It's a family tradition that boys join the army, but I broke with that and attempted to become a priest instead."

"Attempted?"

"Sadly, it didn't work out. Now I am wondering what to do with my life, having wasted ten years trying to become a priest."

"I doubt it was a complete waste of time. You will have learned much during the course of your studies, but I would guess you did not leave much time between leaving school and starting your religious career."

Inigo was surprised by the doctor's perception.

"You are correct about that. I should have taken a year off, possibly two, then maybe I would not have wasted a decade of my life."

"I don't doubt that many who aspire to be priests soon realise they have made a mistake, but why did it take you so long?"

"I don't know. I was all right until a few weeks ago, but… what's that green stuff you're putting on my ankle!"

Lucas laughed. "The old cures are sometimes the best. This is a moss poultice. You'll find that most of the swelling will be gone by tomorrow morning. Are you expected anywhere tonight? You are welcome to stay here if you like, and if you need to make contact with anyone, I have a mobile phone in my car. It's a bit crackly, but there's no landline connection in Hobbswood."

"That would be excellent! I'd love to stay, and I've no

deadlines to meet until the end of next week. But what about Wellington? He's a well-behaved dog."

Inigo reddened as he thought back to the afternoon, but usually the mastiff could be relied upon in company.

Lucas answered, "I'm sure Ivy will be able to arrange something for him. Inigo, you are welcome to stay for three or four days. You certainly won't be able to continue hiking before then, and I would enjoy some educated company."

"Are you sure? It seems a dreadful imposition."

"With all due respect to the worthy people here, I miss intelligent conversation. You would be doing me a favour by staying."

"So be it then."

The doctor concentrated on his work for the next few minutes and Inigo relaxed, knowing he had somewhere to lay his head for the next few days. What a stroke of luck finding someone like Lucas Fairweather in Hobbswood, but again, Inigo asked himself why such a cultured, urbane man should want to live in this backwater. Perhaps he too had a good reason to retreat from the world, but there would be plenty of time to find out more later.

Lucas carefully placed Inigo's strapped foot and ankle into one of his old slippers, which was two sizes larger than Inigo's foot.

"Well, that's all I can do for the moment. Keep your weight off it as much as you can, and I'll lend you a walking stick to help you get around. It's a bit heavy I'm afraid, but it should serve."

"Then I'll go exploring tomorrow, nothing too strenuous, perhaps a look round the woods."

"OK, but don't be overambitious, no more than a mile. I shall be out all day doing my rounds. Is there anything I can bring you?"

"No, thanks, but may I browse through some of your books?"

"Of course." Lucas' brow furrowed as if he was having difficulty with what he was about to say. "Listen, Inigo, I know this sounds a bit silly, but if you decide to follow the track out of the valley towards the Dunwich road, steer clear of the old house at the top of the hill."

"For Heaven's sake, why?"

"That's where Michael Shapmire lives. He's a strange, surly sort, although I have to say he has never bothered me in the five years since I came here. But the villagers seem frightened of him; don't ask me why. They're a superstitious lot and somehow Shapmire seems to cast a dark shadow over their lives, but when I ask them what exactly it is they fear about him, I never get a straight answer. Still, there's no doubting his formidable appearance, so there's no need to confront him unnecessarily. Just thought I'd mention it."

After Inigo had washed and got ready for dinner in his upstairs room overlooking the valley behind the hamlet, he took out his coffee-stained map to look for Hobbswood, but although a few buildings were shown just south of Dunwich Heath, the little hamlet did not apparently merit a name on the Ordnance Survey map. *Strange,* he thought, considering the hamlet had been in existence well before modern maps were produced. It really did seem to be a forgotten backwater.

Dinner was served by a dark-eyed, attractive girl of about twenty who, from the way she swayed her hips, was fully aware of the effect she had on men. Long tresses of jet-black hair cascaded around her smooth shoulders and her tight, rather old-fashioned, green mini-dress seemed to accentuate her stimulating contours. She spoke in a husky, country manner, which stirred feelings in Inigo that could never have been permitted when he was training for the priesthood. Her dark brown eyes seemed to bore through him, as if she could read the desire in his heart, but her real interest was focused on the doctor, who seemed oblivious to her ill-concealed flirting. As he watched the girl offering herself to his host, Inigo became aware of the first twinges of another unaccustomed feeling, one he did not much care for; jealousy.

After the plates had been cleared away and the two men were alone again, drinking Lucas' vintage brandy, Inigo asked, "Who was that girl?"

"Ivy's daughter, Hazel."

"A fine-looking girl," mused Inigo. "Tell me, what do people do for work in Hobbswood? Are they farm labourers?"

Lucas answered, "Some work for tenant farmers, but all the land round here is owned by English Nature, which employs most of the villagers as wardens, foresters, and maintenance workers. I act as their union spokesman when the time comes for wage bargaining with the management."

He looked up at the large, walnut wood-panelled grandfather clock, which stood in the corner of the dining room.

"It's almost ten o'clock and you've had a tiring day. I suggest you turn in now. I shall give you something to ease the pain in your ankle and help you sleep. I hope your room is satisfactory?"

"Very much so. I am sure I'll sleep well tonight."

By the time he had climbed the stairs, Inigo was almost asleep on his feet. He took a last look out of his west-facing window to enjoy the afterglow of purples and pinks cast by the sun in the evening sky, which had set twenty minutes earlier behind a tree-lined hill. On the right, where a track cut through the forest on its way out of the valley, he could just make out a squat, dark building in the twilight, which he guessed was Shapmire's house. What sort of man must he be to have such a baleful effect on the villagers of Hobbswood? Despite Lucas' warning, Inigo, who was not without courage, decided that his morning walk would more than likely take him in the direction of Shapmire's home; after all, an Englishman may go wherever he pleases, especially in England.

The eventful day finally caught up with him. He was swamped by a huge tiredness. He had already bathed before dinner so, after a quick wash and brush of the teeth, he slid into the delightfully cool sheets and was asleep as soon as his head touched the pillow. The sleeping draught prepared for him by Lucas remained untouched.

Inigo awoke with a start. It was pitch black; he could not see a thing. He had no idea of the time, and it took him a few moments to remember where he was. But of one thing he was certain; something had woken him up. He lay perfectly quiet, with his eyes wide open, listening to the stillness of the night, wondering. A silent two minutes passed. Perhaps he had been dreaming after all, but then he heard a noise, soft but clear; the voice of a woman groaning. Was she weeping or in pain? Was she even of this world? He shuddered at the thought, but nothing would surprise him in Hobbswood. Apart from Lucas' reassuring presence, he had felt a little unnerved ever since he had entered the village. But as he lay there listening to the strange, disconcerting sound, another thought occurred to him. Could it be that a spiritual experience might do something to restore his faith and put him back on course for the priesthood? Was this a message from the Almighty, helping him to see the right way forward? He felt he had no choice but to investigate.

He sat up, got out of bed, and felt for his clothes, but before he even reached the door to his room, he realised, with a touch of disappointment, that the woman's voice was definitely of this world and was coming from the other side of the landing. Inigo had led a life isolated from women, apart from his mother, and did not at first understand the significance of the rhythmic moaning. He quietly opened his door, worried that someone was in trouble, but then quickly retreated again, humiliated by his own foolish naivety as the truth dawned on him at last. How could he be so stupid! Intermingled with the candid sound of Hazel's lovemaking, he was able to hear her expressions of affection, and although he knew he should not be listening, he found himself standing by the open door like some sort of pervert, knowing no-one could see him in the dark.

Hazel's moaning became louder and more intense, and Inigo began to wonder if his initial concern might have been at least partially right, because it seemed as if the muted undertone of pain he thought he had heard, was gaining in strength. After a few more minutes, he was certain, for now the ecstatic moans had become cries of agony. But what should he do? If he interfered, only to find he had misinterpreted the situation, he would be obliged to leave immediately, and had he not been told that lovemaking for the first time is often painful for a woman?

"You're hurting me again!" wailed Hazel.

Clearly it was not her first time.

"Get down, bitch!" growled a low, evil, almost inhuman voice. It was certainly not Lucas'.

Hazel cried out again, "No! Stop it! Please!"

There followed a muffled shriek, as if her face was being pushed into a pillow, then silence. Was she dead? Where was Lucas? Surely, he must have heard? Inigo braced himself to intervene but stopped when he heard Hazel's voice again. Now she sounded perfectly relaxed.

"I do wish you wouldn't do that. It's what queers do, and it hurts like hell!"

There was no response, but clearly Hazel was not seriously hurt, so Inigo returned to bed having witnessed, if only audibly, the dreadful sin he had been warned against at school — sodomy.

Sleep would not come. Anger, inadequacy, and shame burned in Inigo's soul. He hated the jealousy that simmered within him, but the desire that gnawed at his body refused to depart. And of whom was he jealous? He did not even know. For the male voice he had heard did not belong to Lucas, he was certain of that. Then who could it have been? One of the villagers, perhaps? But Inigo could not imagine Lucas permitting such goings-on to take place in his household. Then a dark, chilling thought entered his mind; *Michael Shapmire*. What if Shapmire's influence extended further than Lucas was prepared to admit? Maybe the doctor himself lived in fear of the shadow cast by the mysterious occupant of the black house on the hill. Could Hazel's cruel lover be Shapmire? Was the price for his tolerance of the lives of the Hobbswood residents the freedom to use their women as he wished? He had read of such things occurring in the Middle Ages. This seemed to make some sort of sense, but it meant that Shapmire had the power to invade the doctor's house at will.

At last, Inigo managed to escape into a disturbed sleep where he was visited by a series of vivid, unconnected dreams, none of which he could recall in the morning.

III

When Inigo joined Lucas for breakfast it was past nine o'clock.

"Did you sleep well?" enquired the doctor.

"Not really. My ankle throbbed and kept me tossing and turning for a while. Then I imagined I could hear things. Did you notice any strange sounds during the night?"

Lucas looked up from his scrambled egg. "No. Once my head hits the pillow, that's it. It would take an earthquake to waken me before dawn, but I know these old houses creak and groan a bit, especially during a hot summer when the timbers dry out more than usual."

Inigo spooned some grapefruit segments into a breakfast bowl and asked, "Is there anyone else resident in this house? I thought I heard noises coming from one of the upstairs rooms."

"It must have been that sleeping draught I gave you. It is quite strong and sometimes creates spectacular dreams." An edge suddenly entered the doctor's voice. "You did take it, I presume?"

"Oh yes," lied Inigo, obeying an inexplicable urge to conceal the truth. "That must have been the cause. No doubt my imagination was stirred by an eventful day, a sprained ankle and a powerful sleeping drug."

Lucas became his relaxed self again. "I'm sure you're right, and how is the ankle this morning?"

"Still tender, but the swelling has almost gone, and the throbbing pain is no longer there. Your moss poultice seems to have done the trick."

Lucas got up from the table and finished off his coffee.

"I probably won't be back until quite late. I'm on duty at the Halesworth medical centre this afternoon, but Ivy will fix you lunch and we'll dine together again this evening. Feel free to use my library, humble though it is, and when you go out, do not go too far. Keep close to the village in case your ankle plays up again."

Inigo recalled the hostile reception he had received the previous day.

"If that happens, I shan't expect much help from the village if the man I met yesterday is anything to go by."

"Don't be too hard on Seth Greenwood. He was the village headman before I arrived and still feels responsible for everybody's welfare. He is very old fashioned and regards the modern world as something to be avoided, or at best ignored. You were an uninvited stranger in his eyes, but now you've stayed with me, I think you'll find his attitude will have improved."

"Pleased to hear it," acknowledged Inigo, less convinced of Greenwood's change of heart than the good doctor.

Lucas smiled. "Just wait and see, you'll find I'm right. I'd better be on my way now. See you this evening."

He stopped at the door. "And remember what I said about Shapmire."

Shortly after Lucas left, Ivy appeared, bringing in a platter full of Suffolk sausages, bacon and eggs.

"There you are, young sir," she said as she placed the large breakfast in front of Inigo. "That'll build up your strength. You look as though you could do with some filling out, if you don't mind my saying so."

"Thank you, Ivy. I shall try to do your fine breakfast justice. I know I'm rather on the skinny side."

"Slim, I would prefer to say, sir."

"That's very generous of you."

He watched her rotund frame disappear towards the kitchen and thought, *Well, her attitude's definitely changed. Perhaps Hobbswood's not such a bad place after all.*

Chapter Two

By the time Inigo emerged from the doctor's house, it was half past ten. Yet again, the sky was cloudless, and the hot June sun was already beating down remorselessly on the parched earth.

The ditches were all bone dry and the danger of wildfire breaking out in a county that had not seen rain for six weeks was becoming a worry. He hobbled down the garden path towards the unmade road, which ran through the middle of the village.

"Good morning, young sir. I trust you are feeling better today?"

Inigo turned and saw that the good wishes came from none other than Seth Greenwood, who was watering his garden again.

"Yes, thank you, just a little soreness around the ankle, that's all."

"A fine-looking hound you have there. Is he a hunting dog of some kind? I do not recognise the breed."

Inigo looked down at Wellington, who was busy snuffling at his walking stick, considering whether or not he should urinate on the strange object. He was a city dog whose only concept of hunting was chasing squirrels across Regents Park.

"He hunts when he gets the chance," answered Inigo, not wanting to tarnish the mastiff's image. "But the English mastiff is primarily a guard dog."

"You don't have trouble with burglars then?"

"It would be a very brave or foolish burglar who'd tangle with Wellington."

Seth nodded and asked the obvious, "Going for a walk then?"

"Just a short one to exercise the ankle."

"Then I hope to see you later."

Lucas had been right; the locals had certainly changed towards him, but whereas Ivy's attitude seemed genuine enough, Seth was being overfriendly, as if he had been ordered to be nice. But while his voice was warm, his eyes remained cold.

Inigo was not, by nature, a forceful character, but he had inherited a certain obstinacy from his mother, which manifested itself as stubbornness when he was asked to comply with things he did not agree with. Consequently, Lucas' warning about steering clear of Shapmire's home had precisely the opposite effect to that intended, and Inigo stalwartly set course on a route that would take him past the dark house at the top of the wooded hill.

As he limped slowly along the track that neatly divided the hamlet in two, he noticed a faint but unpleasant odour, which seemed to permeate the area. It was not that most characteristic of rural smells, the overflowing septic tank, but something more pungent. It reminded him of the time a rat died behind the central heating pipes in his room at the seminary, only to reveal its presence days later through a powerful stench as the corpse began to rot and attract large, black flies. Still, the odour was not that bad, and Inigo soon forgot about it as he listened to the distant cries of sea gulls gliding overhead and the enticing sound of the cool North Sea lapping against a sandy beach somewhere to his right.

Apart from Lucas' house, all the dwellings in the village were simple, flint-built cottages of the Victorian era, any one of which would have made a perfect retirement home for city-dwellers like Inigo's parents. The tranquillity and natural beauty of this part of Suffolk would be an ideal setting for one's twilight years, or perhaps an extended relaxing holiday, but, thought Inigo, what on earth would a young person do for entertainment in such an isolated spot? Hazel had obviously found one answer, but no one except possibly a nature lover or an author would choose a place like this to settle in. Yet, Lucas had. Probably, concluded Inigo, the fault lay in himself rather than Hobbswood; his spirit had always been restless.

After it left the village, the track swung sharply to the west as it met the incline of the valley's side. Other than Seth, none of the other villagers was about; presumably they were at work in the forests or the nearby fields. The trees closed in again as Inigo began the slow climb towards Shapmire's house, but he told himself, his main purpose was to reach the top of the hill where he could enjoy the view and consider his future while he ate the picnic prepared for him by Ivy.

In the past, when the forest was better maintained, the pines had been underplanted with rhododendrons, brought back from the foothills of the Himalayas by Victorian explorers a hundred years ago. These had matured well on the sandy soil and were now taking over large swathes of the forest floor, creating a stunning array of blood-reds, rich purples, and delicate whites, even though, in mid-June, they were just past their best. The large blooms seemed to illuminate the shadows cast by the trees, like multi-coloured beacons lifting Inigo's spirit with their abundant beauty. Wellington snuffled furiously amongst carpets of moss and ferns with large green fronds, which thrived in the dappled shade of the forest, competing with the Himalayan invaders. But as Inigo laboured up the gravel track, he began to have second thoughts about what he was doing as a sense of foreboding began to claw at him. A feeling of trespassing into the domain of a dark power far greater than his, troubled him. Perhaps, he said to himself, it would be sensible rather than cowardly if he were to turn round now and walk down to the sea shore instead; only a foolish wasp would challenge a spider in its own web. But even while he deliberated on his change of plan, it was already too late, for as he rounded the next spur of rhododendrons, Shapmire's house came into view on his left. Now he could not go back in case the occupant was watching through one of the dirty windows. He would have to carry on or admit defeat even before a challenge had been made.

The dark, shuttered cottage was similar in style to those in Hobbswood, except that it was in poor condition and the garden was completely overgrown. It obviously had not seen a lawn mower in years, never mind a fork and spade. The green paintwork on the shutters and doors was equally neglected, and had it not been for Lucas' warning, Inigo would have assumed the cottage was derelict. But as he hobbled closer, he thought he saw a wisp of smoke coming from the ornate, mock-Tudor brick chimney. But surely there was no need for a fire on such a hot day?

Inigo slowly approached the unkempt front garden, each step harder to take than the last. His stomach churned with nervousness and the hair on the nape of his neck rose in fear. He felt sure that a pair of dark, malevolent eyes was observing him from behind the unwashed windows, yet by the time he had drawn level with the front gate, which hung at an angle on a single hinge, no one had appeared. He found himself almost praying that Wellington would not let out one of those bloodcurdling wolf howls he sometimes indulged himself in for no particular reason other than it felt good, but the mastiff seemed happily preoccupied, exploring a cluster of mole hills close to the forest edge.

Now the cottage was behind them and the next turn would take them out of sight of the obstacle that had threatened to spoil Inigo's morning. He was certain he would avoid the cottage on the way back; just a few more strides.

"Hey, you!"

Inigo span round in response to the stentorian command. There, standing huge and black beside the broken garden gate, almost as if he had suddenly appeared from out of the ground, was Michael Shapmire. He was an awe-inspiring figure, standing at least six and a half feet tall and clad in a long, black cloak, which covered his gigantic frame from shoulders to feet. Despite his fear, Inigo could not help wondering how Shapmire could bear to be dressed like that on such a hot day; he must have been boiling under that cloak. He was even wearing gloves! The long, raven-black hair, which fell to his shoulders, added to the impression that he had somehow slipped three hundred years through time. He would not have looked out of place in Oliver Cromwell's army of religious fanatics, which had terrorised all who stood in its way in the mid-seventeenth century.

But now he had been confronted, Inigo still had his pride, rather too much according to his old tutor at the seminary. He would respond in similar vein.

"Are you speaking to me?"

Shapmire pointedly looked round the clearing and said, "I cannot see anyone else here, so work it out for yourself."

"Well, what do you want!" snapped Inigo, ignoring the sarcasm.

Shapmire stepped over the garden gate and walked slowly towards him.

"I seldom see strangers in Hobbswood. What brought you here and by what route did you come?"

Inigo's voice sounded thin and reedy compared to Shapmire's deep boom, but he managed to keep it steady as the dark shape came threateningly nearer.

"And what business is it of yours?"

A confident smile crossed the huge man's lips, as if he found Inigo's defiance amusing.

He looked down at him from his great height and answered arrogantly, "Because I make it so. Strangers are not welcome around here, so what brings you to Hobbswood?"

"I have told you already, it's none of your business. You have no business threatening innocent passers-by." Inigo turned to leave, unsure of what would happen next, when Wellington, who had become bored with the mole hills, bounded towards Shapmire.

For a dreadful moment, it appeared as if the mastiff was going to attack the huge figure that was threatening his master, but instead, the faithless dog jumped up and wagged his tail as if Shapmire had always been his one true master.

"Here, Wellington! Come along now!"

But Wellington was deaf to Inigo's commands and nuzzled Shapmire's black-gloved hand as if a juicy bone was hidden there. The large man bent down and stroked the mastiff's broad, fawn head as Inigo looked on helplessly, his earlier bluster now deflated by the usurpation of the affection of his closest friend. Mockery shone through Shapmire's vivid blue eyes. He whispered something to Wellington, who instantly lay down in the waiting position, with his muzzle between his front paws.

"It's a shame you do not respond as well as your dog. He knows this is no place for him."

"Permit me to know what is best for my dog," replied Inigo stiffly. "Both he and I shall go where we please. You may be able to startle rustic villagers, but you do not impress me."

"More's the pity for you," answered Shapmire as he stroked Wellington on the shoulders, who then, apparently released from whatever spell had been cast over him, trotted unconcernedly back to his master.

Then drawing himself up to his full height, Shapmire looked Inigo directly in the eyes, as a hunting tiger might to a tethered goat. Inigo could not move. It was as if the mesmeric blue eyes were inspecting not just him, but his soul, too. Then, suddenly, he was released as Shapmire turned and walked back to his cottage without uttering another word.

As the door slammed shut, sprinkling flecks of dried-out green paint onto the doorstep, Inigo exhaled a large sigh of relief and glared at his shameless dog.

"So much for faithful hounds! What came over you?"

Wellington gently butted the back of his master's knees, signalling it was time to resume the walk, and as they rounded the next bend in the track, the scruffy cottage disappeared from view. Inigo told himself he had just about won his face off with Michael Shapmire, but something deep inside him warned that there was more to come.

II

The picnic was eaten, mostly by Wellington, in the shade of a gorse bush on top of the low hill that overlooked the village. From this vantage point, Inigo could see the calm, blue water of the North Sea. Close to shore were some small fishing vessels seeking plaice, skate, and the popular local speciality, longshore herrings, and in the far distance, an oil tanker was waiting to enter one of the East Anglian ports. Everything seemed so normal and completely at odds with the confrontation he had just experienced. If the weather held fair, he would try to take a swim, but that sort of exercise might have to wait a day or two depending on his ankle, which was beginning to hurt again after his walk up the hill. Ivy had thoughtfully included a half bottle of Beaujolais, from Lucas' cellar, with the picnic, which Inigo consumed rather too quickly. So he lay down to relax for a while and soon both he and Wellington were sound asleep as the fine red wine and hot summer weather had their effect.

But Inigo's dreams did not reflect the peaceful atmosphere of East Suffolk. Lurid scenes of events that happened three hundred or more years ago, when intolerance and bigotry stalked the land, passed through his mind in a series of loosely connected scenes, like snapshots from a camera. First, he saw a small group of naked men and women being herded like cattle towards a simple timber-constructed building with a thatched roof, which, from the cross-shaped windows, was probably a chapel. Even though a terrible fate awaited them, they comported themselves with quiet dignity as they silently followed their tall, well-built leader to the building. Their captors, who were clad in the plain black garb of seventeenth century Puritan fanatics, mocked and gloated over the fate of their victims. One of these vicious zealots even wore a clerical collar, and it was he who seemed to be orchestrating the diabolical events about to unfold. Nearby, small groups of ordinary people were watching.

Some of them were weeping, for they were relatives of the victims, but were too terrified to speak out or object lest their turn should come next.

The scene suddenly changed. The thatch on the small building was on fire. The zealots laughed at the screams of the poor souls burning to death inside, congratulating themselves on their grizzly work, and looking for approbation from someone or something that was located behind Inigo's viewing point. Even before he turned to look, Inigo was sure of what he would see. Standing on the remains of a broken wooden cross was a tall, black-cloaked figure, which wore the broad brimmed hat characteristic of the time. Inigo felt certain it was Shapmire, but when he tried to look into the dark figure's face, the image dissolved into flames.

He woke up with a start. He was sweating profusely. The sun had moved across the sky so that the gorse bush no longer shaded him. He looked at his watch; it was just after four o'clock. Wellington was still sleeping, growling quietly as he chased some imaginary furry creature across the open spaces of Regents Park. At least his dreams were untroubled. Inigo sat up and tried to replay the disturbing images through his mind, but they were already fading, as dreams often do. Then he thought back to his clash with the occupant of the cottage at the top of the hill and realised, with something of a shock, that he could not remember anything about Shapmire's face; the memory had faded, just like his dream. Was he bearded or clean shaven, broad-faced or long? Except for the long black hair and piercing blue eyes, he could not recall anything. This was remarkable because, after such an unpleasant experience, he would have expected every detail of his antagonist's face to be indelibly etched into his memory. He got to his feet and prodded Wellington with his walking stick.

"Come on, old boy, it's time to move on."

He was answered by a massive yawn as the mastiff began an ungainly struggle to stand up. Inigo, too, was a little unsteady, but that probably owed more to the Beaujolais than tiredness.

The only way back to Hobbswood was along the track Inigo had used earlier, but before he reached Shapmire's house, he had decided to avoid another confrontation; one meeting with the huge man was quite enough for the present. When he was within, as best as he could judge, two hundred yards of the cottage, he plunged into the pine forest on his left, aiming to re-join the track further down the hill and well beyond Shapmire's home.

Wellington thought the detour was a great adventure, but after his behaviour on the previous day, he was kept firmly on the lead. Although the pines were not especially mature, perhaps thirty or forty years old at most, the rhododendron undergrowth had been allowed to spread unchecked, blocking the avenues between the linear ranks of the trees. Inigo was obliged to follow narrow deer tracks, which frequently led nowhere, and soon the simple plan to bypass Shapmire became rather more complicated as he was forced further and further away from his intended route.

Occasionally, he came across ancient oaks and beeches, which pre-dated the surrounding pines by hundreds of years, like stiff old men amongst groups of supple, spritely youngsters. But there was no opportunity to appreciate the contrasts of nature for a man who was struggling through the dense undergrowth with a walking stick in one hand and a straining mastiff in the other.

After nearly half an hour of stumbling and tripping, Inigo at last reached a small clearing, where he could sit down and rest for a while before resuming his search for the track to Hobbswood. It was early evening and half the clearing was in shadow. As he sat down to take the weight off his throbbing ankle, he thought how pleased Shapmire would have been if he knew of the inconvenience he had unwittingly caused. Inigo's irritation at his own weakness began to dissipate as his natural curiosity became aroused by the clearing around him. It was located in a forest within a forest, for it was bordered by broad-trunked oak, beech, and ash trees, which, themselves, formed an island of ancient woodland surrounded by young pine.

He could not remember how long it had been since he had left the pine plantation behind. He had been concentrating on fighting his way through the undergrowth, but there was an atmosphere about this place, a sense of deep melancholia, such as he recalled experiencing only once before, when he visited the battlefield of Culloden on a school trip. A superstitious person might have said that once upon a time something had happened here which was so unpleasant that an after-shadow of sadness still endured in the fabric of the forest, in the smell of the still air, and indeed, in the very soil itself. Inigo was not of that sort of mentality, but nonetheless, he decided to move on just as soon as the ache in his ankle eased a little.

The floor of the clearing was made up of soft leaf mould, which supported a thin covering of bracken, but as his weight slowly depressed the spongy bed, Inigo felt something hard beginning to press against his left buttock. He shifted his position, brushed away the brown, fibrous compost, and uncovered the corner of a slab of weathered sandstone. Having studied geology at school to advanced level, he knew enough to understand that this type of rock was not indigenous to the area, and as he scraped more soil away, he could see that it had been fashioned into a symmetrical shape by human hand. After ten minutes, and despite some enthusiastic help from Wellington, Inigo managed to excavate an almost entire gravestone, upon which was a badly eroded but still readable inscription.

Here lyeth the mortal remains of Thomas Messynger, late Pastor of the chapel of Saynt Michael, borne in the Year of Our Lorde 1620 to Nicholas Messynger gent and his wife Mary, and who's soule divided from his bodie on mid- summer's day in the Year of Lorde Protector Cromwell 1658. May the mercie of Our Lorde Jesus Christ take unto himself a troubled soule who faced the Great Darkness alone.

A postscript had been added in an undisciplined hand, as if written in a hurry.

Lorde, why forsaketh thee thus your faithful? In the hour of our need where were you?

The sad little inscription disturbed Inigo, particularly the postscript. What terrible trial had Thomas Messynger been faced with? It must surely have been the cause of his early death at only thirty-eight, and where was the chapel of Saint Michael? The Ordnance Survey map showed no chapels, ancient or modern, within miles of Hobbswood. But as Inigo looked round the clearing again, the answer became obvious. Where there was one gravestone, there were likely to be more. A graveyard would certainly be within the curtilage of sacred ground. The clearing had to be the location of the chapel, but it must have been so thoroughly destroyed that not a trace of it remained above ground level to draw the attention of the surveyors of the Ordnance Survey.

I'll speak to Lucas about this place, thought Inigo. *He may know something of the story behind poor Thomas Messynger's demise.*

Although the pain in his ankle was still undiminished, Inigo staggered to his feet and braced himself for the next phase in his battle with Hobbswood's forest; his summer stroll was turning into something of a nightmare. But after only a few more minutes of fighting with springy rhododendron boughs and stumbling over bramble suckers, which were strewn through the undergrowth like hidden tripwires, the forest became less dense. More light penetrated to ground level, and at last, less than fifty yards away, Inigo came upon the welcome sight of the gravel track that led to Hobbswood.

III

When a dishevelled Inigo arrived at the doctor's house, Lucas had already returned. He was not pleased.

"You'd better remove that boot immediately and let me look at the damage," he said as he led Inigo to his study. "We agreed on a short walk, not a cross country marathon."

Inigo obediently removed his boot, wincing as he pulled it across his damaged ankle, and placed an almost black foot on the stool beside the large study table.

Lucas was horrified as he inspected the sorry sight.

"What can you have been thinking of! You've retarded your recovery by at least three days. The swelling is worse than yesterday."

"I took what I thought was a shortcut through the forest," replied Inigo meekly. "But I got lost instead."

"Well, after you've bathed, I'll bandage your ankle again, but tomorrow you must rest. No if's or but's. No walking at all. Is that clear?"

"Perfectly clear. I thought I might go down to the beach and have a dip. It's not far."

"All right," agreed Lucas. "But only to the beach, and no diversions or variations."

As Inigo got up to leave the study, he said, almost as an afterthought, "By the way, I met Michael Shapmire today."

Lucas raised his eyebrows in surprise, "Did you, indeed? I would be interested to know what happened but have your bath first and we'll talk later."

A hot bath and a fresh bandage served to relieve the pounding ache in Inigo's ankle sufficiently to enable him to enjoy a pre-dinner gin and tonic. He sat with Lucas in the small, flower-scented conservatory at the back of the doctor's house, watching the large, red sun dip towards the hill where he had eaten his picnic earlier in the day. Lucas was eager to hear about the encounter with Shapmire and seemed to have forgotten about his instructions being so wantonly ignored by his patient. He asked many questions about the meeting, which exposed how little detail Inigo could recall, but surprisingly, the doctor showed little or no interest in the forest clearing and Thomas Messynger's gravestone.

"I've certainly never heard of a chapel or any place of worship in Hobbswood," he said. "If one ever existed at all, I'd be surprised. At best, it can only have been a simple, timber-framed structure, probably no bigger than a hut. Hundreds of chapels like that were built by the strange religious sects that sprung up in England in the seventeenth century after they were banned from mainstream religious worship. The East Anglian counties had more than their fair share of these. The folk here are a very independent-minded breed, but nearly all these chapels were abandoned after Cromwell's time and fell into disrepair."

"But," insisted Inigo, "something terrible happened there, I could sense it so strongly. And what about the postscript on Messynger's gravestone? It must mean something."

Lucas took a long pull at his gin and tonic and sighed. "This is where you and I will not agree, Inigo. I do not believe in disembodied evil, or good for that matter, as the great religions tell us. I am a straightforward humanist. In my view, the atmosphere you felt in the clearing came from within your own mind, which was predisposed to the dramatic after your difficult experience with Shapmire, assisted perhaps, by too much Beaujolais."

"So I was pissed then!"

"Now, now, I didn't say that, but I do believe that everything that happens to mankind, whether for good or bad, stems from within ourselves, nowhere else. I have no reason to believe that a titanic struggle is taking place in the cosmos between the forces of light and dark, which use us merely as their tools. That debases mankind far too much. There is, however, a massive, vested interest in persuading us otherwise in the form of parasitical church hierarchies, which live off the credulity of their so-called 'faithful'. To me, the faithful are simply the gullible, or the misled."

"So you're an atheist?"

"Yes, are you offended?"

"Of course not. Every man and woman is entitled to his or her view. The trouble is that I have grown up so accustomed to thinking the Christian way. It's imprinted on me like the circuit on a computer keyboard. Although my faith is going through a crisis, hearing such views as yours first hand, rather than hearing them second hand from a teacher with an opposing view, still comes as a bit of a shock. I don't think I've ever met an atheist before."

"Not that you're aware of, Inigo. Even I tend to keep quiet about my atheism because it offends the Christian faithful, who are still the vast majority of people in our country, even if they often don't behave in a very Christian manner."

"That's true enough, most don't even bother to go to church on Sundays any more."

"But you must not think I have anything against Christianity *per se*, Inigo, as long as it is spelt with a small 'c' and is restricted to describing a certain unselfish way of behaving. The social support it espouses is admirable and history records innumerable cases of the good that has stemmed from it. But there is a darker side when Christianity, or any of the other major religions, becomes subsumed into fanaticism. Look at Northern Ireland, for example. The continuous catalogue of murders there are all in the name of two sides within the Christian faith."

Inigo found himself springing to the defence of his erstwhile faith, and almost before he realised it, he had picked up the challenge.

"The Irish conflict is more deeply rooted than English people will ever understand. I knew quite a few Irish scholastics at the seminary. They said that the real problem is nationalism, true Irish against Anglo-Scottish implants. The religious differences are more a convenient labelling of the two opposing sides because the Irish tend to be Catholic and the Anglo-Scots to be Protestant, but religion is not the root cause in itself."

Unimpressed with Inigo's logic, Lucas asked, "What about the Turks and Armenians in nineteen-fifteen? Don't you think that religion was at the heart of that massacre? A million Armenians died. Or the Crusades? Surely you must agree they were religious wars?"

"I do not have all the answers, but religion is all too often made a scapegoat for more sinister, primitive motives. My personal opinion is that race was at the root of the Turkish Armenian conflict."

"Race and long memories," acknowledged Lucas, as he topped up his drink with rather more gin than tonic. "We English have enjoyed an invasion-free history for more than nine hundred years. As a nation, we've forgotten how to hate, though Herr

Hitler came close to reminding us."

"An all-male boarding school, followed by the seminary, meant I never really got a chance to experience the real world. I've led a cloistered life. There cannot be many twenty-eight-year-old male virgins wandering around Britain these days."

"Nothing to be ashamed of, Inigo. Unlike the rest of us, you still have one of life's greatest gifts to enjoy for the first time. Something to anticipate with delight."

Lucas got up and went into the dining room to open another bottle of gin, and as he returned, he asked offhandedly, "You're absolutely sure about it?"

"About what?"

"About being a virgin."

"Of course, I bloody am! It's hardly likely I'd be mistaken about something like that!"

"Sorry, I didn't mean to keep going on about it." The doctor sat down, topped up both their drinks again and silently watched the radiant sunset for a short while.

Then he turned to Inigo and said, "I forgot to mention, there's a village meeting at Seth Greenwood's house this evening. So, after dinner, I'll pop out for a while, if that's all right with you."

"I'd like to come too. I saw Seth this morning and he seemed a different man to the one I met before. Your prediction about his change in attitude was right."

"The meeting only concerns the next round of wage bargaining with English Nature and a few other boring local matters."

"I don't mind," said Inigo. "It would give me a chance to meet the rest of the villagers. It's about time I did."

"I agree, but not this time. The locals will feel inhibited with

51

a stranger present, particularly when the subject of wages is discussed. I'm sure you understand. There'll be plenty of time to meet them later; I'll make sure it happens. For the present, as your temporary doctor, I recommend another early night, seeing that you overexerted yourself so much today."

"Very well, Doctor, I'll do as you say this time."

Before he went to sleep that night, Inigo offered up a prayer for Thomas Messynger's soul and then meditated for a while. Despite his crisis of faith, he still found serenity in meditation, the higher form of prayer used by priests and teachers in all the great religions. On this occasion, he felt especially comforted, as if a powerful but beneficent mind was listening to his prayer. After about half an hour, the sensation became so strong that he even found himself pausing to await a reply. But none came, as far as he could tell, unless it was the solace that seemed to calm his unsettled spirit. Even though there were many questions about Hobbswood still to be answered, Inigo slept well that night.

Chapter Three

Inigo awoke early to a day that promised to be the hottest yet of that subtropical summer. He felt alert and refreshed and jumped out of bed, ready to begin the morning, remembering a split second too late not to put his weight on his injured ankle. After he picked himself up off the floor, noting that the pain was less than it might have been, he surveyed the view from his window.

The long, early morning shadow cast by the doctor's house covered most of the back garden, but it was visibly shrinking as the sun rose higher in the sky. He looked at his watch; quarter past four, yet at this time of year, it had already been full daylight for half an hour. Half a mile away, in the hollows at the base of the plateau called Dunwich Heath, the last few pockets of wispy ground mist were rapidly vaporising. Above all, the blue, blue sky warned of the heat yet to come.

Inigo washed, shaved, and read for a while, knowing no one else would be up and about yet. For the first time since his accident, he was bursting with energy; today would be the day he'd have that long awaited swim. At half past five, he decided to venture downstairs and enjoy the garden until breakfast time, but he found Ivy already in the kitchen, getting organised for the new day.

"You're up with the lark, young sir. How is that poor ankle of yours?"

"Much better, thank you, Ivy. I don't think I'll be needing the walking stick today."

"Don't overdo it again, sir, and obey doctor's orders. Sprains do not heal overnight."

"I shall certainly behave more responsibly," smiled Inigo, flattered by Ivy's matronly concern for him. "I think I shall take a stroll down to the beach for a while and catch up on some long overdue reading. Where's Wellington?"

"Your dog is in the back yard, chained to the gate post."

Inigo's brow creased ominously. "Chained? All night!"

"I had to restrain him, sir, he was terrorising the hens," replied Ivy apologetically. "Two didn't lay this morning."

That explanation had more than a ring of truth about it, so Inigo could not be too angry.

"Very well. I'll take him with me after breakfast and release the hens from their tormentor. Is there no other arrangement that can be made for Wellington? I would rather him not be chained up, and it will only be for one more night. I shall be on my way tomorrow morning."

Ivy suddenly became agitated. "You are leaving tomorrow?"

"Yes, I have enjoyed my stay here, but I must not take advantage of Lucas' hospitality any longer."

"Does the doctor know?"

"Actually no, I've only just decided."

Ivy shook her head and frowned. "I think the doctor is expecting you to stay for at least two more days, sir."

"His moss poultice has worked wonders. I'm sure I can reach Walberswick tomorrow if I rest up today; it's only a few miles. Don't worry, Ivy. I'll speak to Lucas later."

Ivy bustled into the kitchen to bring some breakfast plates and Inigo, surprised at the housekeeper's obvious concern about his early departure, browsed through some old maps laying neatly stacked on a shelf beside the door to the hall. Most were modern, like the standard Ordnance Survey 1:50,000 he carried in his ruck sack, but there was one lying at the bottom of the stack that caught his attention. It looked very old, so old he hesitated to touch it, but soon curiosity got the better of him. He gently eased it out from the maps above and carefully opened it out on the trolley beside the dining table. The yellowed vellum was warm to the touch, almost like still-living skin, but at first glance, the faded brown lines were unrecognisable, bearing little resemblance to the modern map of the area. Westleton and Walberswick were clearly shown, but confusingly, Dunwich was shown as a large town when, in fact, it was barely a hamlet and a pub. To judge from the accompanying script and archaic spelling, the map was drawn in the mid to late sixteen hundreds, about the same time as Messynger and his flock were killed.

After a few minutes' scrutiny, Inigo had one of those 'eureka' moments when he recalled that this part of the coast was subject to severe erosion. So, if the coastline were to be redrawn about a mile inland, the map suddenly made sense. He scanned the area southwest of Dunwich and although not identified by name, he saw a group of black dots that could only be a representation of the dwellings at Hobbswood. More interesting still, just to the north of Hobbswood, in the middle of the forest, a small cross was marked.

"Saint Michael's chapel," he whispered to no one in particular.

It was strange that Lucas did not know about it, but then why should he? His interest in the map was probably more for its antiquarian appeal than for its contents. Inigo now knew he would have to return to the site of the chapel before he left Hobbswood. An inexplicable urge to find out more about Thomas Messynger's fate took hold of him; he was determined to get to the bottom of the three-hundred-year-old tragedy if he could. Maybe by doing so, he could somehow publicly acknowledge Thomas' evident bravery and give the unfortunate cleric the credit he deserved. Thus, justice might be done, even if it was three centuries too late.

Inigo and Wellington left for the beach before Lucas came down for breakfast. Again, Inigo noticed a faint smell of decaying rat as he walked through the village, but there was still no obvious source. Some villagers he had not seen before waved cheerily to him as if they had known him all their lives. The gravelled path that led down to the beach was almost overgrown with gorse and broom. The locals clearly did not use it much, but the sandy cove, which opened out at the end of the path, seemed well worthy of frequent visits.

The beach had the shape of a crescent moon, with a headland jutting into the sea at either end. Apart from the deep gully, which flanked the path, the landward side of the beach was bounded by cliffs eighty feet high or more, composed of the crumbling clay and shingle which predominates along the Suffolk coast. The tide was in, lapping round the headlands, and cutting off the beach from all land access except from Hobbswood. *The villagers have a private beach, but it was not appreciated by the looks of it,* thought Inigo as he sat down on a patch of shingle near the water's edge, where Wellington was tentatively placing a huge front paw in the calm, blue sea.

There was no onshore wind. The sea was like a mill pond and very inviting. Rooting in his ruck sack, Inigo pulled out a theological treatise by an obscure Renaissance cleric, looked at the cover, and put it away again.

"I'm on holiday," he said to Wellington, who had by now

backed away from contact with the unfamiliar sea. "Work can wait."

The mastiff watched his master lie back and close his eyes, then deciding the sun was too hot, he slowly padded to the back of the beach and settled down in the shade of a gorse-covered overhang in the cliff face.

Inigo dozed for half an hour or so but then the overpowering heat of the sun forced him to stir, even though it was not yet eight o'clock. He rubbed his eyes and looked appraisingly at the cool, blue sea. He had no swimming trunks, but there was no one around, so it should be safe to strip off and enjoy a swim. Although unathletic on dry land, he was a strong swimmer and had won trophies in school competitions. 'Fishy Boscabel' had been his nickname, which even followed him to the seminary.

In just a few seconds, he was standing stark naked at the water's edge. He looked down at his long, pale legs, which bore an uncanny resemblance to two sticks of blanched celery, and ruefully concluded that no amount of sun tan could put them in the class of those Wimbledon tennis players who graced the turf of the world's premier tournament. He stepped into the sea, catching his breath at the sudden contact with the sea water, which was always colder than it looked, and waded in up to his thighs. Soft tendrils of sea weed wrapped round his ankles and something with claws scurried across his left foot as he prepared to immerse himself totally. After a quick glance back to check on Wellington, who was still peacefully asleep under his gorse bush, Inigo plunged into the water.

The initial shock, which sent a delicious tingle down his nerve endings, soon dissipated and he struck out firmly from the shore for a full two minutes. Then stopping to tread water for a brief rest, he surveyed his surroundings. His powerful crawl had taken him well clear of the headlands that confined Hobbswood's beach, and from this vantage point, he could now observe at least eight miles of Suffolk coastline.

To the south, looming dark and threatening, was the low, grey, rectangular structure of Sizewell 'A' nuclear power station. Beside it, and just as unnerving in its way, was the shining white dome of the recently constructed Sizewell 'B', which had been the cause of angry protests from those who were already well served with electricity. Between the power stations and Hobbswood, the coast was forested almost down to the shoreline. The remains of tree trunks lay at crazy angles on the beach, where they had been toppled by the latest bout of coastal erosion, but doubtless this was familiar to the distant, multi-coloured figures walking the coastal path. To the north, barely half a mile beyond the headland marking the limit of Hobbswood's beach, was Dunwich, packed as usual with holiday makers and the trinket sellers who were there to exploit them.

Medieval Dunwich, the capital of the Anglo-Saxon kingdom of Anglia, had long ago succumbed to the voracious advancing sea, and Inigo guessed he was probably floating somewhere close to the centre of the old town. Now, all that was left of the capital of Anglia were the remains of Dunwich priory, once a home for the Franciscan Order, and a last, single gravestone from the original, long-lost churchyard, which was perched atop the cliff near the fish and chip shop in the car park at the seaward edge of the modern town. One more bad winter would probably see the gravestone topple into the sea and follow the others to watery oblivion.

Inigo was pleased to see the real world, so near. Hobbswood disturbed him. Even Lucas must be a bit odd if he could find contentment in such strange surroundings. The proximity of picnickers, bawling children, and incompetent yuppie windsurfers was comforting, and Inigo determined that he would not be dissuaded from his decision to leave the next morning.

How little he knew himself.

II

While Inigo daydreamed of inconsequential matters, the incoming tide gradually drifted him back towards the beach. Suddenly, a female voice broke into his soporific contentment.

"Mr Boscabel! Mr Boscabel!"

It was Hazel, standing beside his discarded clothes. He waved and began to swim towards her.

She called out, "I've had to move your clothes further up the beach because the tide's coming in. Is the water warm?"

"Beautiful!" he shouted back.

His eyes widened as she took off her blouse and skirt. Her well-formed body was, unlike his, no stranger to the sun. Her skin was tanned a pleasing golden brown, but his voyeuristic pleasure turned to astonishment when she took off her skimpy bra and panties with a lack of inhibition one might expect from the removal of a hat.

A naked Hazel neatly stacked her clothes beside his and stepped into the sea. Inigo, who was now only twenty yards away, felt he should avert his eyes, but he managed to overcome his ingrained shyness because the girl was clearly at ease in his presence. It seemed as if this child-like creature had never been taught the meaning of modesty; her openness pleased and troubled him at the same time.

He had never seen a naked woman before, except for furtive looks at the top shelves in newsagents' shops where the rude magazines like Playboy were stocked, and despite the counter-influence of the cool sea water, the effect on him was immediate and unambiguous. He was as hard as Cornish granite. He watched, stared almost, as Hazel wobbled unsteadily on a shingle bar just below the surface of the water then, throwing shyness to the winds, he swam a little closer and splashed her. Hazel's shrieks of laughter only served to excite him further, but before any physical contact was made, she plunged into the water and began the most extraordinary breaststroke, which seemed to require twenty or more strokes for every yard of forward movement. Such exertion could not be maintained for long and soon she came to a stop, shoulder deep, in the sea.

She panted, "It's always colder than you expect isn't it, Mr Boscabel."

"You must call me Inigo."

The invitation was immediately accepted.

"I was watching for quite a while before I called out to you, Inigo. Where did you learn to swim so well?"

"It just came naturally. I've always been at home in the water."

"It must be wonderful to be able to swim like that. No one has ever taught me."

"Would you like me to teach you, Hazel?"

"You would spare the time?"

"Of course."

"Now?"

Inigo's manhood was at bursting point, but at least it was well hidden beneath the water.

He managed to sound calm as he said, "Why not? Shall we begin with the breaststroke?"

And so, the lesson began. He explained how to take longer, more assured strokes while, at the same time, using the legs more efficiently, but progress was limited because Hazel lacked the confidence to allow her face to touch the water.

At last, trying to sound as casual as possible, he said, "If I hold you up so your face stays well clear of the water, you could practise the correct strokes and gradually work your way from there."

A little smile plucked at the corners of Hazel's broad, generous mouth.

"All right, Inigo, what do you want me to do?"

He waded close up to her and said, "Just start swimming as I told you and leave the rest to me."

She pushed off again, and at the same moment, he nervously placed his right hand under her flat stomach and his left under her chin so that her face remained above the water. The firm, female flesh felt good, but the distraction of seeing the complete back view of Hazel's body brought the lesson to a premature halt when Inigo lost concentration and allowed Hazel's chin to drop. She suddenly jerked to a halt and coughed up a mouthful of sea water. The physical contact was ended.

Between coughs, she suggested they return to the beach for a while to dry off.

"There's a grassy patch at the back of the beach. We could go there, seeing that neither of us has a towel. If we lie down wet on the beach, sand will get everywhere."

Inigo's hopes were confirmed; he was being invited to make love to her.

She led the way and Inigo followed. His mind was racing with excitement and nervousness. Was it really going to happen to him at last? As they left the water, the obvious physical evidence of his hunger for her embarrassed him, but Hazel was untroubled. She directed him to a grassy bank a couple of feet above the general level of the beach and not far from the slumbering Wellington. It was screened by bracken and broom. An ideal place to become a man at last, thought Inigo, too innocent to have heard of 'first-time failures'.

They lay down together side by side, with Hazel on her back soaking up the sun. She sighed with pleasure.

"We'll be dry in no time. I think this must be the hottest summer I can remember."

Inigo propped himself up on his left elbow, now unashamedly looking at the beautiful girl beside him.

"How many summers do you remember, Hazel?"

"Nineteen; that is my age, but I suppose I cannot recall the first few summers."

"Have you always lived in Hobbswood?"

"Yes."

"Do you go out much?"

"I go out every day."

"Yes, but what I meant was, do you leave the village, visit towns, see other people of your own age?"

Hazel frowned as if Inigo had said something strange.

"But why would I want to do those things? All I need is here. I have the fields, the forest, the sea, and my cooking. Surely that's enough. Mother says my preserves are the best she has ever tasted, better even than hers. She has warned me about the world outside. It is evil and corrupt. I am fortunate to be free of it all."

Inigo replied gently, "I would guess your mother knows no more about the outside world than you do. Aren't you just a little curious about what exists beyond the boundaries of the village?"

Hazel thought for a moment, then answered, "Well, perhaps just a little bit."

Inigo cursed his lack of experience. The conversation,

though interesting, was not what he needed at the moment. But he was sure Hazel wanted him. How should he begin? How did the film stars do it? He could not bear the thought of spoiling things now by being too gauche, yet the longer he delayed, the more he feared his courage might fail him. He already sensed that his fine erection was beginning to wilt a little. Nerves perhaps? If only she would make the first move, he was sure he would be all right. But had she already made it and he had missed it? He decided it was down to the man to take the initiative. Her hair! That was it; he would begin by stroking her long black hair. He tentatively stretched out his left hand and started to fondle the long, raven tresses.

"Ouch!" squealed Hazel.

Inigo swore to himself. His fingers had stuck in one of the many tangled knots caused by the swim. The erection was softening rapidly; disaster was beckoning.

He whispered apologetically, "Sorry about my clumsiness."

She shaded her eyes against the sun and looked at him. Then she smiled, took hold of his hand, and without further ceremony, placed it between her thighs.

The erection was immediately restored. *Thank God,* thought Inigo as his fingers came into contact with the delightful, warm dampness. Everything was going to be all right. He began to move closer as the special, wonderful moment approached.

Suddenly, a large, warm muzzle shoved him in the back. He fell across Hazel in an ungainly heap, the moment of truth shattered. He turned round angrily.

"Wellington! Bugger off!"

But the mastiff showed no inclination to move until Inigo jumped to his feet. Fortunately, Hazel saw the funny side of it as an irate, naked Inigo, led by his rapidly failing erection, pursued his huge dog across the beach. Eventually, Wellington was reluctantly persuaded to return to his gorse bush, but just as Inigo began to walk back towards Hazel, he heard a low growl behind him. He spun round. This growl was not a game; it was deadly serious.

"What is it, boy?"

Wellington was looking up at the cliff above them. His large, amber eyes were cold and hostile as he stared at a moving bracken frond halfway up the cliff, but there was no breeze.

Inigo walked slowly back to Hazel and said quietly, "Someone is watching us."

Considering the lack of inhibition she had displayed earlier, her reaction was startling. She was terrified.

Inigo tried to reassure her.

"It's not all that bad, Hazel. Whoever it was could not have seen much. Sunbathing in the nude is not so terribly wrong, the French do it all the time. It's not as if we've actually done anything."

His attempt to calm her was ineffective. She quickly scrambled to her feet and ran to the place where she had left her clothing. He followed, thinking murderous thoughts about the Peeping Tom.

"Hazel, surely we can meet again later?"

"You don't understand," she said as she hurriedly struggled into her clothes.

Inigo, utterly confused, asked, "What don't I understand? For Heaven's sake, explain before you rush off. Is it your mother or father? Will they be angry?"

"No."

"Your boyfriend then? Surely you must have one?"

"No."

She bent down, picked up her shoes, and looked at him directly in the eyes.

"Listen well to me, Inigo Boscabel. Hobbswood is a bad place for you. Do not stay here."

"What do you mean by bad?"

"Dangerous. Today is Midsummer's eve. You must be far away from here by tomorrow night."

"Hazel, surely you can tell me more?"

"I have said too much already. I must go now. Do not follow me."

She ran across the beach and disappeared up the track, leaving Inigo frustrated and angry, standing by the water's edge. At least his ankle was feeling better, so he went for another swim to cool his unfulfilled desire.

The day was ruined. Inigo could no longer relax, so instead of basking in the afternoon sun, he decided to return to the village to look through Lucas' library. There he might be able to uncover more information about the chapel of Saint Michael and the fate of its last pastor. As he walked back up the path from the beach, he pondered on what Hazel had said. How could danger threaten him in sleepy Hobbswood? True, the villagers were certainly an odd crew, but the few he had seen seemed friendly enough now they understood he was staying with the doctor. Yet Hazel's fear had been genuine. He knew he could not leave without making sure she would come to no harm. If there was to be retribution for their mild indiscretion on the beach, he must be present to take his share. Furthermore, someone would have to admit to spying on them. He would have plenty to say to that someone.

III

After a quick bath and a change of clothes, Inigo entered the doctor's study. He had been given unrestricted access to the book collection, some of which looked as old as the house. It was like stepping back in history. The smell of polished wood and dry, powdery leather reminded him of his old headmaster's office, a hallowed place where one was only invited for a very special reason, usually punishment. Many of the books were classics; the complete works of Shakespeare, Marlowe, Milton, and all the great Victorian novelists. There were obscure medical treatises and assorted journals, but on the far wall, near the door to the dining room, the section that attracted Inigo's interest consisted of three shelves of very old, calf-bound books which, from the accumulated dust and cobwebs, had not been touched for years.

He crossed the study, picked one up from the top shelf, brushed off the dust from the pale brown cover, and taking care not to damage the brittle spine, opened it. To his delight, he was holding an early edition of John Bunyan's *Pilgrim's Progress*, which would be worth a small fortune to a book collector. After a quick glance through the sepia pages, he tried to put it back but the other books, which were tightly wedged together, had eased sideways a little and had reduced the space left for Bunyan's masterpiece. He decided to remove three more and then try and force all four books back together, but all he achieved was to push the book at the left edge of the gap back so far that it fell off the shelf and into a large hole in the wooden panelling at the back of the bookcase. The hole was about at eye level, so hoping it had not been caused by rats, he pulled the books out again, put his hand through it, and began to feel around for the missing volume. His fingers pushed through dust and dense cobwebs, but the gap behind the panelling was large, and he began to think that the only way to recover the book was to remove a section of the panelling and do the job properly.

Inigo stretched, squeezed, and groped for at least five minutes, but then he recoiled as his fingers came into contact with something soft. After a moment's reflection, he realised that whatever it was, it could not be alive because it was cold to the touch. So, taking a deep breath, he put his hand down the back of the panelling again and stood on tip toes to enable him to use the full length of his arm. He soon found the soft object again, and after a brief fingertip survey, he deduced that the object was thin and cylindrical. Gripping the end tightly between his thumb and forefinger, he pulled it out of the panelling and into the light of day to reveal a dusty, faded, red leather tube, which was held shut by a seal of amber-coloured wax. It was obviously very old, and Inigo surmised that it might have been lost at the time the panelling was first installed.

He brushed away centuries of accumulated cobwebs, dirt, and brick dust and sat down at the long study table to examine his find. The cylinder was about a foot long and two inches in diameter. At one end there was a metal cap, which looked to be made of bronze, but this could only be opened by breaking the seal, which was still intact. The seal itself was imprinted with symbols that might be some sort of pictogram writing. The spiky shapes reminded him of runic, but he had enough knowledge of that form of writing to realise that any relationship between the two scripts, if there was one, could only be very distant. The red leather casing was wrapped around a hard tube of metal, which had more than likely kept the contents in a reasonable state of preservation.

Inigo looked at the strange seal again and wondered. He wanted to break it and open the tube, but should he not wait for Lucas to come home so that he could share in the excitement? But almost before he knew what he was doing, he had split the seal and was easing off the cap.

As soon as the cap was removed, Inigo felt tired, not just sleepy, but seriously drowsy, as if he was going to faint. He was not ill, but he was fighting to stay awake. Struggling to keep his eyes open, he pulled out a roll of yellow parchment from inside the tube. Perhaps it was the long swim or the strain of the meeting with Hazel that was catching up with him, but it seemed odd, uncanny almost, that the near unstoppable desire for sleep had begun at the very moment the seal was broken. He put down the metal tube and carefully unrolled the parchment with a reverence that he would have given to a first edition of Darwin's *On the Origin of Species*. Then, through drooping eyelids, he began to read.

Proclamation

I, Sefton Lightwell, Gent. Magistrate and Wytchfinder for the Commonwealthe of England do herebye announce my finding. After full and diligent investigation in the parrish of Dunwich in the countie of Suffolk, the discoverie of devil worshippe and other nefarious activities that runneth against God's law. By the power invested in me by the Lorde Protector, I now do sentence the leader of this conspiracie, one Thomas Messynger, and his evil acolytes to be burned in the chapel that witnessed their misdeeds, this sentence to be carried out tomorrow, mid summer's day in the Year of Our Lorde 1658. May God have mercie on their soules.

The study darkened, the cheerful afternoon sunbeams faded, and suddenly Inigo was wide awake. The heavy, lined curtains had been closed and he could not understand why he had not noticed that before. Then he realised he was standing, though he thought he had been sitting; something strange was happening to him. He found himself standing beside the door to the dining room, looking back into the study where he could now see a group of people who seemed unaware of his presence. All were dressed in the plain black attire of the Commonwealth period, except for a man who stood at the far end of the long wooden table looking towards Inigo but without seeing him. He was clad in the buff uniform coat of a cavalry officer in Cromwell's New Model army. His buckskin breeches and brown leather cavalry boots exuded quality, yet despite his martial appearance, the collar round his neck identified him as a cleric. Like the remainder of the company seated round the table, he was clean shaven, though his black hair was long enough to touch his shoulders. And although his narrow face and aquiline features hinted at the hauteur of nobility, the large, brown eyes suggested a compassionate nature.

But the dark rims round his eyes and his set jaw indicated that this man was under severe stress. Opposite him, seated at the other end of the table with his back to Inigo, was a large, black robed figure wearing a broad brimmed Puritan hat. Between the two protagonists, sitting on the left side of the long table, was a middle-aged, near bald recorder with his goose quill at the ready. Finally, a row of four men of unmemorable appearance sat

70

opposite the recorder, each with the close-cropped hair typical of the Puritan sect. The large, black robed man began to speak, and although the language was archaic seventeenth century English, the voice seemed familiar.

"And now, Thomas Messynger, the time is come when I shall be delivered of my verdict. I have given full weight and balance to all the evidence which has been placed before me, and by the judgement of these four God-fearing men," he acknowledged the four Puritans sitting opposite the recorder with a slight nod of the head. "My duty stands clear. Thomas Messynger, leader of the fallen in our midst, envoy of Satan, I find you guilty of wytchery and worshipping the Dark One and his minions. Have you aught to say, as is your right as a freeborn Englishman, before I pass sentence upon you?"

Apart from the scratching of the goose quill, there was silence as the disgraced cleric gathered himself for a last show of defiance. He folded his arms in a gesture of contempt for those assembled before him, the light from the candles on the table flickered in his eyes. His voice was mellow and cultured.

"Master Lightwell, you have found me guilty on evidence no honest jury would even consider. Your distortion of the truth is a marvel to behold!"

"The wytchfinder is inquisitor as well as judge," interrupted Lightwell. "No jury is needed in cases of wytchcraft, but I have offered you the opportunity to bring forth witnesses in your own defence. You have arrogantly spurned this act of mercie on my part at your peril. The Lord Protector has full confidence in his wytchfinders."

"I doubt the great Oliver even knows of your sordid existence," sneered Thomas. "But I warn you, he knows of me. It is those bastards, Lambert and Fleetwood, who act in his name whence you derive your authority."

A gasp of horror at such frank language came from the rest of the gathering. Lightwell quickly signalled the recorder to stop writing, and then turned on his victim, venom lacing his voice.

"You do forfeit your right to speak, yet in faith I would feign deny a condemned man from saying his piece. You may continue."

Nods of approval from the four men sitting opposite the recorder signified their acknowledgement of the witchfinder's compassion despite intolerable provocation.

"Master Lightwell," continued Thomas undaunted. "I know not who or what you are, but a wytchfinder you are not. Beside you, the notorious Matthew Hopkins would appear as an angel of mercie. I did come to Hobbswood at the request of the Pastor of Blythburgh to clear out a nest of evil, not by the threat of eternal damnation, but by the promise of salvation through prayer and good honest preaching. A hard struggle it was, and grief and pain it caused me. I have fought with General Fairfax at Marston Moor, and with the great Oliver at Naseby, where I stopped a musket ball in my shoulder, the scar of which you claim to be the mark of Satan. I fought and overcame the wild Scots at Preston, and again at Dunbar, to protect our parliament from tyranny and to allow freedom to worship as one chooses. But in all those great campaigns, never was I so troubled as I was in Hobbswood this past year. Yet in truth I believed I saw progress in recent months. Some Hobbswood folk began to attend divine worship in the chapel of Saint Michael, which I built with my own hands. In a few more months, I believe the followers of Satan would have fallen before the sword of the Lord, which I wielded in my unworthy hand on his behalf. But then you came here, Master Lightwell. Who called you, I know not. At first, I welcomed you as an ally in the great fight, but you cared not for the teachings of Jesus Christ. I now see, much too late in the day, that with your arrival my quest perished. Consequently, in this small corner of Suffolk, the Dark One will triumph for now but mayhap the day will come, long after my ashes have been scattered in the wind, when the great cause of Light will prevail. Even as I speak, I feel the presence in this very room of one who will become the instrument of the Lord's vengeance."

A shiver went down Inigo's spine as Thomas seemed to look directly at him. The four witnesses glanced round uncomfortably. Had Messynger somehow sensed Inigo's presence in the room, or was he merely seeking comfort from his faith?

The witchfinder responded, "Are your insane, idolatrous rantings now finished, Thomas Messynger? This court has been exceeding tolerant."

Thomas looked at his four accusers one by one, all of whom avoided his searching gaze.

"All I ask for is mercie to be shown towards my flock. Any fault you find in them is my doing. Now, Master Lightwell, I am finished."

Lightwell, relief plainly evident in his voice, hastened the trial's conclusion.

"Then all that remains is for sentence to be passed."

The witchfinder stood up to pronounce the sentence. He was well over six feet tall.

"Thomas Messynger, late Captain of Horse in the army of the Commonwealth, out of your own mouth have you revealed the depth of your corruption.

"Only the complete elimination of your evil influence would be a true and righteous verdict from this trial. It behoves me, Sefton Lightwell, Wytchfinder of Suffolk, to deliver protection for the fayethfull of Hobbswood against the plausible tongue of Satan, who, without doubt, speaks through you. I see your base appeal for mercie for your followers as a means to lead their soules into the fire of Hell. That shall not happen! It is meet, therefore, that the soules you have corrupted should be cleansed before they meet their Redeemer so that they may still have a chance to achieve everlasting life. That chance will not be offered to you. Wherefore, I declare they will join you in the flames of your own evil chapel. Thus, you shall be taken hence to your chapel, you shall be incarcerated therein, along with your misguided followers, while around you the chapel shall be burned to the ground and the ashes scattered to remove all traces of its existence. May the Lord have mercie upon us all. Take him away."

The four accusers stood up and escorted an ashen-faced Thomas towards the door.

Inigo found himself shouting, "Stop! This is all wrong! Is there no true justice in this land!"

No one could hear him. He began to shake; his neck started to roll.

"Inigo wake up! Wake up! Are you all right?"

All at once, the room became light again, the candles were gone, and evening sunlight flooded through the windows where the curtains had been drawn back. Instead of Sefton Lightwell, Inigo found himself looking into the eyes of a worried Lucas Fairweather, who was shaking him by his shoulders.

"Inigo, what's happened? I thought for a moment you were dreaming, but you were sitting bolt upright with your eyes wide open; you seemed terrified."

"Not terrified, Lucas, but angry," replied Inigo as he slowly recovered his senses. "I don't exactly know what came over me. One moment I was unrolling a seventeenth century proclamation by a so-called witchfinder, then the next I was witness to the conclusion of Thomas Messynger's travesty of a trial. I suppose I must have fallen asleep after reading the proclamation, but I don't really understand how that could have happened. I found it in a hole in the panelling behind your bookcase. Where is it, by the way?"

"What?"

"The proclamation. It was written on faded yellow parchment."

Lucas glanced round the study. "There is no parchment here. That must also have been part of your dream."

"But there must be! It came from behind the books over there," said Inigo indignantly, pointing to the shelf where he had discovered the John Bunyan book.

Lucas walked over to the shelf and drew his forefinger across the spines of the books. Then blowing the dust away from his finger, he shook his head and sighed.

"But these books haven't been moved in years. I've never even looked at them; they're covered in dust."

"But I moved and dusted some of them only a few minutes ago, unless…" his voice faded away.

Lucas finished the sentence for him, "Unless that was also part of the dream. Either someone has gone to a lot of trouble to mislead us, or you have had a daytime nightmare. These things do happen. Have you been under any form of stress lately? Is anything troubling you?"

"No," then Inigo reconsidered his response. "Actually, maybe just a little."

Lucas sat down opposite him. "You'd better tell me about it.

Take your time and don't hold anything back."

After overcoming a few qualms, Inigo decided to tell his friend all that had passed with Hazel earlier in the day, but when he finished, he wondered if he had made a big mistake. Lucas seemed distant, deep in thought, his brow furrowed in concentration.

Inigo broke the silence, "Lucas, what is it? Have I offended you in some way? If so, it was unintentional."

The doctor's pale eyes locked on to him like radar on a target. Suddenly, Inigo wondered if he was facing the dread green-eyed monster, jealousy. Had his brief, unfinished fling with Hazel alienated his only friend in this weird village?

"Are you sure it went no further than you said?" asked Lucas in a deadpan, almost metallic, voice.

"Of course! Why should I lie about a thing like that? I would far rather have told you a story about a fine conquest which ended my virginity, but it didn't happen. I admit, I would have made love to Hazel if I'd had the chance."

At once the warmth returned to the doctor's face.

He relaxed and smiled. "Well, I can't see that anyone in the village should complain. Hazel is an attractive young lady, and these things happen. Why else are we made as we are?"

Relieved that the cordial relationship between them had been restored, Inigo said, "Even so, Hazel was truly frightened, as if some abominable retribution would strike her down. And why should she warn me of danger? What could possibly happen in sleepy Hobbswood?"

Lucas became alert again. "You did not mention that before. Any threat should be taken seriously. Now think carefully. What exactly did she say?"

"I cannot remember the exact words, but they were

something about today being midsummer's eve, and that I should leave before tomorrow night."

Lucas drummed his fingers on the study table, as if weighing up a delicate matter.

"Inigo, perhaps you should do as Hazel says and leave tomorrow. I believe the people here are harmless enough, but I do not presume to understand them fully. I, too, am a stranger in their midst, though they seem to have accepted me. But they live very close to nature and believe in magical superstitions that you and I would not take seriously."

Inigo's chin jutted out, always a prelude to obstinacy.

"Actually, I did intend to leave tomorrow morning, but I shall be damned before I allow a mob of primitive nature worshippers to hound me out of here with my tail between my legs. Anyway, I am determined to make sure Hazel doesn't suffer because of me. If there's retribution to face, I must take my share. I shall stay another day and night, if that's all right with you, Lucas."

"Bravo!" laughed the doctor. "Spoken like a true Englishman. You are welcome to stay as long as you like."

Chapter Four

After a dinner of roast lamb and new potatoes, Inigo took Wellington for his late evening walk along the track that led to Shapmire's house. He was deeply troubled. The brief flash of hostility he had seen in Lucas' eyes, and the failed attempt to end his virginity with Hazel, were bad enough, but the fate of a brave man who had been murdered more than three hundred years ago by a band of religious bigots was, at that moment, of capital importance to him.

Furthermore, he had no idea if he had dreamed the trial, seen ghosts, or had been present at a time-warped replay, but of one thing he was certain, the events he had observed in Lucas Fairweather's study had really happened. Obviously, Lucas was unaware of the memories stored in his house. But why, pondered Inigo, should he have been chosen, rather than the doctor, to be a witness to the injustice served up by Sefton Lightwell upon poor Thomas Messynger and his followers. Surely he was not being asked to avenge Thomas in some way? If he was, he could not see the means by which he might affect something that had occurred so long ago, but maybe he could at least find a way to put the record straight.

Inigo looked up at the clear, twilight, summer sky. The sun had just set and already some of the major stars were clearly visible in the east. A sea mist was forming as the daytime temperature cooled, and the path he had used to go down to the beach in the morning, was now plunged into a thick, grey fog which was beginning to penetrate inland along the low-lying stream beds, like ghostly fingers reaching from the salty depths.

Soon, he arrived at the overgrown little path that led to Thomas Messynger's gravestone. It forked right from the main track and disappeared into the forest, which was now at that strange, silent stage when the daytime creatures have returned to their nests and burrows, but the night dwellers have yet to awaken. He paused to consider which direction to take, but Wellington made the decision for him by trotting purposefully along the path towards Thomas' grave. That at least meant another confrontation with Shapmire would be avoided.

But, almost immediately, Inigo began to reconsider the decision as the densely planted pine forest closed in around him. The pleasant summer twilight was replaced by an oppressive gloom, and when he almost undid all of Lucas' good work on his ankle by tripping over a concealed bramble and sprawling full length on the forest floor, he decided it was time to return to the track. He was about to call Wellington back when a low rumble from the darkness ahead made him think again. It was the chilling sound of the mastiff growling for the second time that day.

Inigo felt perspiration form on his forehead as he slowly, stealthily, walked a little further along the path, which now curved to the left. Then he found the great fawn mastiff, legs braced apart, and hackles raised, looking intently to his front. He gently stroked the powerful neck and shoulders, noting the tension in the muscles. He had only seen this once before in Wellington, which had been the prelude to his pursuit of a Great Dane that had unwisely challenged him at the gates of Primrose Hill the previous summer. But that had just been sport for the mastiff; now he was deadly serious.

Inigo was not sure if he was frightened for himself or more

frightened of what Wellington might do.

"Steady boy," he whispered. "I'm with you."

As he spoke, he saw a light perhaps a hundred and fifty yards away which lit up the forest around it in a faint glow. As best as he could judge, it came from the clearing where Saint Michael's chapel had once been, but after his recent experience in Lucas' study, he had no wish to precipitate further encounters with inexplicable phenomena. He attached the lead to Wellington's studded leather collar and tried to retrace his steps, but the dog refused to move. He pulled hard, but two hundred and twenty pounds of obstinate mastiff was sixty pounds more than he could bring to bear on the other end of the lead; they were going nowhere. He became worried rather than angry, for the mastiff had never defied him before in this cold-blooded, determined way. He pulled again, but with no effect.

Suddenly, a cry of pain, a woman's cry, echoed through the forest. Wellington lunged forward, dragging his master with him, and faced with the choice of investigating further or abandoning his best friend, Inigo resigned himself to the inevitable. Once on the move, Wellington did not try to bound ahead but instead advanced at a strong, steady, fast walk that had a discipline about it that Inigo had not seen before. Normally, Wellington had just two speeds, fast and stop, but now his master was seeing a new, frightening side of the English mastiff for the first time, something bred into the breed since ancient times which no amount of modern, scientific cross-breeding could completely eliminate. He did not know what to expect.

Soon, they left the pines behind and entered the much older, broad-leaved forest trees where, thankfully, Inigo could see that the light was cast by a dozen or so gas lamps placed in a circle around the clearing that contained Messynger's grave. At least these were modern appliances, so there would be no repeat of the spectral scenes in Lucas' study. A group of figures was gathered inside the gas lamp circle, but one of them stood to one side, a little apart from the rest.

Inigo and Wellington were now only ten paces away from the edge of the clearing. Fervently regretting his intrusion upon what was obviously a secret meeting, Inigo pulled on the lead once more. This time, to his surprise, the mastiff obediently stopped and waited. He did likewise.

The gathering consisted of about twenty villagers, some of whom Inigo recognised. There was the tall, thin carpenter whose face was so lined it might have been chiselled out of mahogany. Beside him stood the squat farm foreman; his hands were like two great plates which, when clenched, looked capable of hammering six-inch nails into seasoned oak. Seth Greenwood was there too.

Seth walked over to the solitary figure and said angrily, "You well knew what you were doing! You were willing to endanger our release by indulging your carnal pleasure with no thought of the wishes of our Great Lord. Years of waiting would have been wasted had not worthy Magnus Locke seen you in time."

The thin carpenter bowed his head to acknowledge Seth's compliment.

The lone figure spoke between sobs. It was Hazel.

"It was not as you say. I felt sorry for him. He is so innocent; it seems so unfair. He does not deserve the fate you have in store for him."

Seth could barely control himself. His voice became shrill with fury, "That only makes it worse! Forgiveness I might find for simple, ill-controlled lust of the flesh, but you acted with premeditation. This is the reward betrayal deserves."

He raised his right arm and struck the girl a mighty blow across the face with the back of his hand. Hazel staggered but did not fall.

Wellington growled, but Inigo whispered, "Steady now, we must wait a little longer. I need to hear more before we move."

Meanwhile, Seth continued to vent his wrath on Hazel.

"The fate of all of us depends on tomorrow night. Well you know that! Our fathers, our fathers' fathers and generations before them could only dream of the opportunity that has come before us. Yet you took it upon yourself to endanger our hopes of freedom. It is right you should receive your just punishment on the hallowed ground of Our Lord wherefore he may witness our treatment of those who displease him. Have you aught to say in mitigation before punishment is administered?"

Hazel shook her head, so Seth continued, "So that you remember well this lesson, you will receive three lashes of the whip from all those present here. Strip her!"

While eager hands began to pull at Hazel's dress, Inigo tried to recall a quotation he had heard somewhere, which went something like 'Now is the time for all true men to stand up and be counted'. *What bright spark dreamed that one up?* he thought. Despite the risk, he was certain he would never forgive himself if he stood by and allowed Hazel to suffer alone. He looked down at the powerful creature beside him; at least he was not on his own.

He knew he must show no fear, so taking a deep breath, he said, "Come on, Wellington."

He strode boldly out into the clearing.

"Wait!" he shouted.

His voice sounded high pitched and thin in his own ears; fear must have tightened his vocal cords.

"You will leave that woman alone and you, Seth Greenwood, will answer to the police for common assault."

Daylight was gone now. The gas lamps threw strange, criss-cross shadows across the floor of the clearing in various densities of grey. The gathering, which moments before had been noisily tearing off Hazel's dress, was shocked to silence as twenty pairs of malevolent eyes turned on Inigo. He was committed; now was no time for hesitation. Walking determinedly through an almost physical barrier of hate, but with the formidable Wellington at his side, he confronted the Hobbswood villagers with a show of arrogant disdain.

Seth Greenwood started to move menacingly towards him but immediately stopped when the mastiff began to growl.

"How long have you been spying on us?"

Reassured by Wellington's fearsome aspect, Inigo replied confidently, "Long enough to understand the depths of your depravity. You are all like the dinosaurs, redundant in the modern world. Black magic and superstition no longer matter now, as it used to when people knew no better, but still you cling on to outdated, vicious beliefs that use a distorted form of faith to indulge perverted sexual excesses. You are prepared to inflict pain, and no doubt, rape on this helpless girl for a worthless, extinct cause. I do not doubt that, in your case, Seth Greenwood, this is merely an excuse to release your sadistic perversion under the cover of religious righteousness, and maybe it's the only way you are able to get your thrills, but at least this time you shall be thwarted. Hazel will now return to the shelter of Doctor Fairweather's house with me, and tomorrow we shall see what the police have to say about your degenerate behaviour."

Seth signalled to some of his comrades, who moved to block

the path back to Hobbswood, while the others edged threateningly closer to Inigo. Hazel did not move. She remained stock-still, like a rabbit transfixed by car headlights, seemingly unaware that her rescuer was at hand. Inigo now appreciated the full extent of his peril; there was murder in Seth's eyes. The outside world seemed far, far away.

Sensing his master's fear, Wellington lurched forward emitting deep, ferocious barks, intermingled with slavering, white fanged snarls, which would have even done justice to the Hound of the Baskervilles. Inigo's right arm felt as if it was about to be wrenched from its socket, but he hung on for dear life because the mastiff was his only means of escape. The threat from Wellington was quite enough to halt the sinister advance of the villagers.

"Stay back!" warned Inigo. "If I let him loose, blood will flow!"

He was by no means sure that it would, but it sounded good.

He shouted to Hazel, "Come on! You don't have to put up with this. Don't be afraid, you're safe with me. I'll take care of you."

He had no idea how he could look after her, but that was unimportant just at this moment. He knew he must save her and himself from her tormentors or face death where he stood. Hazel seemed to snap out of her trance and ran to him, neatly side-stepping a lunge from Ambrose, the farm foreman, who tried to block her way. The top half of her dress had been ripped away and her nose was bleeding, but otherwise she was unharmed.

"Get us out of here, Inigo!" she pleaded. "They have evil in their hearts."

Under the cover of an angry, baying mastiff, Inigo and Hazel slowly walked towards the forest path that connected

Messynger's clearing to the main track out of Hobbswood. The four villagers who stood between them and escape prudently stood to one side as the slavering fangs drew near.

Inigo heard Magnus Locke mutter, "What about tomorrow? He must not get away."

"Have no fear, Magnus," answered Seth grimly. "There is no escape out of here for him."

Worryingly, the locals seemed far more concerned about keeping him in Hobbswood than punishing Hazel.

Inigo and Hazel stumbled rather than ran down the dark path and soon they had left the ancient, broad-leaved trees behind and were amongst the pines again. Looking round, Inigo could see no signs of a pursuit. The Hobbswood folk seemed confident he would not escape, yet how could they be sure he would not turn right when he reached the track and run all the way to Southwold police station? Even before the thought was fully formed in his mind, he already knew the answer. *Shapmire!* He would have to pass Shapmire's house in the dark.

There was no way he would do that, especially on this night of all nights! He slowed to a walk.

"OK, Hazel, they're not following us. We can stop running now. My ankle's had enough, and we'll soon be at Lucas' house."

Her reaction was not what he expected. "I cannot go there, Inigo, it would be madness!"

"Listen, Hazel, Lucas is not part of all this. We'll be safe with him until tomorrow morning, and then we can go to the police. Lucas is our friend."

She pulled away from him, almost crying with terror.

"No! No! I must get away."

Without another word, she fled from the path and plunged into the trees, leaving Inigo confused and angry for the second time that day. Yet again, Hazel's behaviour seemed at odds with all logic, but panic affects people in different ways, and he felt he could do no more for her now. The white knight had fought gamely for his fair damsel, but only minutes after rescuing her, he had managed to lose her again.

He headed back to Lucas' house, fervently hoping that the doctor had not been called out for the night. The sense of relief he felt when he saw that the house lights were on was almost overwhelming.

II

"Good gracious! What on earth's happened?" exclaimed Lucas as he opened his front door to a bedraggled looking Inigo. "You look like you've been dragged through a hedge backwards!"

"Not far from the truth," panted Inigo. "You won't believe what I've just seen. I'm lucky to be alive still!"

Lucas took a step back from Wellington's white, foaming muzzle and said, "Take your dog through to the back yard while I pour you a brandy. You look as though you could do with one."

"Thanks. Is there anything for Wellington? He's more than earned his supper tonight."

"There might still be a bone left in the kitchen from the lamb joint we had earlier if you care to search for it," replied Lucas as he disappeared into the study.

The doctor was not, and never could be, a dog lover.

It did not take long for Inigo to unearth a leg and shoulder bone from the rubbish bin in the kitchen. Wellington grabbed them in his huge mouth with delight. His master took him into the back yard and looked at the harsh iron post that Wellington had been tied to the night before. He could not see much because it was so dark, but there was just enough light to outline a wooden chestnut post that had been hammered into the ground to form the hinge of the gate to the hen house. Inigo decided to secure Wellington to this instead of the iron post; it was a decision that was to save his life.

Five minutes later, a contented mastiff was gnawing at the

remains of a shoulder of lamb while his master sat swilling Remy Martin in Lucas' study.

Inigo quickly emptied his glass, and as the doctor replenished it, he said, "Lucas, we must call the police. There might be serious trouble here later tonight. I've upset the village."

He went on to recount all that had happened in the clearing by Saint Michael's chapel and ended with an apology to his host.

"I do hope I have not prejudiced your position here. You are now, in effect, giving shelter to an enemy of Hobbswood."

Lucas topped up his own brandy and smiled. "Don't worry about that. Tonight, I shall personally bolt all the doors and lock the windows. No one will enter without your express permission."

He looked at Inigo through a doctor's eyes, appraising his state of mind.

"I can see you've just been through a traumatic experience, but is there a possibility you may be over-reacting? I've known for some time that the villagers here worship the old gods rather than the Christian one. It's something of a tradition in Hobbswood, but don't you think that calling out the police is, well, a little over the top?"

"But, Lucas, they were about to strip and whip Hazel if I had not intervened. No amount of eccentric old ways can justify that sort of behaviour in twentieth-century England. It would probably have ended in gang rape."

"Very well. But on a practical note, I don't think the Southwold police will appreciate being called out tonight to attend a crime that did not actually occur. Under the circumstances, why not leave it until tomorrow? I have to go to Southwold anyway, so you might as well come with me and we'll go to the police station together. They will be more inclined to take this seriously if the local doctor is with you to back you up. I expect they will send a constable here to give the villagers a lecture and a warning, but don't anticipate much more than that."

"Well, at least that will be something," agreed Inigo, disappointed by Lucas' mild reaction.

"Anyway, it might be as well if you leave Hobbswood before tomorrow night in view of what you heard in the forest clearing. Although I don't put any store in the villagers' primitive beliefs, it's better to be safe than sorry. I'll drive you to your next stop, if you like."

"Thanks, Lucas, but I'm on a walking holiday. Even so, I really would appreciate a lift past Shapmire's house. I'll walk once we reach the Dunwich road. It sounds like you do take the villagers seriously then?"

"Not the black magic nonsense, but people may still behave strangely because of what they believe. There is no Dark Lord, but if Seth Greenwood and his friends think there is, then it makes sense for you to leave here before the solstice."

"Which is tomorrow?"

"Indeed it is, the twenty first day of June. The solstices and equinoxes have always held significance for primitive societies."

"What about Hazel? What will happen to her?"

Lucas shrugged. "I will do what I can for her, but it's likely she will take a beating whether you stay here or not. Neither the Suffolk police nor I can watch over her forever."

"Surely her father will protect her?"

"It's not as simple as that, Inigo. You see, marriage, as you and I understand it, is not recognised in Hobbswood. Men and women tend not to pair off formally. Relationships are, at best, loose, and frequently a woman may be sexually active with three or four men at the same time without causing a stir in the village."

"That sounds pretty uncaring to me. It seems that women are treated like sexual chattels."

"Indeed, and it also causes complications with regard to paternity. When a baby is born, one of the village men will acknowledge the child as his for the purpose of the birth certificate. I have delivered half a dozen Hobbswood children myself, and I'm positive that most of the official fathers are not the genetic fathers, so the parental bond is not as strong as you might expect."

"Who is Hazel's official father?"

"Mycroft Stone, the woodsman, but judging from her appearance, Seth Greenwood is more than likely her real father."

"Then that makes Seth's behaviour in the forest even more reprehensible! It's hard to credit that such things can still happen in this country."

"The old ways are more widespread than you might think, Inigo."

"But surely such free and uncaring parenthood was never popular, even in the distant past. People don't change that much."

"Certainly, modern historians don't say much on the subject, probably because they don't know, but I believe such practices stem from a time when villages like Hobbswood were the norm rather than the exception. Most small communities had a village idiot who was probably the result of too much inbreeding. East Anglia had its fair share. Remember that roads were poor and sometimes impassable in winter for long periods of time until the coming of the railways. Some of the more isolated villages saw no strangers from one year to the next. I suspect what you and I regard as a loose moral attitude was Mother Nature's way of mixing up limited gene pools as much as possible."

Inigo smiled. "Lucas, you have the ability to make even the

most bizarre behaviour seem normal, but sometimes even your avuncular cynicism is simply not enough. What I saw tonight was pure evil, which, in my opinion, has been handed down from generation to generation. Such were the folk who murdered Thomas Messynger, conveniently using the worship of Satan as the reason for their degenerate, murderous ways."

Lucas read the conviction in Inigo's eyes and spoke gently, "I do not disagree with much of what you say, though I do think you're letting the nightmare you experienced in my study influence you rather too much. The only difference of substance between us is that I believe evil resides in Mankind alone, not in some mysterious dark force."

"So, for you, religion has no value at all?"

"I did not say that. It has no value for me, but that is not the same as saying religion has no value at all. Take your Catholic sacrament of confession, for example. Whoever thought that up distilled in one simple ceremony a process that psychiatry has been trying to emulate ever since."

"Which is?"

"Shifting the burden of guilt. Even Freud never managed that. A Roman Catholic can rob, rape, and murder, but if he goes to confession and promises to try not to do any of those things again, he is absolved by God's representative on earth, a priest. Then he can go on his way, free of guilt, and with an afterlife in Heaven back within his grasp. Bloody wonderful! If I were religious, I would be a Catholic for the sake of confession alone!"

"That's a rather simplistic view, Lucas," replied Inigo, irked that an outsider should mock the faith he had grown up with and only recently lost, but a sharp rap at the front door immediately put an end to the discussion.

The fear, which had been gradually fading from Inigo's mind, suddenly returned.

"What are you going to do?" he asked nervously.

"Nothing to worry you. I've already assured you of that. I'll open the front door and see who's there, and if I think there is any sort of threat, I'll shut it again. Stay here and I'll leave the study door open so you can hear what's going on. If the worst comes to the worst, there are a couple of walking sticks with heavy ivory heads in the hallway."

Lucas went to the front door and Inigo heard him unlatch the heavy, brass chain. There followed some quiet conversation, which was inaudible from where Inigo was sitting, but a few moments later he leaped from his chair as the doctor returned to the study accompanied by Seth Greenwood.

"It's all right," said Lucas reassuringly. "Seth asked if he might have a few words with you. I shall stay in attendance until he leaves."

Inigo remained standing and glared balefully at the village headman. "Well, say your piece then."

Greenwood lowered his eyes in an attempt to show humility.

"I want to apologise, sir, for my own part and on behalf of the village. We meant no harm and deeply regret startling you. I expect our country ways must seem unfamiliar to a sophisticated city dweller like you."

"Bollocks to your country ways! I heard you order your followers to strip and whip Hazel in the name of some evil lord who you intend to placate tomorrow night."

Seth's mild response was not matched by the fury in his eyes. "Indeed, sir, you are mistaken. No such words were uttered, I assure you."

"Then why secretly assemble in the middle of a forest if not to carry out your wicked work?"

"We just worship nature in our own way, as our forefathers have done for hundreds of years. The spirits of the air, the sun, the sea, and the earth; these are the gods we worship. A country person would understand." The mask of friendliness briefly slipped as he added, "Not some meddling busybody from the city."

Seth's hypocrisy only fanned the flames of Inigo's anger further.

"You depraved wretch! I know what I saw and heard, and I shall see you pay for what you did to Hazel."

Before the meeting got worse, Lucas intervened, "We have clearly reached an impasse. There is no point in continuing this discussion. Seth, I will see you to the door."

When Lucas returned to the study, Inigo said, "That man's a downright liar!"

"But a plausible one."

Weary of the doctor's determined attachment to reason and logic, Inigo snapped, "Do you take me for a liar, then! You can't have it both ways. One of us must be lying."

"I am sure you are not lying, Inigo. I know you believe what you say, but I wonder if you might unwittingly be embellishing your story a little, what with the dark shadows around you, the story of Thomas Messynger fresh in your mind and so on. It could easily prey upon the imagination, and I am only trying to see it from the point of view of the police tomorrow morning. It does sound rather like a story from a fairy tale."

"I see," answered Inigo stiffly. "I am sure Hazel will support what I say."

"I doubt it. Remember, she will still have to live here after you are long gone. Without her to back you, just imagine how things will look if you report this to the police. It will be your word against twenty villagers, who will no doubt claim that all was peaceful until you arrived, lost and uninvited."

"Maybe you're right, about the police I mean," agreed Inigo. "But could you not see the visceral hatred in Seth's eyes?"

"Actually, no. He seemed genuine enough to me, but to be fair, I'm only a general practitioner, not a psychiatrist."

Inigo did not immediately reply. He was disappointed that he had lost the confidence of his friend, if only partially, but then another thought entered his stressed mind, a black, frightening thought.

"What if Shapmire is at the root of all this? The clearing in the wood is not far from his house."

Ever the voice of reason, Lucas replied, "Hardly, Inigo. The locals fear Shapmire; they do everything in their power to avoid going near him."

"All the more reason, then! The Mexican Indians lived in abject terror of their gods. They were always placating them with human sacrifices, as the Spaniards found out to their cost. The Aztecs even resorted to ritual cannibalism to please their hideous spiritual masters. Have you not read Bernal Diaz' account of Hernán Cortés' invasion of the Aztec Empire?"

"Can't say that I have," sighed Lucas.

"Well, Diaz actually marched with Cortés and saw at first hand the depths men will plumb, in order to avert the wrath of vengeful gods."

Lucas raised his eyebrows in mock surprise. "Surely you are not comparing the rustic villagers of Hobbswood with the Aztec Indians?"

"In a way, I am. Seth and his companions seem to live in terror of their master, whoever that might be, just as the Aztecs did, and just like the Aztecs, they are prepared to make the ultimate sacrifice for him, which in the case of Hobbswood, is me!"

At last, Lucas seemed reluctantly to acknowledge the possibility of Shapmire's involvement. "Well, I cannot deny that Shapmire does seem to have an almost unnatural hold over Hobbswood, but to equate him with a vengeful, man-eating Aztec god still seems a little fanciful."

"Perhaps," said Inigo, pleased that he had at last seemed to have broken through the doctor's irritating insistence on empirical evidence before agreeing to anything. "But Shapmire is here for a purpose, I'm sure of it."

"Well, whatever it is, Inigo, I shall make sure he stays well away from you. Another brandy before you turn in?"

Inigo smiled and held out his glass.

Chapter Five

As soon as he opened his eyes, Inigo knew he had drunk too much brandy the night before. It took him a few seconds to focus on the wrist watch lying on the bedside table. Half past nine! He had slept for more than ten hours. He wanted to turn over and go back to sleep, but the sooner he left Hobbswood the happier he would be. Only Lucas stood between him and the wrath of the village, but there was no telling how much longer the good doctor could protect him.

Outside, all was quiet; there were no irate villagers clamouring at the door, and the night had passed peacefully, as far as Inigo knew. The events in the forest now seemed remote and unreal, rather like a bad dream, but the pain in his right shoulder and arm, caused by restraining Wellington's massive frame, confirmed that last evening had been no fantasy.

He slowly got to his feet and sat on the edge of the bed; the room seemed to be slowly spinning around him. His stomach was in that state of limbo where it is impossible to judge whether or not it will reject its contents, but with a great effort, he managed to drag himself across the bedroom to the wash basin. The face that peered at him from the mirror was, despite the sun tan, sallow and drawn. It seemed ten years older than yesterday morning, but a wash and a shave would hopefully improve its appearance a little, even if the red-rimmed eyes remained dull until later in the day. At least his ankle was feeling better.

By the time he had dressed and packed his rucksack, it was

quarter past ten. Everything had to be done slowly or not at all. Bending down to put on his walking shoes was almost impossible, and for a while the laces seemed to wriggle before his eyes like a nest of worms, but at last he was ready to leave his room and search for Lucas. He managed to negotiate the stairs and reach the dining room without hurried recourse to the bathroom. The breakfast table had been cleared, not that Inigo cared; food was furthest from his mind. But there was no sign of the doctor or anyone else. He felt a pang of fear, in case Lucas had left and gone to Southwold without him. Almost running into the study, he looked out of the window and saw, to his relief, Lucas' car still parked outside.

He was turning to leave the study when he noticed the leather tube containing Sefton Lightwell's proclamation on the table. Lucas had found it! At least that proved Inigo had not simply day dreamed Thomas Messynger's trial. It would be interesting to hear Lucas try to rationalise his way out of that one. Despite his delicate state, he decided to take another look at the proclamation before he left. He unrolled the yellow parchment to re-read Thomas' death sentence, and as he looked at Lightwell's small, spidery signature, he noticed the signatures of the four witnesses written at the foot of the document for the first time. He could not understand why he had not noticed them before, because either there was an incredible co-incidence or something more sinister was going on. The names were Magnus Locke, Mycroft Stone, Ambrose Samphyre, and right at the bottom in a barely legible scribble, Seth Greenwood. All four names were still in use in Hobbswood. Perhaps it was a tradition to hand the same name down from generation to generation; that at least would be a more rational explanation than the dark alternative forming at the back of his mind. He quickly rolled up the parchment and put it back in the tube. It was time to collect Wellington and leave.

The sight that met Inigo when he entered the back yard made his blood boil. Wellington was still tied to the chestnut post where Inigo had left him, but someone had kicked away the water bowl his master had placed beside him. The mastiff, who was shackled in the hot sun, had badly chafed his neck while struggling to reach the upturned bowl, where he thought he would find water. Inigo picked up the bowl, filled it from an outside tap, and placed it beside his dog, but Wellington did not drink. Instead, he looked at something behind Inigo's left shoulder and began to growl. Before he could turn, Inigo was felled by an expert blow to the back of his neck and hit his head hard on the concrete floor of the yard. Just as he was slipping into unconsciousness, he felt his arms being roughly dragged behind his back and a rope tightening round his wrists. Wellington barked helplessly as his master was injected with a hallucinatory drug and dragged back into Lucas' house by his ankles.

And now Inigo began to dream, but these were dreams, the like of which he had never before encountered. Multi-coloured images flashed before him like a nightmarish picture show, but the colours were all wrong. Flame red and orange skies, purple clouds, and yellow seas. He found himself standing on a deserted coast composed of black, volcanic sand. A huge storm was raging. The wind sounded like the howls of thousands of lost souls crying from the depths of despair. He looked out to sea where a gigantic wave whipped up by the storm was building. There was no escape. It was already breaking as it rushed towards him, threatening to engulf the coast. But when it finally broke, the wild sea was transformed into myriads of kaleidoscopic beads and the white foam into fire, which opened into a huge, dark pit where winged and horned creatures of medieval demonology awaited him. Heironymus Bosch, their creator, stood by the pit, smiling as he painted more winged devils that awoke from his canvass and floated upwards from his brush.

Then, suddenly, Inigo felt himself falling into the pit. Deeper and deeper he went, far beyond all hope of return, until the flames gave way to an inky blackness. At last, he reached the bottom, where all was still and quiet. The floor was clammy, the silence oppressive. He could see nothing in the absolute darkness, uncontaminated by light. It was so dark; he could not be sure if his eyes were open or shut. That same smell of decaying rat that hung over Hobbswood was present, but as he stood in the blackness wondering what to do, he sensed the smell was getting stronger. He was not alone. Something obscene, malevolent, and hideously evil was approaching in the dark, crawling nearer and nearer, intent on devouring him. He could not tell whether it was coming from the left or right, front or back. He was helpless, yet he dared not wait, but nor could he flee in case he ran straight into the arms of his predator. This was pure, cold terror, terror that could destroy a man's soul, terror he would never forget. Then there was nothing.

Gradually, consciousness returned. Not physical awakening, for Inigo had been injected with a large dose of a heroin derivative, but a change in awareness that released him from his drug-induced nightmare into the dreams of more normal sleep. Now he was standing beside the chapel of Saint Michael. It was a clear, moonlit night. Thomas Messynger, hands tied behind his back, was being herded into the chapel, along with his followers, by some of those Hobbswood villagers who remained impervious to his ministrations. Sefton Lightwell was standing at the edge of the forest clearing, overseeing what was happening, but his face was still obscured by the broad-brimmed, black hat of the

Puritans. Messynger, who was the first to reach the chapel, stood to one side of the entrance, encouraging and trying to raise the spirits of his doomed flock. When they were all inside, he shouted to the witchfinder.

"Who are you, Sefton Lightwell! You are not Satan himself, for I would have sensed his presence before now, but you are surely from his evil family. Mayhap you are one of his powerful warlocks I have heard tell who live in the remote parts of our great land, spreading fear and pestilence."

Lightwell answered in the quasi-religious vernacular popular with sectaries at the time, "Fool! Knowest thou not the awesome power ranged against thee? It be not of this world."

"Then name yourself, if you dare, so that my vengeance may seek you out before you wreak more havoc."

"Thy pitiful threats trouble me not," sneered Lightwell. "For who will remember thee after tonight? As for my name, it may not be spoken except by my priests, but this I will promise thee. When the flames begin to burn thy flesh and the smoke chokes thy lungs, then I shall reveal myself to thee so that the last living thought confronting thee shall be of thy conqueror."

Then turning to his black acolytes, he commanded, "Place him inside the chapel with the rest of his doomed followers!"

Lightwell's servants gripped Messynger, but he momentarily threw them off with a mighty shrug of his powerful arms, like a lion shaking off a pack of hyenas.

"You believe you have won, Lightwell, but I sense your downfall is present here even as we speak. Enjoy your victory while you can because you will be brought down by another, and sooner than you think."

The chapel door was bolted shut and torches put to the simple wooden structure. Within seconds, flames began to lick upwards and very soon the tinder-dry thatched roof was alight. Above the crackle and roar of the conflagration, Thomas' flock could be heard reciting the Lord's prayer, but it was not long before the communal praying broke up into coughs and retching as the smoke began to penetrate the victims' airways. The lucky ones died of smoke inhalation, but those of a stronger constitution survived long enough to endure the burning of the flames. Blood-chilling shrieks pierced the night air, and Inigo recalled he had seen this part of the dream two days before, just after the confrontation with Shapmire. Now the pieces of the jigsaw seemed to be falling into place.

Sparks and flames roared upwards into the night sky. It seemed that all within the burning chapel must now be dead, but just as the roof began to collapse, a final shout arose from the funeral pyre. Although distorted with pain, it was clearly the voice of Thomas.

"Get thee back to Hell!"

Then came a name, which sounded a bit like Bethlehem, but could not have been.

Damn, thought Inigo, *I should have been listening more attentively,* but as he racked his brains trying to make sense of Thomas' last words, which had identified the true name of the enemy, the flames disappeared. Everything went black, except for a few pinpoints of light.

They were stars; he had awoken and opened his eyes. His head pounded furiously.

II

Inigo was lying down on grass made damp with dew in the cool, clear, summer night. His head was pressed against something cold and hard. His ankles were tied together, but his hands were free. Around him, he could hear the murmur of suppressed voices. He struggled up to a sitting position.

A voice from behind called out, "He's awake."

Inigo turned to see Magnus Locke, the carpenter, standing behind him. He blinked and looked round, trying to orientate himself, and soon realised he was in the forest clearing of Saint Michael, the very place he had just been dreaming about. The cold, hard object that was now digging into his back was Thomas Messynger's gravestone and to his right, close to the forest edge, was a table covered with a black cloth. On closer scrutiny, Inigo could see it was, in fact, an altar, complete with a golden chalice, two black candles on either side, and an inverted crucifix in the middle. Standing beside the altar was Seth Greenwood.

In the centre of the clearing, the rest of the villagers stood talking quietly round a log fire, which crackled merrily, counteracting the cool of the night. Hanging in the trees, illuminating the great oaks and beeches like fairy lights, were twenty or so gas lamps. The entire gathering had an air of normality about it, rather like a bonfire night outing, or a midsummer party, but Inigo knew that he was witnessing the precursor to something horrible instead. The normality only seemed to make it worse. Apart from the black altar, there were no bizarre appendages, such as the black hooded cloaks, pentagon symbols, or mysterious chanting he had seen in horror films. Everyone was wearing simple daytime clothing and behaving in a way that an average onlooker would consider not in the least remarkable.

Seth Greenwood addressed the gathering like a pleasant school teacher rather than a practitioner of the black arts.

"Gather round, everyone, let's make a start. We do not have all night. Magnus, bring Mr Boscabel a little nearer so he can see what's going on."

"What are you going to do to me!" shouted Inigo, as Magnus dragged him towards the fire, hopping like a rabbit because of his tied ankles, but Seth ignored him and continued to organise his congregation.

A metallic reflection coming from the altar cloth caught Inigo's eye. Any hopes he may have secretly harboured that these people would draw back from the ultimate crime were expunged, for laid out neatly beside the golden chalice was an ornate, thin-bladed dagger, about eight inches long, and a small axe. Both were made of polished silver and looked more like a surgeon's tools than instruments of death. Somehow this made them even more frightening.

As soon as Seth was satisfied that his congregation, who now stood in two neat lines facing him, was ready, he went to the back of the altar and put on a garment similar to a priest's robe. On its back, the robe bore complex, whirling abstract designs wrought in red and gold, like the wild Celtic patterns Inigo had seen on European Iron Age shields during his archaeological studies. After lowering his eyes in a short, silent prayer, Seth returned to the front of the altar, and with his back to the villagers, started to speak in Latin. Inigo was surprised to hear a rustic village leader speaking liturgical Latin, but his surprise turned to anger when he began to recognise prayers which were familiar to him from the Catholic Mass. A strange mixture of fear, fury, and frustration tore at his heart, each competing to take over his mind, but soon deep sadness and disappointment prevailed as the last flickering embers of his faith died away.

If there really was an all-powerful, all-seeing God, then how could he allow such evil to be perpetrated in glorifying Satan, his arch enemy? Was the Darkness actually stronger than the Light after all? Had the great religions of history been simply conning their faithful followers for thousands of years? It certainly looked like it now. Or was Lucas right, in claiming there was nothing beyond this world? But even now, Inigo could not quite accept that. And what of these ignorant, misguided murderers in Hobbswood? They were no more than fools led by fiends such as Greenwood and Locke, eager to satisfy their sick lust for blood and physical gratification. But, reflected Inigo, Mankind's greatest lust has always been for power, and there is no power greater than control of minds. People like Seth had learned how to gain that power over simple folk by pretending to have access to forces outside the familiar surroundings of this earth, and by weaving a web of mystery around themselves that impressed and frightened the uneducated. Many of the great tyrants of the past had used these psychological weapons, which often seem like inspiration to lesser men.

Yet even though he was alone, facing imminent death and abandoned by his faith, the spirit within Inigo Boscabel was still undimmed. More than three hundred years ago, Thomas Messynger had yelled defiance to the last and Inigo was determined to do no less. Although Thomas eventually lost his battle with his enemy, it had not been without purpose, for Inigo began to feel that Thomas' fortitude was somehow transmitting itself through the centuries to him. It was almost as if his spirit was watching, just as Inigo had witnessed earlier in Thomas' trial and last moments on this earth. That thought brought some comfort. Perhaps he was not entirely alone after all. Thomas died branded as a criminal, and now Inigo would not be able to put the record straight as he had hoped. But if he could only conjure up the same spirit of defiance, then maybe, in a hundred years or so, another Thomas or Inigo might draw enough strength from him to overcome the evil in Hobbswood.

All these thoughts rushed through his mind in just a few seconds. In the cold light of day, he would have called them fanciful, but to a man staring death in the face, they provided the last moments of life with a purpose. God or no God, he was certain of one thing; he would not allow a black Mass to be performed in front of him without hindrance. Physical interference would be impossible because of the bonds that tied his ankles and the close proximity of Magnus Lock and Ambrose Samphyre, but he still had his voice and air in his lungs. When death is certain and nothing more can be done to avoid it, fear can sometimes be replaced by peacefulness, or even, as in Inigo's case, recklessness, knowing that the consequences no longer matter. He would make Thomas proud of him, but for the moment, he bided his time.

The atmosphere in the clearing became especially solemn as Seth approached the black Mass equivalent of the transubstantiation, the changing of the bread and wine into the body and blood of Christ. Everything was quiet, except for Seth speaking the ritual words in a priest-like monotone. Inigo briefly wondered what was going to be used for this part of the blasphemous ceremony because there was no bread and wine on the altar, but then he reminded himself there was no need for such things; he was going to be the sacrifice. He had already decided he would not go quietly.

So, offering up a short prayer for forgiveness out of habit rather than faith, he took a deep breath and yelled, "You're all fucking bastards!"

A moan of horror arose from the congregation. Seth spun round, rage distorting his face. *Brilliant!* Inigo thought.

He shouted again, even louder this time, "Wankers! The whole bloody lot of you! Wankers! Wa-a-a-ankers!"

A huge fist hit him in the face, loosening his front tooth and splitting his lip. The fist belonged to Ambrose, the farm foreman.

"Again, Ambrose! Harder!" shouted Seth.

The next punch cracked Inigo's nose, but the disruption had been so successful that, despite the pain, he still managed another 'wanker' before a third blow pummelled him into silence.

Having something to do helped fight the fear. He started to plan more interruptions for other solemn parts of the ritual. While he did so, he scanned the faces of Seth's followers and was pleased to see Hazel was absent. At least she had made her escape, but what on earth had happened to Lucas? He probably had no idea of what was happening on his own doorstep, and if he ever found out about Inigo's fate, he would probably end up in a shallow grave in the forest. But Lucas was no fool; he would certainly be wondering about Inigo's sudden disappearance without his dog. If he suspected foul play, he would go to the police.

All too soon the moment of truth arrived. Inigo's heart sank when he saw Seth leave the altar and walk slowly towards him carrying the chalice and axe. Magnus gripped him firmly by the shoulders from behind. Inigo had thought he had a little longer;

until the black communion at least. He was not quite ready for the end.

Suddenly, his bravado slipped away. He really did not want to die. His heart began to beat hard as Seth approached with the evil looking axe in his right hand. Now he began to feel more than fear. Abject terror tore at his guts. The veins in his forehead pounded, his pulse accelerated, and he suddenly realised he would do anything to avoid this; anything!

"Magnus," he whispered. "Is there any way out of this? I'll do whatever is required of me."

There was no time to feel shame. He just wanted to live.

"You were lost the moment you came to Hobbswood," answered Magnus. "You will die tonight, nothing can stop it."

Seth was just a few paces away. Instinctively, Inigo began to struggle. Terror lent him extra strength. He could not believe he was about to be killed. He started to sob and shout at the same time.

"No! Please! I'll do anything! Mum, help me!"

He fought even harder as the axe was raised. Ambrose came to Magnus's aid and together they held him tight, but Inigo continued to fight. Every last second was a second more of life.

Seth shouted, "Hold him still!"

Two more villagers ran to help Magnus and Ambrose and at last Inigo was held fast. Seth grabbed his left arm.

"Mr Boscabel, your time is still some minutes away. All you are required to do at this moment is to hold out your left hand. Soon, you will wish you were dead because instead of a quick end, you have earned yourself a slow, painful death. But I will yet show mercy if you refrain from any further interruptions."

Ambrose held out a white, marble butcher's slab and placed Inigo's left hand, palm downwards on it. Then he pulled the little finger away from the adjacent one so hard that it was almost breaking. A split second later, Seth brought down the axe hard and neatly severed the finger at the second joint from the nail.

Inigo let out a mighty howl, which shattered the silence of the black summer night – a howl of shock from the sudden pain, tinged with anguish at the prospect of oblivion. But it was also a howl that was heard half a mile away, in the back yard of Lucas Fairweather's house.

III

Throughout that long, hot, summer day, Wellington had been tugging fretfully at the rope that bound him to the chestnut post, but as the sun began to set, he curled himself up as best he could to await his master's long overdue return. The mastiff had, however, weakened the structure of the post, which was partly infested with woodworm, so when he gave a mighty heave in response to Inigo's distress call, he snapped it about six inches from the top. The back yard gate was only three feet high and no obstacle to a dog of Wellington's dimensions. The great beast was free.

Meanwhile, having neatly decanted some blood from Inigo's open wound into the chalice, Seth returned to the altar with the dismembered finger. Ambrose, somewhat pointlessly in view of Inigo's imminent death, tied some coarse twine around the finger stump and pulled it tight to stem the bleeding. Through misting eyes, Inigo stared ruefully at his disfigured hand. All thoughts of disrupting the ceremony were temporarily forgotten, until he heard Seth resume his prayers again. Seth was carefully cutting away pieces of the flesh from the finger with the silver dagger and placing them in the chalice with the blood. He casually cast the bone into the grass behind the altar.

With growing horror, Inigo watched Seth bow low over the chalice to utter the words of greatest sanctity to the Catholic Church, the words of Jesus Christ himself. The black priest was about to consume the contents of the chalice in a disgusting, cannibalistic mockery of Christianity.

"*Hoc est enim corpus meum.*"

Meaning 'This is my body.'

Inigo no longer had the courage to challenge the ceremony. He had just faced death, or so he thought, and had humiliated himself by begging for life. Now he would have to face it all over again.

The best he could do was to shout, "You're all murderers!"

Another mighty punch from Ambrose knocked him to the ground in a barely conscious state, leaving him unfit for further disruption. Seth turned to face his congregation for the prayer called the Agnus Dei, the Lamb of God, which is said during the Catholic Mass when the priest holds up the consecrated bread and wine for all the faithful to see just before the communion. Seth's words were, of course, different.

"*Ecce Antichristus, ecce Antichristus sanctus.*"

Inigo began to wonder if he could find the courage to yell more abuse when a movement in the trees behind the altar stopped him. Some in the congregation saw it too. An irritated Seth turned round to see what was disturbing his followers. After a few seconds, he seemed to go rigid, then he fell to his knees as a tall, dark figure slowly walked into the clearing. The villagers quickly followed Seth's example, but Inigo struggled to his feet to get a better look at this strange newcomer who clearly engendered respect from the Hobbswood folk.

He briefly wondered if he was dreaming again. The tall figure, which was clad in a long, black cloak and a Puritan hat, looked for all the world like Sefton Lightwell, but as it came closer, Inigo realised that Lucas had put in an appearance at last. Hope came flooding back. How ingenious to dress up as the object of local adoration; only Lucas could think of that. If the ruse worked long enough, the cost to Inigo of this night's evildoing might yet be restricted to the loss of his little finger. He dared not speak for fear of blowing Lucas' disguise, so he waved and pointed frantically to the bonds round his ankles, gesturing in a sawing motion, and then pointing towards the dagger on the altar.

But Lucas seemed not to understand. He walked straight past the altar without a second glance and stopped beside the kneeling Seth Greenwood, from where he slowly surveyed the bowed heads of the villagers.

Lucas, for God's sake, don't push your luck, thought Inigo as the seconds ticked away.

At last, the doctor saw him, but Inigo's frustration increased as Lucas walked towards him without picking up the dagger from the altar. Precious seconds were being wasted.

"For God's sake, get the dagger before they see who you are," whispered Inigo as Lucas came to a halt in front of him.

But when their eyes met, Inigo's blood ran cold as the awful truth dawned on him. The face was indeed Lucas', but this was not Lucas Fairweather.

A face is much more than the sum of its parts, more than a collection of the features which constitute it. Character, personality, the very essence of the human person, show through in a way that is universally accepted in a day-to-day sense but cannot easily be described. Perhaps the almost infinite variations in facial expressions form the vehicle through which the personality reveals itself, but to analyse these simple yet subtle functions we take for granted is well-nigh impossible. Because of this, Inigo knew that the man who was looking, staring at him almost, could not be Lucas Fairweather, though the facial features were certainly his. It was the eyes more than anything else that revealed the change. The colour was still pale grey, but there was an icy coldness about them which had not been there before.

Inigo said quietly, "Sefton Lightwell?"

The reply came in a hard, metallic voice that was not Lucas Fairweather's, "You may call me that, if you wish."

The thin lips widened into a humourless, mocking smile. "Welcome to your destiny, Inigo Boscabel."

"What have you done to Lucas!"

The tall figure chuckled unpleasantly. "Lucas Fairweather, Sefton Lightwell, they are both the same."

"Rubbish! I know Lucas. He does not believe in your mumbo jumbo. He's an avowed atheist and humanitarian. He'd have no truck with murder. He's a doctor, for Christ's sake."

"For whose sake?" chided the tall, dark figure. "Think you not your expletive is out of place in this company?"

The archaic English confirmed in Inigo's battered mind that he was addressing Sefton Lightwell, though he did not know how this could be.

"You cannot be Lucas Fairweather. He is my friend!"

"It suited me well for you to think so," came the reply.

"Then who the hell are you! You cannot be Lucas, nor can you be Sefton Lightwell because he lived more than three hundred years ago!"

Sefton raised an eyebrow. "Ah, so the sacrifice hath spirit. So much the better."

Turning to Seth, he said, "Thou hast done well. This night, thou shall reap thy reward."

Seth, still kneeling, answered, "Thank you, Lord. You have been living amongst us all these years, yet we knew it not until tonight."

"It was meet that it was so, for thereby others also remained ignorant of my presence. Now, you may complete the ritual."

While Seth turned back to the altar to continue his prayers, Sefton Lightwell resumed his conversation with Inigo. Now his language was less archaic, almost modern.

"I shall miss you, Inigo Boscabel. Your intelligent conversation was a pleasing change from the company of these bovine country folk."

"Miss me? Am I going somewhere?"

"Do not play the simpleton with me. It becomes you not. Well, you know that in a short time, your blood will flow freely from your veins."

Hoping to appeal to the logical side of Sefton, or Lucas, or whoever it was who stood before him, Inigo said, "You are an intelligent man. Is it really necessary to commit murder? Your priest has already taken some of my blood, not to mention some flesh and bone besides. Is that not enough for you?"

"I shall require all eight pints. Everyone must drink to ensure salvation."

"Salvation!" snorted Inigo. "How can killing me help you? And even then, what can you offer that cannot be achieved by less violent means?"

"Much the same offer as is made by your priests and bishops," answered Sefton affably. "Life after death, of course, but in addition I offer pleasure instead of penance in this world."

"But what sort of life after death? Surely oblivion is preferable to eternal life in your master's service."

"You had a taste of it, I think."

"When I was drugged?"

"Yes."

"But that was a decent into Hell. I was terrified. You can

hardly call eternal fear, salvation."

"You would have felt no such fear had you been one of my followers."

"Would following you save me now?" Inigo was angry with himself for asking that question, but he needed to know if he had a choice.

"No, for you there is no escape. You have a particular attribute that is needed for this sacrifice. It is your body I require, not your soul."

"What attribute? What makes me different?"

"You represent the lamb of innocence. Your blood will release my flock from its prison here in Hobbswood, for you are untainted with experience. You are a virgin. If your God cannot save a chosen one such as you, then tell me, what is his protection worth? Why should anyone worship him?"

Inigo's despair was complete. He had no answer to Sefton's question.

Unable to hide his disappointment in his own faith, he said, "So that's it. When I told you I had never known a woman, I condemned myself to death."

"Perhaps, but I had already begun to sense you were different from the occasional lost traveller that sometimes strays into my domain. Your fate was already sealed when you stumbled into Hobbswood."

The background murmur of Seth's prayers came to an end. The time had come. Sefton nodded towards the altar, where Seth picked up the dagger and waited.

"Prepare yourself, Inigo Boscabel," said Sefton.

In a last, desperate attempt to save his life, Inigo demanded, "If you are as powerful as you say, then why must I die? What is the release you spoke of? Who is it that has the power to hold you here? Is it Jesus Christ himself!"

"Speak not that name here!" snarled Sefton, reverting to the seventeenth century English he used when speaking to his followers. "Thy defiance shall avail thee nought, as Thomas Messynger discovered when his time came upon him. Thou shall depart this world as he did, beaten unto pitiful desperation in the full knowledge of the triumph of his enemy."

The cold, grey eyes seemed to glow with a baleful, fanatical light, the voice shook with the exultation of victory as he shouted, "Take the sacrifice to the altar. Tonight, we shall be free!"

As Ambrose Samphyre's powerful hands gripped his arms, Inigo looked up for the last time at the beautiful, starlit sky. Was eternity out there somewhere? He would soon know for this really was the end. He hoped it would not be too painful. Twenty-eight years old, he had achieved nothing. He might just as well never have been born. What an epitaph! Thomas Messynger had at least made his mark in the world before he died. Inigo knew it was useless to struggle, but he could not go calmly to his death like the martyrs of yore. He lashed out with his elbow, scoring a direct hit on Ambrose's nose, who heartily regretted not binding his captive's hands as well as his feet. But Sefton simply gripped a pressure point near Inigo's neck, which quickly subdued any further resistance. Inigo was roughly frog-hopped to the black altar, where Seth was waiting with the gleam of victory in his eyes and the dagger in his hand.

Someone called out a warning. Sounds of rustling undergrowth and snapping twigs came from the trees on the far side of the clearing. Sefton released his grip on Inigo long enough for him to turn his head and see Wellington burst from the forest, snarling and slavering like a hound from Hell.

A voice from behind Inigo shouted, "Hold that damned

animal!"

But no one was brave enough or stupid enough to try.

"Wellington! Over here!" called Inigo, just before Sefton's strong fingers squeezed the pressure point again, forcing him to his knees.

The huge mastiff saw his master in distress and bounded towards the dark creature that seemed to be inflicting the pain. But Sefton Lightwell, for all his great power, real or imagined, had been caught by surprise. He did not wait for the clash with the advancing fangs but fled to the cover of the woods, along with Ambrose, Magnus, and the rest of his terrified flock. Seth Greenwood was the fastest and clawed his way up an oak tree, while the rest of the gathering scattered in all directions as a brood of hens might before a hungry fox. For a crucial minute, the altar was left unattended. Inigo hopped over to it, grabbed the dagger that Seth had dropped in his panic, and cut through the bonds around his ankles. Then slipping the dagger into his belt, he picked up the small axe to wield should his flight be challenged and recalled Wellington. There was no immediate response from the mastiff, so Inigo staggered towards the place in the tree line where Wellington had first made his spectacular appearance, as this was likely to be the best escape route.

He stopped at the forest edge and called the dog again. He could see that six or seven of the villagers were already coming after him. He tightened his grip on the axe shaft. Just as he was about to call yet again, Wellington reappeared at the opposite side of the clearing and headed straight for him. Two deep barks were enough to stop the pursuit in its tracks. The villagers threatening Inigo's escape turned and ran away. A dozen long bounds brought Wellington, panting, to his master's side and together they plunged into the forest.

116

Behind them, someone shouted, "Ambrose, bring the gun!"

Inigo found he was unable to run properly because the blood flow to his feet had been restricted all day by the rope tightly binding his ankles. The best he could manage without falling was a fast walk. The odds were still against him.

He could hardly see a thing once they left the light cast by the gas lamps, but there was no time to stop and consider which direction to go. Master and dog simply followed the route of least undergrowth, or wherever gaps in the trees allowed them to pass. Low branches smacked against Inigo's face and body, leaving bloody cuts and scratches across his skin. He was still dressed in the short-sleeved shirt he had put on in the morning. He yelped as a bramble bush tore at his injured left hand, and a second later, he was tripped by a tree root and fell head first onto the forest floor.

Soon they left the great oaks and beeches behind and entered the pine forest, where the undergrowth was less thick, but although that meant they were not travelling in a circle, Inigo had no idea in which direction they were headed. He risked a brief halt to take stock, but quickly resumed their flight when he heard the sound of the pursuit coming up close behind them. It seemed to be coming from his right so, at the next firebreak, he turned left, hoping this would take him to the Dunwich road.

The regularly planted pine trees let in a little more starlight than the heavy leaved, deciduous forest, but although he was able to quicken his speed a little, the villagers were definitely closing in on him. They, of course, knew these woods well and were doubtless using shortcuts to head him off. He was still weak from the effects of the drug and the binding of his ankles, but try as he might, he could go no faster.

Wellington, who was a few paces ahead, suddenly let out a

puppy-like yelp, in marked contrast to the aggression he had been showing earlier. He lurched forward, wagging his tail furiously. Seconds later, Inigo collided with a hard, warm object that was invisible in the dark. Yet again, he went tumbling to the ground but this time the axe slipped from his grasp as he fell.

He lay on the ground trying to recover his senses but was suddenly blinded when a torch clicked on just above him. A large boot stepped on his right wrist before he could retrieve the axe. All seemed to be lost, and as his eyesight slowly became accustomed to the light of the torch, he saw a huge, menacing figure towering above him. In his wild, directionless flight from the clutches of Sefton Lightwell, he had run straight into the arms of Michael Shapmire!

Chapter Six

"You will not be needing that," said Shapmire as he kicked the axe out of range of Inigo's clutching fingers.

Inigo began to fumble in his belt for the silver dagger, but a large, gloved hand stopped him.

"Or that. Get up quickly and come with me."

As he got to his feet, a tumult of disorganised thoughts raced through Inigo's mind, which culminated in one overriding question. By going with Shapmire, was he simply exchanging one danger for another? Behind him was certain death, ahead lay the unknown; there was no real choice. At least Shapmire was his enemy's enemy, therefore that might make him an ally despite his frightening appearance.

Wellington growled and his hackles rose as the sound of the pursuit came nearer. Shapmire spoke again, but this time with more urgency.

"Hurry or they will be upon us."

He turned and trotted along an overgrown path, followed by Inigo. Wellington padded happily beside the big man, oblivious of the disapproval of his master, who struggled to keep up with them. The path led to another firebreak where Shapmire stopped and pointed to a distant light through the trees.

"That is my cottage. We will be safe there, but our pursuers are closing on us fast. Can you go faster?"

"A little, but my ankles have been bound all day and I'm struggling to feel any sensation in them."

"You must go faster, or we'll be caught. Push on and I will cover your back."

"I will do my best."

"Good. We are almost in my domain, but now the darkness favours the enemy. Let's go!"

They ran the last few hundred yards to the house. Inigo was faint from pain and exhaustion. He managed to glance back and saw torchlights flashing behind them, but the lights had definitely halted some way before the track that led to Dunwich. They were safe for the moment at least.

When Shapmire opened his creaky front door, Wellington bounded in as if he had lived in the cottage all his life. Inigo paused in the overgrown garden to regain his breath. Now that the adrenalin was no longer pumping, his limbs felt leaden, and he could hardly put one foot in front of the other. Even so, he had enough mental energy left to register surprise when he entered Shapmire's dwelling.

Because the outside was so unkempt, he expected to be faced with the sort of squalid, smelly, primitive abode, with no modern conveniences, that you might associate with a tramp or a squatter. Far from it. The interior would have graced the centre pages of Ideal Home magazine. Most of the single storey cottage consisted of a single large living room, which was lavishly furnished. The off-white carpet looked like best Axminster and the dark oak furniture was highly polished and cared for. The beamed ceiling and white plaster walls were typical of most East Anglian cottages, but the ornamental bronze wall lights must have been imported from France or Italy. The crimson-coloured lampshades cast a warm glow, which seemed to welcome Inigo as he stumbled over the threshold, but the glow was hardly necessary because, although it was midsummer's night, a blazing log fire cracked in an old brick inglenook fireplace that covered most of the right-hand wall.

Shapmire saw Inigo stare at the fire and said apologetically, "I feel the cold."

"So does he," replied Inigo, pointing to a supine mastiff who had already stretched himself out in front of the fire.

"What has happened to your hand?" asked Shapmire.

Inigo looked at his bloody stump.

"Seth Greenwood cut my finger off as part of the sacrifice during his perverted ritual in the forest. It was the starter before the main course of a black communion with me as the intended victim."

"Are you in pain?"

"Yes."

Shapmire pointed to a door beside the inglenook.

"Go to the bathroom and wash the wound. When it is clean, I will attend to it. Is there anything I can get you? Tea? Coffee? Something a little stronger perhaps?"

"A brandy would do well," then remembering his hangover he added. "But just a small one."

While Inigo washed his stump in the pristine bathroom, staining the white towel with blood, he found himself wondering about his benefactor. Something was not quite right; the cottage was too perfect. He recalled the scholastics' rooms at the seminary. His own was typical; books stacked in irregular heaps on the floor, bed unmade all day, mugs unwashed for weeks at a time, and an assortment of sticky coffee rings and streaky drip marks on the desk, which testified to years of constant sleeve wiping. Above all, there was the all-pervading smell of burnt toast in the corridor outside. This was how single men lived. Yet in Shapmire's home, all the cushions were in place on the settees and chairs, and the china was clean and neatly placed in an illuminated display cabinet. There was not even a discarded newspaper in sight.

Inigo's mother was almost paranoid about tidiness, but even she would have been hard pressed to match the standard of Shapmire's housekeeping. The whole place looked, Inigo tried to form the words in his mind, sort of unlived in. The cottage seemed to be how the perfect home should be but in practice never is. After cleaning his stump, he washed his hands and grimy face, then he returned to the living room where Shapmire, still clad in his heavy, black coat, was gently stroking a snoring Wellington, whose jowls were frothy from the bowl of water he had given him.

"Do you live alone here, Mr Shapmire?"

"My name is Michael. The answer to your question is, yes. Why do you ask?"

"Your home is kept so beautifully tidy. I wondered if I detected a woman's touch."

Shapmire smiled. "Regrettably there is no woman here."

He looked round the room. "I did not realise this place was anything special. Do other people live differently then?"

"They do where I come from, but then I suppose a seminary full of single men is not typical."

"I suppose not," agreed Shapmire.

Inigo was bursting with questions. He walked to the window next to the front door, pulled the curtain a little to one side, and peered into the darkness.

"I can't see anything of the villagers, but they are determined to get me back though. Should we not barricade the doors and windows?"

Shapmire looked up from the sleeping mastiff and said

quietly, "Quite unnecessary. Drink your brandy and try to relax. I told you that this is my domain. You are perfectly safe here."

Inigo was not yet convinced. "You did not see the looks of hatred on their faces when I escaped. They are desperate for my blood."

A note of impatience entered Shapmire's voice, "They will not trouble you here. Believe me, Inigo, they would not dare to cross into my domain."

"You know my name! But we have only met once before, and I know I did not tell you my name then, Mr Shapmire."

The big man settled himself into a luxuriant, burgundy-coloured padded chair and smiled. "We did not get off to a good start, did we? For that I was at fault. At the time, I thought you had come to Hobbswood to become a permanent resident."

"Would that have made a difference?"

"Certainly."

"Then when did you find out I was just passing through?"

"On the evening of our first meeting, when I sensed you meditating. Then I understood you were not part of the Hobbswood evil. Since then, your presence here has been of great concern to me."

Inigo thought back to his second night in Hobbswood when, during his meditation, he had experienced a strange sensation of someone listening to him. But now, instead of answers, Shapmire was creating more questions in his mind.

He said, "How could you have sensed my meditation? I don't understand. And what exactly is the evil you speak of, Mr Shapmire?"

Shapmire stood up and stretched his large frame.

"Enough questions for now. For the present, all you need to know is that we are on the same side and that you are safe when you're near me. And would you please stop calling me Mr Shapmire and use my real name instead."

"All right, Michael," replied Inigo hesitantly.

"That's better. You've been through a terrible trauma, which you must recount to me in every detail, but that can wait until tomorrow after you have had a long sleep. Now, I shall attend to your hand before you retire with your brandy."

Michael took hold of Inigo's left hand, then turned round so that Inigo's nose was almost touching the large, black back, his left arm firmly wedged between Michael's chest and elbow. This was exactly how Inigo's mother used to remove splinters from his hands when he was a young boy so he could not see the needle enter the skin, but that had not stopped him peeping over her shoulder when he had grown tall enough. This time, all he could see was Michael's coat, but he felt no fear. The nervousness he had previously felt in the presence of the big man had already been replaced by an inexplicably strong confidence, which he could not really justify; not yet at least.

Michael removed one of his gloves and placed it on the coffee table. A second later, Inigo felt his hand being encased in heat, as if it had been put into an oven. But this heat did not burn, rather it radiated a powerful warmth, which penetrated his hand like an X-ray beam so that the flesh, sinew, and bone were warmed equally without scorching the skin. The sensation was as pleasant as it was startling. A minute later, Michael replaced his glove, released Inigo's arm, and turned round. Inigo stared at his injured hand dumbfounded. The open wound where his finger had been cut off was healed, as if the injury had occurred years ago. The skin had grown over the stump and had knitted as neatly as any surgeon could have sown it.

He looked up at Michael and gasped. "But how can you do

this?"

"A technique I learned a long time ago. Never thought I would have to use it again."

"But surely what you have just done is well beyond the scope of current medical knowledge?"

"Beyond western medical knowledge, perhaps, but there are many wonderful medicines and cures in parts of the world that you would consider primitive."

"Ah," nodded Inigo sagely. "You have spent time in the tropics? Is that why you feel the cold so much?"

"Certainly, I am accustomed to much greater warmth than the English climate offers."

Michael handed Inigo his as yet untouched brandy and continued, "I know you have many questions, and I shall do my best to answer them in the morning, but now you must sleep. You may use my room for I still have much to do before this night is over."

Michael's bedroom was as perfectly kept as the rest of the house, indeed it looked as if it had never been used. Suddenly, the adrenalin stopped; Inigo felt safe at last. Finally, exhaustion caught up with him, and within seconds of his head touching the pillow, he was fast asleep.

The brandy remained untouched.

II

Inigo awoke to his new surroundings in some confusion. Which of the previous day's events had been real and which were merely the result of drug-induced hallucination? He looked at his disfigured left hand; regrettably that had been real enough. There was no pain though, nor were there any after-effects from being drugged. Whatever else he might be, Michael Shapmire was a natural healer. Inigo looked at his watch. Ten thirty! Michael had thoughtfully left a bag of essential toiletries next to the watch, so Inigo was able to bathe, shave, and freshen up, though the effect was somewhat tarnished when he had to get back into the torn and crumpled clothes of yesterday.

At eleven o'clock, he emerged from the bathroom. Another blisteringly hot day was in prospect, but the interior of the cottage was pleasantly cool. There was no sign of Michael or Wellington. Perhaps he had taken the dog for a walk. Inigo was suddenly aware that he was ravenously hungry. He had not eaten for a day and two nights, so he went into the kitchen and found some bread, milk, and cereal. Yet again, he was perplexed to see how correct everything was; no plates to wash up, and all crockery neatly stacked. Even the knives, forks, and spoons were carefully placed in their individual sections in the drawer by the sink. His host seemed to be a slave to orderliness, yet Michael had none of the mincing ways about him that can often accompany such a personality.

After a bowl of cereal and four slices of toast, Inigo decided to investigate his surroundings further. To his surprise, there was no lock on the front door so, leaving it on the latch, he went outside to inspect the overgrown garden. The first thing he noticed was the absence of the decaying rat smell that permeated the village. On the contrary, a delightful blend of scents greeted him because, apart from the weeds, most of the plants were herbs. There was a stand of pink hollyhocks and a clump of sunflowers near the gate, but most of the front garden had been taken over by a blue carpet of borage. A few patches of purple sage and lemon thyme were still holding their own in the more shaded recesses. It was obvious that this had once been a carefully managed plot of land, presumably before Michael's arrival. As he bent down to pick a thyme leaf, he became aware of a deep rumbling sound coming from some long grass near an old shed, which he immediately recognised as the snores of a contented mastiff.

"Wellington!" he called, and the rumbling stopped.

There was movement in the grass, and moments later, the great fawn dog emerged, wagging his tail, with tongue poised for a slobbery lick. After the obligatory wet welcome, Inigo heard footsteps coming up the track. He spun round, fear racking his stomach, but relaxed again when he saw Michael's large frame come into view.

"Good morning," boomed Michael. "I trust you slept well?"

"Yes, like a log, thank you. And you?"

Michael swung open the creaking front gate. "I do not need much sleep. Have you been up long?"

"No. I was just about to have a look round your garden."

Michael stopped in the gateway and surveyed his garden.

"Explore, you mean; it's a bit of a jungle, is it not? I do not seem to have the time to tend it properly."

"Perhaps you could spend a little less time working on the inside of your cottage," suggested Inigo tentatively, partly because he remembered he had left the kitchen in a bit of a mess. "And more on the garden. You must do more cleaning than my mother!"

"Is that a lot, then?"

"Certainly," replied Inigo, surprised at Michael's apparent ignorance of his own remarkable standards.

"Very well, I will start clearing the weeds this afternoon, but I do not have much knowledge about gardening."

"I may be able to help there. I used to help out in the garden at the seminary."

"Good, but before we do anything, we need to talk. Have you breakfasted yet?"

"Yes, thank you."

"Then I will make some tea, or coffee if you prefer, and we can discuss what to do about last night. There is a piece of lawn at the back of the house, which I manage to keep cut, and a garden table and chairs in the old shed if you care to set them up."

Ten minutes later, Michael was pouring out the tea from a round Georgian silver teapot while Inigo stroked Wellington's soft, large ears. The plate of biscuits provided by their host had not gone unnoticed by the mastiff.

Michael said, "I love tea. It's almost an addiction for me, especially PG Tips. I prefer the simple brands. I find the more exclusive brands like Earl Grey taste more like wet smoke than tea."

With that, he gulped down a cupful of the steaming liquid and had already poured another before Inigo had taken his first sip. It was still boiling hot. He winced as he felt it burn its way down his throat and into his stomach.

"Michael, you must have an asbestos mouth. I've just scalded mine."

"Tea should be drunk as hot as you can bear it. Have some more milk to cool it down a bit."

Tossing some digestive biscuits to Wellington, the large man continued, "Now I need you to tell me everything that has happened since you arrived in Hobbswood. Spare no details, however unimportant they may seem to you, then together we shall work out a course of action."

"I will do my best, but I was drugged for some of the time. The boundary between dreams and reality is decidedly blurred in my memory."

"Then you must tell be about your dreams, too. They may be significant."

It took Inigo three hours to recount his story, including the bizarre images of his strange dreams, but whenever he mentioned Thomas Messynger, Michael seemed to become particularly attentive and asked detailed questions which Inigo tried his best to answer. While he was talking, Inigo considered leaving out the incident on the beach with Hazel, but when the time came, he found himself unable to dissemble as he looked into Michael's large, azure eyes.

By the time the story had been told, the sun had entered the western sky and the two men were sitting in the shadow of one of the two Scots pines that formed part of the boundary of Michael's property.

Michael got up and moved his chair back into the sun, and as he did so, he muttered to himself, but loud enough for Inigo to hear, "So that's how he did it!"

"Did what?"

Michael replied with a question of his own, "What do you believe is the root cause of your brush with death?"

Inigo had to think for a few moments before answering.

"I suppose it was the result of a few, powerful, perverted minds gaining control of others in an incestuous little society where the counter-influence of the outside world is more or less negligible. The perversion can only be satisfied through bloody and cruel acts, which, in Hobbswood's case, have taken the form of black Masses and satanic rituals. I have to admit that the show Lucas Fairweather put on was impressive. At one time, I really began to believe I was talking to a re-incarnated Sefton Lightwell, Witchfinder of Suffolk, though in the cold light of day, I realise I cannot have been. If I, with all the advantages of living in London and a private school education, found myself falling for Lucas' trickery, what chance do isolated rural villagers have of remaining free from his influence?"

"Very little, I would have thought," agreed Michael. "But tell me more about Lucas. Are you sure he is the source of the evil and not Seth Greenwood?"

"I am now, though he fooled me completely until last night. The odd thing is, Lucas told me he has lived in the village for about five years, but I gained the strong impression that Hobbswood has been rotten far longer than that. Yet I distinctly remember that, at the climax of the black Mass, when Lucas appeared out of the forest dressed up as Sefton Lightwell, Seth Greenwood and the others were surprised not so much by the appearance itself, but by who had appeared. While he was busy grovelling in the dirt, Seth mumbled something about their lord dwelling amongst them without their knowledge."

Michael gave Wellington another biscuit and said, "You do not think there could be more to this than vicious rituals and perverted minds?"

"You mean real Satanism?"

"Possibly."

"Before last night, I might have agreed with you, but not now. I wasted ten years of my life training to be a Jesuit priest, but late in the day I lost my vocation and began to have serious doubts about my faith. That is why I am on holiday, to take a long break and think about things. After last night, I have come round to agreeing with Lucas about one matter at least. There is no God, no Devil and no afterlife. How could any god worth his salt allow one of his own to be subjected to what I went through last night?"

"There are many who have fared a great deal worse and still retained their faith," said Michael.

"Then more fool them."

"You think Thomas More, Chancellor of England, was a fool and others like him? And did you not say you had already lost your faith before this happened? Therefore, strictly speaking, you were no longer one of God's own, as you put it."

"Then forget me for a moment. What of all the good people like Thomas Messynger, who retained their faith to the end but were still given up to the darkness? And what of all the other countless tragedies in the world, like the six million Jews murdered by Hitler and his Nazis? If there is a God, he does not care about us."

Michael shrugged. "It might depend on your view of God."

"Are you a believer then, Michael?"

"Yes, though I do not use the word God, but Creator. My expectation of the Creator is very different to your expectation of God."

"That's just semantics. Whatever your view, you cannot explain why God, or the Creator as you call him, neglects his own creation and allows evil to continue to triumph over good. It's illogical."

"Your God and the Creator are not the same. The Creator is the Lord of our universe. Your God is just one of its creations, as are we all."

"It?"

"Male and female are unusual life forms in our universe, which is why the Creator takes special interest in this world. Elsewhere, life can procreate without the complication of sex."

"You make it sound like the Creator has no control over the development of life."

"It only creates the conditions in which life might form but does not interfere with how this happens. If it did, it would nullify billions of years of evolution."

"But why should he bother with all this?"

"It, not he. I cannot answer that question, but perhaps it is to do with companionship. The Creator cannot do everything. It can certainly create life directly if it wants to, but that would only be a pale reflection of itself. Any form of sentient life has what you call a soul, which is in fact a small part of the Creator, but the way life has evolved here is unusual. The division into male and female creates unpredictability in the procreation of new generations, which is not controlled by the Creator. This results in originality, which, I believe, must be of priceless value to the Creator. Each one of you has a soul that chooses who continues after death and who simply dies with the body. The personality that lives in a way that pleases the Creator will conjoin with the soul and return to it to be a companion forever. The personalities of those who do not, sadly the majority, will die with their bodies. Their souls will return to the Creator unused."

"So there is no Heaven and Hell?"

"Correct, just Heaven and oblivion."

Inigo's mind was ablaze with excitement. This was a faith that seemed to make sense.

"But how can the Creator be sure that, in our world, evil will not overcome good?"

"It can't be sure. You speak of good and evil, which are human terms, but if we speak in terms of the Light and the Dark, it will be easier to explain. History here teaches us that the victories of the Dark tend to be ephemeral, within the long-term ascent of Mankind from the primordial sludge. The Light always returns stronger than before. Democracy is the key, for it allows the Light to flourish. True, it has seen many failures and disappointments since its inception by the ancient Greeks, but it should be judged upon the whole and not on the transient moments of downward cycles.

"It is also the only guarantee we have against self-oblivion in global war, and we should be grateful that it took a firm root in free societies before the advent of weapons of mass destruction. You can count on the fingers of one hand the number of times true democracies have gone to war against each other. It is tyranny and fanaticism we must guard against."

Inigo knew that no amount of scholarly debate would change Michael's views. His personal conviction was immovable, but unlike some of the radicals at the seminary, there was no extremism about him. It was as if his moral certainty was based on some well-hidden deep knowledge rather than blind, unquestioning faith alone. Inigo began to wonder if his own faith was really as dead as he thought, or maybe there was still a faint glow somewhere amongst the dull grey embers. He dared not hope lest he be disappointed again. For him, the only way to progress was to be demolished in intellectual debate by a believer. He had hoped for just such a perverse defeat at the hands of the seminary teachers, but it had not happened. Ultimately, he had been forced to react against the unreasoned conviction he had been taught at school and the seminary, but which all the worldly evidence around him cried out against. Yet could this obscure but immensely impressive country man have the answer? Time would tell.

He stood up and Wellington, sensing the possibility of a walk, struggled up too in typical, ungainly mastiff fashion.

"Where are you going?" asked Michael.

"To Dunwich post office to phone home and then to the police station. All my belongings are still in Lucas' house and I'm not going back there alone. Is the nearest police station at Southwold?"

"Yes."

"Have you got anything I can use as a lead for Wellington? I left that in Lucas' house, too."

Michael went to the garden shed, and after some rummaging about, returned holding a piece of strong nautical rope.

"You should be able to fashion something out of this. I wish I had a car so that I could drive you to Southwold. It's a good two hour walk from here along the coastal path, but I don't even have a driving licence. Never seem to have had the need."

Inigo left, wondering what sort of man could live on his own in the middle of the countryside without a car.

III

Inigo rang his mother from the phone box outside Dunwich post office, but he decided not to worry her about his experiences in Hobbswood. In truth, the decision was not his own because Wellington, who had insisted on squeezing into the phone box with him, broke wind with the full power and fury only a mastiff can muster. Faced with the choice of truncating the conversation or being gassed, Inigo selected the former option and bolted from the confined space as soon as he could decently put the phone down without startling his mother.

The sweet old lady who was waiting patiently outside to use the phone next smiled and said, "It's all right, dear, there was no need to hurry your call because of me."

Just before he reached the bend in the road that would take him out of sight of the phone box, he glanced back sheepishly to where the nice old lady was glaring at him furiously through the window, but there seemed no point in returning to offer an explanation. Meanwhile, the source of the trouble strode on unconcernedly towards the beach.

As Michael had predicted, the walk to Southwold took about two hours. Inigo used the coastal path past Walberswick, crossed the iron footbridge over the River Blyth at Southwold harbour, and walked down Southwold's busy high street towards the police station.

Wellington was in one of his territorial moods and seemed

determined to urinate on every lamp-post and gateway within sniffing distance, but eventually they reached the red brick, single storey police station at the far end of the town a few minutes before four o'clock. He had considered phoning the police from Dunwich and saving himself a journey, but the allegations he intended to make needed to be done in person.

Southwold police station was only manned part time. Constable William Teach, Bill to his friends, was packing away his papers, ready to lock up at four, when a tall, lean, scruffy-looking individual entered, preceded by an enormous dog. Thankfully, the animal was well secured on a sturdy rope lead but even so, the constable was content to be separated from it by the high, wooden counter that divided the reception area in two.

Fervently hoping that the new arrival could be dealt with quickly, the burly, middle-aged policeman asked, "How can I help you, sir?"

"I have a serious complaint to make against some of the residents of Hobbswood village."

Oh Gawd! thought Teach. *So much for a prompt departure,* but always the dutiful professional, he tried to keep the air of resignation out of his voice.

"What sort of complaint, sir?"

"Attempted murder."

The policeman sat up and looked at Inigo appraisingly. Although scruffy, the newcomer did not strike him as the sort who would bring such a serious charge spuriously.

"You'd better come into the office, sir. That dog, is it safe?"

Inigo pushed the memory of last night's snarling beast of death to the back of his mind and answered, "I know he looks formidable, but he wouldn't hurt a fly."

"Then you can bring him through with you. Great Dane, is

136

he?"

"No, an Old English mastiff, the world's largest and oldest breed. The mastiffs are recorded as going back at least as far as the ancient Babylonians."

"The Baby-who?"

"At least as far back as two thousand BC in the Middle East."

"Well, I've never seen one before. I don't suppose you get many burglars around your house."

After providing the required identification details, Inigo recounted the story of what had happened in Hobbswood for the second time that day, but this time he kept the account strictly down to earth. Descriptions of dreams and hallucinations were unlikely to impress the Suffolk constabulary, and apart from his severed finger, there was no tangible proof of a breach in the law.

When he finished, he noticed the constable looking sceptically at his injured left hand.

"Looks like an old wound to me, sir; it's healed perfectly. If that happened last night, don't you think it would still be scabbed up?"

"Well… er… yes, but Mr Shapmire treated it with some medical technique he discovered when he lived in the tropics and healed it almost instantaneously."

The policeman raised an eyebrow. "Really?"

Got a right one here after all, he thought. His first impressions were usually reliable, but they seemed to have failed him this time. He decided the strange interview should be terminated.

"Now, I don't know what your game is, Mr Boscabel, but I should warn you that wasting police time is a criminal offence. You'd best be on your way."

"But I'm only telling you the facts," objected Inigo.

"Never mind all that. Now I'll tell you a few facts. I've been based at Southwold for more than twenty years, and in all that time, there's never been any trouble in Hobbswood. Suddenly, a complete stranger arrives telling stories of black magic and witches, but the only evidence he brings is a wound which is at least six months old. Doctor Fairweather is a well-known and respected member of local society, he even delivered both of my grandchildren. Do you really expect me to believe he's some sort of grand wizard just on your say so? I think you begin to take my point Mr Boscabel."

Inigo shrugged. "I suppose so."

"Very well then. I suggest you leave here before I change my mind about charging you with wasting police time."

Inigo knew there was no point in arguing any more, but he was not prepared to abandon his personal effects at Lucas' house.

He tried to sound suitably apologetic, "I am sorry about what I said, Officer, I expect I must have imagined it all."

Teach frowned at the thinly veiled sarcasm, but Inigo carried on undaunted, "But I really am nervous about returning to Hobbswood on my own. All my personal belongings are still in Doctor Fairweather's house. Would you please come with me to collect them? I promise I shall cause no further trouble."

Constable Teach was on the verge of sending Inigo away with a flea in his ear, but a lifetime in the force had helped him to develop a nose for troublemakers. The young man sitting opposite him did not fall into that category; he was genuinely frightened.

Teach looked at Wellington and said wryly, "All right then, but I've only got a Ford Escort."

Twenty minutes later, Teach turned off the Leiston road and

headed down the track that led to Hobbswood. Beside him, Inigo fidgeted nervously while Wellington, who filled up the rest of the car, rested a friendly black muzzle on the policeman's uniformed shoulder. They passed Michael's house on their right and drove slowly down the hill towards the village. The potholes seemed to become craters as the extra weight in the back of the car magnified the bumps in the track and Teach fretted for his suspension every time they plunged into the next rut. But the reliable Ford did not fail them and soon they stopped outside Lucas' house, none the worse for their journey.

Inigo felt strange. It was only a day since he had been here, yet it seemed far longer than that. There was no one about, but as he stepped out of the car, he could sense hostile eyes watching him. Wellington, too, was unsettled. He growled quietly in the back of the car as he watched his master and the policeman walk towards the doctor's house. Unlike Inigo, the mastiff had always known who the enemy was.

The constable knocked at the front door and while they waited for a response, Inigo looked back at the village. How calm and peaceful it seemed! No wonder his story was difficult to believe. A sudden movement from an upstairs window caught his eye, but the sun was shining directly on the window pane, so the reflection made it difficult to see who or what it was. Inigo recalled Lucas saying that the house actually belonged to Ivy, he was just a long-term tenant, and then, with a twinge of conscience, he realised he had given little thought to Hazel's fate. Although she had not been at the black Mass, she could not hide forever.

Because of her inexperience of the outside world, she would inevitably return to her mother, who had also been absent from the ritual. Both of them would be in danger after last night's fiasco. There was no point in voicing his concern to the constable. Teach's patience had already been stretched to the limit, but Inigo could not just forget the girl who had risked so much for his sake.

Lucas himself answered the door.

"Inigo! Thank God you're all right! I thought you might have damaged your ankle again. We've been looking for you everywhere."

Inigo wanted to say, 'I bet you have', but he did not want to alienate Teach, so he just said, "Have you?"

"Yes, the entire village has been out searching for you most of the night. Constable Teach, how good to see you, and thank you for bringing our lost sheep back home. Would you care for a cup of coffee?"

"No, thank you, Doctor, and Mr Boscabel will not be staying. I regret that I am here in an official capacity."

Lucas' eyes widened in apparent surprise. "Really. In that case, how may I be of service, Constable?"

Teach spoke in a strictly neutral tone as he explained, "Mr Boscabel has launched an official complaint against you and some others in the village."

"Has he indeed?" replied Lucas. "What sort of complaint?"

"A serious physical assault, sir, which took place in the forest near here last night. Though I should add that, after some discussion, the complaint has been withdrawn, but I thought I should mention it in case you wish to comment."

Lucas looked perplexed. "I am very pleased you mentioned it, Constable, but you have the advantage of me. I really don't know what Inigo means, but surely there must be some mistake. He's being staying here as my guest for the last few days, and excellent company he is, too. If I have offended him in some way,

140

then it was unintentional, and I apologise unreservedly."

Lucas was so overwhelmingly charming that Inigo decided his only possible response was to accept the inevitable before he was made to look even more foolish.

"It seems that it is I who should apologise to you, Doctor Fairweather. I'll just collect my things and go."

"It could be side effects from those pain killers I gave you for your ankle," suggested Lucas helpfully. "They can cause spectacular hallucinations, especially when combined with alcohol. Inigo, you are more than welcome to stay here until your ankle is fully recovered. I am sure no malice was intended."

Lucas was so convincing that Inigo fleetingly wondered if he could really have been hallucinating, but a quick look at his finger stump removed any doubt.

"My ankle is well recovered now, so it will be best if I continue my journey."

"Very well then," acknowledged Lucas. "Your things are upstairs where you left them."

It did not take Inigo long to gather his few belongings, and soon he and Constable Teach were walking back to the car, accompanied by Lucas.

"Inigo, you are more than welcome to stay here for a few more days. Your ankle could do with a while longer to recover fully, even though it feels all right now."

Laying on the hospitality a bit thick, aren't you, thought Inigo, as he replied quietly but firmly, "No, thank you, Doctor."

He was about to open the car door when something landed in the dust beside his feet. He spun round just in time to see a fanlight window closing on the upper floor of Ivy's cottage. Looking down, he saw a piece of paper wrapped round a stone close to his left foot. He bent down quickly, picked it up, and slipped it into his pocket.

"What was that?" asked Lucas, who had not come too near the car when he saw the large, growling occupant in the back seat.

The jolly tone in his voice was gone.

Avoiding eye contact, Inigo, who was a hopeless liar, replied, "I just dropped something; it's nothing."

He quickly slid into the passenger seat of Teach's car and stared at his feet as the constable turned the car round, but as soon as they reached the edge of the village, he looked back. Lucas was still standing outside the front garden, the mask of friendship shorn away from his face. His baleful expression chilled Inigo to the marrow.

When they reached Michael's cottage, Inigo said, "Just drop me off here please, Constable. I'm staying with Mr Shapmire until tomorrow."

The car seemed to grow six inches taller when Wellington got out, but before closing the door, Inigo tried to make his peace with Teach.

"Thank you for coming with me. I'm very sorry to have been such a nuisance. You won't see me again."

Constable Teach drove home slowly. He was troubled. Something deep inside him was saying all was not well. He might not be Assistant Commissioner material, but he was no fool. Inigo had believed in his allegations, Teach's experience told him that much, and while Doctor Fairweather's lips had smiled, his eyes had not. As for it all being a hallucination caused by pain-killing drugs, Teach was surprised that the doctor should offer such a lame explanation. He would write a full report tomorrow. It was too soon to close the book on this one, he decided.

Chapter Seven

"I thought you might get that reaction," said Michael. "The police must have their evidence."

Inigo gloomily watched Teach's car disappear round the bend towards the Leiston road and sighed, "I suppose so, but I had to try. It angers me to think that Lucas and his murderous gang will get away with their mischief."

Michael shut the front door behind them and went into the kitchen from where he said, "I expect you must be hungry. I'm not much of a cook, so feel free to use the kitchen as your own. Now let me see."

Inigo heard a couple of cupboard doors open and shut.

"There's a Fray Bentos steak and kidney pie, a few potatoes, some French beans, and plenty of eggs," called out his host. "I expect you can do something with those ingredients, but first I'll put the kettle on."

Apart from breakfast, Inigo had not eaten a proper meal for two days; he was ravenous. He could not be bothered to prepare vegetables and just put the steak and kidney pie in the oven before going out to join Michael in the back garden for yet another cup of tea.

Michael asked, "What sort of reception did you get in the village? Was Lucas there?"

"Lucas was positively charming. He made me look like an ungrateful troublemaker in front of the constable, while at the same time being sympathetic and forgiving to me as if I'd suffered a bout of mental illness. I was utterly humiliated. That reminds me," Inigo fumbled in his pocket and produced the paper wrapped stone. "Someone threw this to me from a window as I was leaving, but I didn't get chance to see who it was."

He unfolded the creased paper, looked at the irregular, child-like writing, and read aloud:

Dear Inigo, terrible things are gooin to hapen here, the docter he is real mad, he say he means to kill me tonite, help me if you can pleese;

Hazel

The two men looked at each other in horrified silence. It was Inigo who spoke first as he handed Michael the note.

"Well, it seems it's not over yet. I had better get back to Southwold quickly and report this to the police. We cannot let this happen."

"Of course we can't, but that piece of paper is unlikely to persuade the constable to come out here again today. Did he see how you came by it?"

"No."

"Then in view of his attitude to your story, he will think this is just another prank and arrest you for wasting more of his valuable time. The script could have been written by a ten-year-old."

"Then what do you suggest?"

Michael's eyes became distant, as if he was reflecting deeply. A few moments later, he sighed, stood up, and looked hard in the direction of the village. His view was blocked by the forest, but to Inigo, the large, black-clad man seemed like a huge beast of prey sensing rather than seeing the presence of its enemy.

At last, Michael sat down again and answered Inigo's question, "Direct action. Hazel must be rescued this evening, as soon as it gets dark."

"But she says Lucas will kill her tonight."

"I understand that, Inigo, but I do not believe he will make his move before the last of the daylight has gone. At this time of year, that will be ten o'clock, which means, allowing time for some morbid little ritual where his followers will be permitted to indulge their frustrated lust upon her, Hazel will be alive at least until midnight. You will need to set out at dusk and complete the rescue by quarter to ten."

Inigo's stomach churned. His ravenous appetite disappeared.

"Me? You mean you won't be coming too."

"I regret I cannot come with you. It is difficult for me to explain. It is clear that the only way to save Hazel is through stealth. We cannot go in there like the Grenadier Guards, just the two of us against Lucas and the entire village."

"Of course not, but if there are two of us, then the odds will be halved."

"Inigo, if I accompany you, we will lose the element of surprise because Lucas will sense my presence."

"How exactly?"

"In the same way I sensed you meditating the other night. It is possible, with sufficient training, to be aware of the proximity of certain people without the use of the traditional five senses. I am not talking about mind reading or paranormal phenomena, just an awareness of a strong entity. Lucas has that ability."

"More so than you?"

"Perhaps. He has lived in Hobbswood for more than five years, but I never discovered the truth about him. Somehow, he has been able to cloak his presence from me all that time. It was quite a shock and must have taken great skill. It was not until last night, when he finally revealed himself to his followers, that I belatedly discovered who he is."

Sensing the terror of the previous night closing in on him again, Inigo asked, "Then if Lucas is not who he claims to be, who is he?"

"All in good time, Inigo. Last night, our meeting in the forest was no co-incidence. I was coming to rescue you, but had it not been for your brave dog, I would have been too late again."

"Again? I don't understand. Who or what are you, Michael? Why are you here? Who sent you?"

"I understand you must be curious, Inigo, so I will answer your questions as far as I can. It would not be right to send you into danger without some knowledge of the forces ranged against you, but some things will have to remain unanswered for the present."

A smell of burning came from the cottage. Michael leaped up and ran to the kitchen, only to return to the garden holding a small, round, blackened object.

"I'm afraid this sorry looking mess is all that remains of your pie. I'll see if I can find you something else."

"Don't bother, Michael, I couldn't have eaten it now anyway, but Wellington will when it's cooled down a bit. I'll make myself some sandwiches later."

"I'll see to your sandwiches. You go and prepare yourself for tonight. You'll find some black trousers and a sweater in my wardrobe. You can cut the bottom few inches off the trouser legs and then I'll blacken your face. But before you go, I'll tell you more about Hobbswood and me."

146

II

It was nearly nine o'clock. The sun was low in the sky. Inigo sat in Michael's kitchen, trying to force some cheese sandwiches down his unwilling throat. His host sat opposite him, drinking the inevitable scorching cup of tea. Outside, the sharp bark of a dog fox cut through the hush of the early evening, but no sooner had the echo died away, the forest resumed its heavy, oppressive silence, which seemed to presage a night of terror and final decision, the calm before the storm.

Michael watched Inigo struggling to eat his food.

"Would you care for some tea? I can offer you something stronger, if you prefer."

"I could manage a large brandy," said Inigo, "but I'd better not. I need to keep my wits about me tonight."

"True enough," agreed Michael. "But before you go, I shall tell you something about me."

"And not before time," said Inigo, who was still not convinced about the need to go alone on this mission.

Michael acknowledged the criticism with a graceful nod and began, "The established churches are not the only religious organisations in this world. There are others who choose to carry out their duties in a less ostentatious and usually more effective manner."

"The Freemasons?"

"No, Inigo, I did not mean them, worthy though they are. The group I belong to is less numerous, more secret, and far more ancient than the masons. We have been in existence for," Michael paused, trying to select the right words. "Well, for a very long time, and our purpose has always been to oppose the threat posed by men like Lucas Fairweather."

"You believe in God, and Lucas in Satan?" asked Inigo.

"Not in the sense you mean. It is much less personal, more a case of the Light and the Dark."

"Is there no God, no Devil, then?"

Michael shrugged as if the answer was obvious, "They are one and the same."

Years of Jesuit teaching, instilled from the age of seven, fought in Inigo's mind against Michael's stark statement. How could all that was good and wholesome be contained within the same entity as absolute evil? Surely even atheism was preferable to such a paradox of faith?

Sensing Inigo's struggle, Michael tried to help him.

"I can only tell you what I believe to be true. You must judge what I say for yourself, but you may not know that there are many more gospels recounting the life of Jesus Christ than the four you were brought up to believe in. They throw a different light on Jesus' mission."

"What gospels are these, and what happened to them?"

"There are the gospels of doubting Thomas, Phillip, Mary Magdalene, and yes, even Judas, amongst others. They were suppressed during the reign of Constantine the Great, the first Roman emperor to adopt Christianity as the official religion of the empire. At the time, there were all sorts of versions, variations, and understandings of Christ's message competing with each other. Being a military man, this was too abstruse for the emperor. So, he called the Council of Nicaea, locked up the bishops, and threatened to throw away the key unless they came up with an official version of Christ's teachings that could be taught to all present and future Christians as one clear doctrine. Hence the Nicean creed, which all Catholics follow, and the four official gospels of Matthew, Mark, Luke, and John. All other versions of Christianity would be deemed as heretical and dire punishments would await any who continued to teach them. But with their suppression, much of the value in Christ's teachings was lost."

"I assume you are referring to the Gnostic gospels, but I've never seen any of them."

"Well, what I am about to tell you draws heavily upon the Gnostic gospels."

Michael took a gulp of his tea and continued, "We all exist in the consciousness of a supreme intellect, not the Judaeo-Christian God you talk about, but the Creator. I believe that our entire universe is this supreme intellect. One single, mighty consciousness. If I am right, then your Catholic catechism, which proclaims God exists everywhere is, apart from the name, correct. We are but miniscule, constituent parts of the Creator, tiny microcosms of the supreme intellect. Now, within this universal consciousness there exists Light and Dark, or, if you prefer to speak in human terms, Good and Evil, just as there is good and evil in all of us. It helps our limited understanding if we personalise these opposing forces as God or Allah, Lucifer or Satan, or any of the thousands of other names invoked to describe them throughout human history, but they are all contained within the single, universal entity."

Inigo shifted uneasily, "But from what you say, there is no certainty that Light will ultimately triumph over Dark. There are good and bad people on this earth. So, if we are but microcosms of the universal entity, how can we be sure the Dark will not eventually overcome the Light? Within each person, there are opposing forces pushing us towards good and evil, but because we have free will, we all have the final sanction as to which route we will take. If these forces are equally matched, as they tend to be in us, then the future of creation is just a lottery."

Michael shook his head, "Not quite. The Light has advantages over the Dark. To speak metaphorically, the opposing warriors may be similar in strength, but the weapons wielded by the Light are more powerful. The trinity of Light, the weapons it uses to combat the Dark, are love, knowledge, and order. The weapons of the Dark, are hate, ignorance, and chaos. Love is stronger than hate because it is unselfish and is prepared to sacrifice itself if called upon to do so. Knowledge can grow out of ignorance and in that way defeat it, but ignorance can never be spawned from knowledge and must therefore ultimately give ground. The ascent of Mankind is a good example. Finally, order structures the other two weapons of Light to maximum efficiency, chaos cannot do that. Just compare the crystalline strength of a diamond to coal or graphite, both of which are made of the same material as a diamond, namely carbon, but are less well structured."

Inigo rubbed his chin thoughtfully, creating a white streak on his soot blackened face, and asked, "But how exactly do we fit in to all this? What is our purpose?"

Michael put down his mug of tea and leaned forwards, his bright blue eyes looking directly into Inigo's.

"That, my friend, is the ultimate question. I do not have all the answers, but we must aspire to be companions of the Creator. It has given us souls to make this possible, so if we are small reflections of the Creator, but in the case of the human race, with the added quality of originality as I previously said, then we should support what the Creator wants. The victory of Light over Dark. That is how you will be chosen to go to the Creator when your body expires, or not as the case may be. If it was any other way, discord would enter the natural harmony of life, evolution and progress would have no meaning, and we would inexorably slip back into primeval chaos."

"Michael, I think I understand. The ascent of Mankind is a purpose in itself."

"That is a good way of putting it. And look how far we have come. Remember our conversation this morning, when we talked of the erratic but inexorable advance of democracy. If we can advance that far in just two and a half thousand years, then think how far we might go in another two thousand!"

"Yes, but I still find it difficult to think of the Creator as an 'It'."

"I agree 'It' sounds impersonal, especially in the English language, but if you must personalise the concept, then 'she' has as much value as 'he', perhaps more. The old religions always thought of creation as being female; the mother goddess, nature, and so on. But outside of this world, the concept of male and female sounds equally odd."

Inigo's mind began to return to the dangerous task that lay ahead.

"Michael, you speak with the confidence of one who knows rather than believes. I would like to feel as confident as that before I leave this cottage tonight. Have you any facts or evidence to support what you say?"

"I cannot give you hard facts any more than the teachers at your seminary could. I can only give you logic which makes sense of the world around us. It is, nonetheless, the creed of my Order."

"What is your secret Order?"

"If I told you, it would no longer be secret."

"All right then," said Inigo, irritated by his companion's reticence. "What has all this got to do with Hobbswood, and if I'm going to put my life at risk again tonight, me?"

"Now that is a matter I can be more explicit about. Three hundred and thirty-seven years ago, a terrible event occurred here. You have already discovered something about Thomas Messynger, have you not?"

Inigo nodded and Michael took a deep breath. What he was about to say troubled him deeply.

"Hobbswood had already turned away from the Light before Thomas arrived, but he was a determined young man just back from Cromwell's wars, full of the light of Christ and well-provided with moral fibre, as you are. He quickly sensed the evil in the village, but his teaching and personal example soon began to penetrate some of the darkened souls that lived there. If things had been allowed to follow their natural course, Thomas' mission would have been crowned with success, but unfortunately, an outside influence arrived which tilted the balance away from the Light again."

"Sefton Lightwell."

"Exactly so. Lightwell was of the dark Order that opposes mine. He came to Hobbswood, concealing his true identity."

"He came as a witchfinder."

Michael nodded. "You have already seen much, Inigo."

"I saw part of Thomas' trial, remember. Or maybe I just dreamed it. But whatever it was, I saw a gross injustice."

"What you think you saw really did happen and it should not have been allowed to take place, but Lightwell's disguise was so effective that he was able to murder Thomas before we realised what was happening. As a consequence, the Dark gained a foothold here which my Order has been unable to weaken. The best we can do is to contain it in this small corner of Suffolk and prevent it from spreading. Ever since poor Thomas' death, we have kept a guardian here."

"So that's why the villagers hate you so much, but what would have happened if they had managed to kill me last night?"

"Then I would have failed as the Guardian of Hobbswood, and I very nearly did because of Lucas Fairweather's skill in fooling me. The sacrifice of Inigo Boscabel would have been the catalyst the Dark needed to break free of the stranglehold my Order has had on it for more than three centuries."

"But what if I fail tonight and Hazel dies?"

"That will not be the same. The release of the blood of a male virgin is full of significance, though why the followers of the Dark feel it must take place on the solstice baffles me.

Remember, Inigo, the eating and drinking of the flesh and blood of a male virgin has not always been confined to the followers of the Dark. Most primitive religions believe in something of the sort, and even Jesus Christ said, 'he who eats of my body and drinks of my blood shall have eternal life'. And at the Last Supper, that is exactly what happened."

"But he used bread and wine as substitutes," objected Inigo.

"Did he? Are you sure? I know your Bible would have us believe it so. Certainly, Christianity, to its credit, quickly dispensed with real sacrifices and replaced them with the esoterically bland concept of Transubstantiation, as you Catholics call the supposed changing of bread and wine into the body and blood of Christ. But it is only a pretence that avoids the unpleasantness of a true sacrifice."

"A few days ago, I would have fiercely argued that point

with you," sighed Inigo wistfully. "But now I don't know what to believe any more."

"The power, real or imagined," continued Michael, "that accrues to the person who consumes the flesh and blood of a male virgin has been acknowledged by most societies since the dawn of Mankind. Indirectly, Catholics like you acknowledge this too, although they can never participate fully because their sacrifice is restricted to their Christ. Therefore, there is no point in eating anyone else."

"You make it sound like the menu at a Berni Inn!" smiled Inigo irreverently.

"True," laughed Michael. "After all, we can't have people going around eating each other in this day and age. But..." he became serious again. "The point is that sacrifices strengthen faith, for better or for worse, and as a consequence, the power of prayer amongst the faithful."

"Is that so very important?" wondered Inigo aloud.

"It is of capital importance! Prayer is integral to the conflict between the Light and the Dark. It is the fundamental source of power both sides draw upon."

Inigo finally gave up on his sandwiches and pushed his plate to one side.

"So that must be why Jesus Christ placed so much emphasis on prayer, especially communal prayer. He encouraged his followers to pray together as much as possible."

Michael said, "Christ was a messenger from the Creator, not the Judaeo-Christian God who set himself up to replace the Creator. Communal prayer and meditation are critical factors in the eternal struggle, the very sustenance of the opposing forces. Imagine the setback we suffered in England when King Henry VIII dissolved the monasteries in 1536, those sacred bastions of concentrated communal prayer and deep meditation. Certainly, some of them were corrupt, though only a few, but the few gave an avaricious and near bankrupt king the excuse he needed to destroy their society and steal their property. The dissolution of the monasteries was a mighty blow, which set back the cause of the Light for centuries. The aftermath was a prolonged period of weakness for my Order, during which England suffered civil war, religious fanaticism, and social strife. It need not have been so."

"And Thomas Messynger was killed," murmured Inigo.

Michael stared hard at the kitchen floor and said quietly, "It was during our weakness that the Dark first gained its foothold in Hobbswood, and brave Thomas was left to his fate unaided. I should not say so, but I want revenge for his murder."

"But it can't have been your fault, Michael. You speak as if you were there at the time."

Michael did not answer. His large, blue eyes became sad, but after a few moments, he seemed to recover himself and returned to more immediate matters.

Glancing at the clock on the kitchen wall, he said, "It's time you were on your way, Inigo. The sun is setting."

The fear, which had once again been forgotten for a while, now suddenly returned like an icy claw gripping Inigo's stomach. When he tried to stand up, his legs felt leaden, and his skin was clammy with cold sweat. Both men went through to the living room, where Michael scooped up some more soot from the chimney onto his gloved hand and re-blackened the white streak on Inigo's chin.

"The moon is already up, so at least you'll be able to see, but remember to keep to the shadows."

"I will, Michael. Tell me, do you ever take your gloves off?"

"Yes, but not here if I can help it."

"But it's boiling hot in here!"

"I do not find it so. What of Wellington? Will you take him with you?"

Inigo looked fondly at the sleeping mastiff, whose tail wagged occasionally at some pleasant experience taking place in his doggy dream.

"He's too precious to risk on this venture, and although he has many fine qualities, guile is not one of them; he'll make far too much noise. Before I leave, I'll write down the contact details of my parents in London, so if the worst happens to me, you can contact them, and they will come and collect him."

Soon Inigo, looking like the Ace of Spades, was walking down the moonlit track accompanied by Michael. They had walked about two hundred yards when the big man suddenly stopped as if he had reached an invisible barrier. Inigo looked round but could see nothing in particular to cause this sudden change.

Michael whispered, "This is as far as I go. Beyond here, my power wanes, but even so, if you get into trouble I shall know, and rest assured, I will come to help you whatever the odds may be. Good luck."

This was just the reassurance that Inigo needed. The two men shook hands, and without another word, he set off alone down the track towards Hobbswood.

III

As he trudged down the track, Inigo found himself wondering in disbelief at what he was doing. Five short days earlier, he had been walking his dog in the peaceful Suffolk countryside, considering the future course of his life. What had seemed major problems to him then now paled into utter insignificance. He could still hardly believe the events that had so radically altered his world in such a short time. He felt like pinching himself in case it was all just a bad dream from which he would soon awaken in the safety of his bed in Regents Park. Worse still, having escaped a bloody death by seconds the night before, he was now voluntarily walking into life threatening danger again, like a demented lemming. He must be mad! But he knew he must do this in order to save Hazel or lose his self-respect forever.

Certainly, if he did nothing, he would never be able to look Michael in the face again. But even now, he had no idea if his courage would fail him when it mattered most. Strangely, this was a comforting thought for it meant that he could turn back at any time, having, in his own mind at least, made an effort to do the right thing. Without the knowledge that he could turn back if things looked too dangerous, he would never have set out in the first place.

As he listened to his shoes crunching rather too loudly on the loose gravel surface of the track, he carefully went over the plan he had formulated to rescue Hazel. He would avoid the obvious route leading directly into the village and use the beach path instead, which ought to bring him close to the back of Ivy's cottage, and attempt the rescue from there. But he soon discovered that planning and implementation were two entirely different matters.

It took only a few minutes to reach the place where the beach path left the main track, but before turning off, Inigo paused to look at the village, which lay two hundred yards directly ahead. Lights twinkling in the windows and moonlight reflecting from the glazed pantiles on the cottage roofs gave Hobbswood a dreamy, picture-postcard appearance that belied the seething evil within. Mortal danger lay ahead, and as he began to follow the beach path, Inigo wondered what his colleagues at the seminary would have thought if they could see him now; Fishy Boscabel playing the hero! *Heroes have an uncomfortable habit of getting killed,* thought Inigo ruefully.

After fifty yards or so, Inigo left the path and struck off into the undergrowth on his right. He immediately encountered problems because the gorse grew so thick that he was forced to abandon any hope of following a straight course towards Ivy's house. He soon realised he was being edged away from the village and towards the sea cliffs, which were somewhere to his left. The sound of waves gently lapping against the shore warned him he must not drift any further in that direction. Every now and again, he was able to push back towards the village when irregular gaps in the gorse barrier opened up. But these only led to a prickly dead end a few paces later. To make matters worse, he seemed to be making more noise than a busload of drunken rugby players. He looked at the luminous hands on his watch; almost ten o'clock. He was falling behind schedule.

Determination and incipient panic enabled Inigo to force his way back to the village, but by then his clothes were almost ripped to shreds and he was bleeding from scores of scratches inflicted by the unyielding gorse bushes. He quietly crossed the track where Lucas' car was parked and crept behind Ivy's house, knowing that the doctor might look out of his upstairs window at any time. He slithered over the gate that led to the back of the house and rested for a moment beside the broken chestnut fence post that had held Wellington the night before until the mastiff heard his master's cry of distress. Another half hour had passed; he felt as if he had just run a marathon.

The curtains of the house were still drawn back, so Inigo could see Hazel sitting in her downstairs bedroom strapped to a chair. She seemed to be asleep. In the next room, two men were sitting playing cards like gaolers guarding a condemned prisoner. One of them had his back to the window, but Inigo recognised the powerful frame of the other. It was Ambrose Samphyre. There was no sign of Hazel's mother or Lucas.

Stepping clumsily over a fence, Inigo crushed six or seven prime onions before falling in an ungainly heap in the vegetable patch. He lay still for a few seconds, but despite the disturbance, his presence remained undetected. A tall line of runner beans enabled him to move up under cover to within five paces of the back wall of the house, but a stretch of open lawn separated him from Hazel's window. He would have to crawl the rest of the way in full sight of Ambrose, but he told himself, there was no cause for the farm foreman to look up from his cards and out of the window.

His body was cold with fear as he slowly eased himself out from the cover of the runner beans and began to crawl across the open grass, brushing the ground ahead with his fingertips to ensure there were no booby traps waiting for him. After a minute and a half, which seemed like an hour, he reached the cover of the house wall that separated Hazel's window from her gaolers' and took a short rest before beginning the most dangerous part of his mission. *Now,* he thought, *is the time to turn back if I'm going to.* But having come this far, he found just enough courage to keep going.

When he tapped softly at Hazel's window, the time was a few minutes before eleven. He should have been well on the way back to Michael's house by now. Lucas must surely be coming to collect Hazel at any moment for whatever perverted ritual he had in mind for her and would have every chance of discovering Inigo in mid-rescue. What a bonus that would be for him! Inigo's difficulties were compounded when Hazel failed to respond to his signal. He tapped again, more loudly this time, but a noise from the room next door warned him to take care. Probably Hazel was drugged like he had been, in which case no amount of window tapping would waken her. She was clad in the same tight, flower-printed dress she had worn when he first saw her serving dinner on the evening of his unplanned arrival in the village. Her skirt had ridden up, revealing shapely, sun-tanned thighs, and Inigo was startled to find that, despite his perilous situation, he still hungered for her. Perhaps fear could enhance all the senses, even lust, and now any remaining prudent thoughts of turning back vanished.

He looked along the concrete path that led to the back door of the house for an implement to jemmy open the window, but there was nothing obvious to hand. Then, glinting in the moonlight, he saw an old cement trowel laying close to the water butt beside the back door. That would do. It would be no use as a jemmy, but he should be able to push it between the sash windows and slip the catch locking the top window to the bottom.

Carefully, Inigo slid the point of the trowel into the slit

between the windows and moved it towards the catch. The windows had been open for most of that hot summer, so the catch moved easily. He began to smell success and smiled to himself. If all else failed, he could always try burglary for a profession. The window squealed on its runners as he raised the lower half, but he was committed now. It was do-or-die — literally. Still Hazel remained motionless; she was almost certainly drugged but hopefully not so deeply as to prevent him waking her. She was not heavy, but he could never carry her half a mile uphill back to Michael's cottage unaided. He took a last look at the stars hanging like bright lamps in the sky. A gentle breeze touched his cheek with the softness of a velvet-gloved hand. Then he swallowed, took a deep breath, and climbed over the window sill into the house.

It was a strange sensation. He had never been in a woman's bedroom before, except for his mother's — which did not really count. His dirty, size ten trainers seemed incongruous and out of place beside the dainty shoes neatly placed in a line below the window. A large teddy bear stared expressionlessly at him from the pink quilt that covered the bed, and on the far wall he could see his own reflection in a full-length mirror. He hardly recognised himself. White lines of tension had worn through his blackened face, mingling with blood red scratches caused by the gorse. His eyes were unnaturally bright, reflecting his fear sharpened senses, and he wondered if this was how his grandfather had looked in the Great War just before going over the top. He looked at Hazel again. The feminine scents of perfume and powder brought home to him that he had entered her inner sanctuary. Only a lover could get closer.

He tiptoed across the bedroom towards Hazel, leaving footprints of topsoil on the pale grey carpet, and whispered in her ear, "Hazel, wake up, we must get out of here."

Hazel began to murmur, and Inigo was forced to place his hand across her mouth to muffle the noise. But this only served to startle her, and she lashed out with her foot, knocking over a jar of cream on the dressing table. She opened her eyes, but as recognition began to dawn, the sound of a scraping chair in the adjacent room warned of danger. The falling jar had alerted the gaolers. Inigo quickly wriggled under Hazel's bed, but as he heard someone enter her bedroom, his heart froze; his messy footprints led directly from the open window to his hiding place.

Surely, he must be discovered now.

"What was that noise?"

Inigo recognised the voice as Ambrose Samphyre's.

"I knocked something over on the dressing table when I woke up," answered Hazel sleepily.

"You shouldn't have woken up at all after what the doctor gave you. Still, there's not long to go now, so you might as well stay awake I suppose."

He casually put his hand up her skirt as if he did it every day of the week and sighed. "What a shameful waste. Still, you brought it upon yourself."

He lingered for a moment, then slowly removed his hand and turned to go. As Inigo watched the booted feet walk towards the door, he began to hope he had escaped discovery, but suddenly the feet stopped.

"What's this? How did you manage to open the window? I checked it only an hour ago."

There was a brief pause as he digested the significance of the footprints. Then his voice turned more threatening.

"Or have you had help from someone else? Is that it, my beauty?"

He strode across the room to the window.

Inigo had no time to think. He quickly rolled out from under the bed and stood up behind Ambrose, who had his head outside the window, scanning for the intruder. Summoning up all his strength, he slammed the window hard down onto the broad, muscular neck, briefly stunning the country man. The noise quickly brought the other gaoler running into the bedroom, but Inigo had already slipped behind the door with a large flower vase at the ready. He smashed it over the second man's head, instantly felling him, but already Ambrose was beginning to stir.

"Are you all right?" whispered Inigo as he started to fumble with the knots that bound Hazel's wrists to the chair.

She nodded, but the knots had been tied tightly and he could feel panic welling up inside him as valuable seconds were wasted.

"I'm going to the kitchen to get a knife," he said. "I'll be back in a few seconds."

Hazel was now fully awake and sensed Inigo's panic.

"Hurry, he's waking up!"

He returned carrying a carving knife, which made short work of Hazel's bonds, but by then Ambrose had recovered and was struggling to dislodge the window from the back of his neck, which Inigo had slammed down on him. Hazel threw herself into Inigo's arms.

"You came for me! I just knew you would!"

He managed to disentangle himself from her fervent caresses and warned, "We're not safe yet. Just follow me and run like the wind."

He slipped the knife into his belt, then lifted the window and smashed it down on Ambrose a second time to give them a few precious extra seconds. Then, grabbing Hazel's hand, he ran to the front door, unlocked it and ran out to the gravelled street just as an angry roar announced that Ambrose had regained full control of his faculties again. At the house next door, the front door opened and Seth Greenwood bellowed, "You cannot escape!"

"Piss off!" shouted Inigo as he ran up the street towards the forest, hauling Hazel behind him. But when he looked at her feet, she was only wearing carpet slippers. He thought, *You may well be right, Seth Greenwood, but you'll have to catch us first.*

Mad thoughts careered through his mind as they ran between the cottages lining both sides of the street. Would he be able to use the carving knife on another human being if he had to? What the hell was he doing here, anyway? If he had to make a last stand, would Michael come and help as he had promised?

As they put more distance between themselves and Lucas' dwelling, he noticed that the all-pervading dead rat smell afflicting Hobbswood began to get fainter. Lights were being switched on in all the cottages, but as yet no one stood between them and escape. But by the time they reached the edge of the village, he knew they would be caught as he heard the sound of pursuit gaining rapidly upon them. He looked round and saw Ambrose and Seth only thirty paces behind. Hazel could go no faster, but he could not abandon her. In a fight, she would be of little use against such powerful men as Ambrose and Seth. Soon the fugitives reached the junction of the road and the beach path where, less than an hour before, Inigo had paused to look at Hobbswood in the moonlight. He determined to make a stand here.

"Hazel," he gasped. "Run on to Shapmire's house and stop for nothing. Michael's a good man and he'll protect you."

There was no time for good-byes. Hazel put her head down

and ran as fast as she could while Inigo stopped and turned to face his enemies.

Ambrose and Seth also stopped about ten paces from Inigo. They briefly conferred, then Ambrose approached Inigo, ready to grapple, while Seth moved aside to bypass the fight and hunt down Hazel. In a desperate attempt to buy more time for her, Inigo moved to his right and rugby tackled Seth round the legs, momentarily stunning the tall villager. But the respite was short lived because Inigo had barely got to his feet again when the large-fisted Ambrose was upon him.

Suddenly, bright car headlights were switched on from somewhere behind Ingo's left shoulder, stopping the vicious little battle in its tracks like an illuminated frozen tableau.

"What's going on here, then?"

It was Constable Teach.

Chapter Eight

"Get out of the way, Constable, or it will be the worse for you," growled Ambrose, but Teach was unmoved by the threat.

The sense of unease he had felt after dropping Inigo off at Shapmire's house in the afternoon had not left him. Far from forgetting about it all, Teach had been unable to rid himself of the thought that he had taken the line of least resistance by treating Inigo's complaint so superficially. At the time, the last thing he wanted was a lengthy inquiry just as he was about to go off duty, but he was a thorough and conscientious officer. He knew he should have taken Inigo more seriously. When he had told his wife about the incident during dinner and that he intended to return to Hobbswood in the evening, he felt much more at ease with himself.

"What about your darts match, dear? They'll be expecting you," she had said, but the King's Head's darts team would have to manage without his services on this occasion; he was no marksman anyway.

Teach had driven down the track, past Shapmire's cottage, and parked on the outskirts of the village, not quite sure what to do next. He switched off the engine and lights, turned on the radio, and waited. It was half past ten. At eleven o'clock, he began to doubt the wisdom of his lonely vigil. Nothing had happened, nothing was going to happen, and Hobbswood seemed as quiet and peaceful as any other Suffolk village. Still, he felt much better for having done something.

He looked at his watch. *Ten more minutes,* he thought, *and if all is still quiet, I'll head for home with a clear conscience; pity about the darts though.* The match was against the King's Head's main rival, the White Hart at Blythburgh, a local derby if ever there was one. He could have played after all.

The Book at Bedtime finished on the radio. Teach switched it off and wound down the window to empty his pipe and let some of the fug drift out of his car. His fingers were actually touching the ignition key, ready to start the engine, when he heard a shout from the village. A minute later, he saw a young woman run past his car as if all the devils in Hell were after her. A little way behind her, he could see shadows moving in the moonlight, so he decided now was the time to turn on his headlights. A moment later, he got out of his car to confront an angry Ambrose Samphyre who seemed to have the Devil in him.

"Are you threatening violence to a police officer, Mr Samphyre? That is a serious criminal offence," said Teach coldly.

"Get away from here, Bill, for your own good," pleaded Samphyre, who had known the policeman for many years. "It's out of our control now."

"What's out of control!" demanded Teach, but as he spoke, he saw about twenty Hobbswood villagers approaching him in the light of the car headlamps, armed with an assortment of agricultural implements, and just to his right, Inigo was getting to his feet beside a felled Seth Greenwood. *Perhaps,* he thought, *a temporary retreat might be the best strategy;* at least until the morning, when he could return with the full force of the Suffolk constabulary behind him and sort out this strange affair once and for all.

"All right, Ambrose," he said. "I'll leave you alone for now, but mark my words, there'll be a deal of explaining to do in the morning. Anything you say now may be used in evidence. Get into the car, Mr Boscabel."

Ambrose's placatory tone vanished, "Boscabel stays here, Bill."

"Nonsense! Mr Boscabel is coming with me. He's a key witness."

Inigo started to walk towards the policeman's car, but Ambrose blocked his way. For only the second time in his career, Teach drew his truncheon, but it made no difference.

A recovering Seth Greenwood barked orders to his comrade, "Ambrose! Get the car keys, quickly!"

The burly villager moved with surprising speed, brushing Teach aside, and reaching inside the car, he pulled out the ignition key. Before Teach or Inigo could stop him, he threw it into the undergrowth.

The village mob was less than fifty yards away. There was no time to search for the key, and Teach realised the time had come to fight for Inigo's and his own life. He brought his truncheon down hard on Ambrose's head. The farm foreman fell unconscious at the policeman's feet. Taking his cue from Teach, Inigo planted a perfect right hook on Seth's chin, who crumpled as if he had been poleaxed.

"God, that felt good," he said quietly.

"No time to stop and admire your handiwork," snapped Teach. "We'd better follow that young lady back up the track before the rest of the mob gets here."

The two men ran up the track, abandoning the police car, and hotly pursued by the angry villagers. On his own, Inigo, who always kept himself fit through regular long-distance running, would have had no difficulty staying ahead of his pursuers, but the well-rounded, middle aged constable was not cut out for this sort of exertion.

Michael's cottage was about five hundred uphill yards away, but Inigo and Teach had covered barely half that distance when the sound of pounding feet closed in fast behind them. The wheezing policeman could go no faster, and only a short distance ahead, Inigo could see Hazel labouring up the hill. It seemed as though all three of them would be caught. Inigo glanced back and saw that a tall, young villager, whose name he did not know, had detached himself from the rest of the mob and was within a few paces of running them down. He was armed with a large club, which looked heavy enough to smash a man's head in.

Now Inigo Boscabel's resolve was about to be tested. There was no room for compromise.

He loosened the carving knife in his belt and shouted, "Keep going, Constable. Michael's house is just around the next bend in the track. I'll try to buy us some time."

A pained groan was the only indication that the officer had understood, but Inigo knew he must stop the athletic villager or face the retribution of the vengeful people of Hobbswood. Three lives, including his own, depended on him. Did he have it in him to take a human life? He steeled himself for what must be done.

Taking the knife from his belt, he stopped, turned round, and ran towards his opponent, charging him head on. His club-wielding pursuer, taken by surprise by this unexpected change in tactics, was unprepared. Inigo was able to step inside the arc of the swinging club and grapple the villager to the ground, but not before he had buried the carving knife deep into the stomach of his adversary. He quickly got to his feet and pulled the knife out of the groaning body, not knowing whether or not the wound was mortal, then resumed his flight to Michael's house. The leading villagers slowed to assist their comrade, giving him time to gain a few more yards. He knew that later on he would be shocked by what he had done. Assuming, of course, he survived this terrible night.

Inigo's act of desperation granted him enough time to escape, but only just. He caught up with Teach and Hazel just as they reached Michael's front garden, but the mob, howling with anger, was hot on their heels. Michael had already opened his front door and he emerged swinging a heavy log splitter around his head, which would decapitate anyone coming within reach. The villagers quailed at the sight of this huge force heading towards them and stopped dead in their tracks, enabling Michael to give cover to the three fugitives as they entered the cottage. The red-faced constable collapsed on the floor near the fireplace where, as usual, a fire was blazing in the grate. Hazel fell to the ground just behind him, while Inigo, who was less exhausted but just as frightened as the others, watched Michael slam the door shut and slip the heavy bolts in place.

"Thank God, we made it, Michael," he said. "Now we're safe."

"Not this time," replied the big man grimly. "Get ready to fight for your life."

II

"So what's changed since yesterday?" asked Inigo as he tried to dodge the huge licks of welcome from Wellington. "Why should the villagers fear to attack us last night but not now?"

Michael peered through the window beside the front door.

"Because the Dark has revealed itself to them at last. The people of Hobbswood fear it far more than me. They will attack us tonight, you may depend on it."

Before Inigo could say any more, a large lump of flint smashed through the window beside Michael's head, shattering the glass into razor sharp splinters that scattered across the floor and furniture. Hazel screamed and Wellington slunk to the far wall, shivering, but portly Constable Teach sat up, still red-faced, but ready for action.

He spoke through laboured gasps, "What can I do? Is there a phone here?"

"Unfortunately, not," answered Michael. "We must rely entirely upon our own resources."

He risked a quick look through the broken window and then spoke to all of them.

"There are four windows in this house, three of which must be guarded. I will take this one by the front door, and the Constable can look after the one in the bedroom. Inigo, you guard the one in the kitchen. The one in the bathroom is too small to allow anyone to squeeze through, but we'd better leave Wellington in there just to be sure. Hazel, will you please pick up the broken glass before it hurts anyone and be ready to help where pressure builds up most."

Teach asked, "What do we defend ourselves with? I've only got my truncheon."

Michael nodded towards a cupboard beside the door to the kitchen.

"You will find a few pick-axe handles in there."

The policeman frowned. "Pick axe handles could be construed as offensive weapons."

Michael boomed a deep laugh. "They'll be offensive weapons tonight, I hope. They are my insurance against occasions such as this, but by all means, my dear constable, stick to your truncheon if you prefer."

"Bollocks," muttered Teach as he got up and opened the cupboard door. "That lot out there aren't playing games."

He handed out the weighty pieces of wood to his companions and took up his position in the bedroom, which was at the front of the cottage. Inigo went to the back, put Wellington into the bathroom, and paused in the kitchen doorway to appreciate Hazel's shapely bottom for a moment as she bent down to pick up the shards of broken glass. She saw him looking at her and smiled knowingly, as if to say, 'if we survive all this, you won't have to wait long'.

A second projectile smashed against the back door just behind Inigo. Hazel screamed again and dropped the glass shards she had collected.

Inigo ran to the kitchen window as Michael shouted, "Turn out the lights! There's no need to help them with their aim."

For the next few moments, they stood motionless in the firelight, casting goblin-like shadows against the walls. Hazel abandoned her glass collecting and nestled up to Inigo in the kitchen. He was flattered and put his arm round her shoulders. He could feel her body shaking with fear, but a pulse of excitement passed through him as he let his hand drop to her hips.

"Don't worry," he whispered. "We'll get through this all right, I promise. Michael knows what he's doing; all we have to do is follow his orders."

Hazel put her arm round his waist and squeezed.

"I feel safe when I'm near you, Inigo, but after all this is over, what shall I do? I cannot go back to the village. My mother has no love for me, never has. Why else would she stand back and allow Lucas to have his way with me all these years?"

"But Hazel, you are only young. Surely, he cannot have been lusting after you for years."

"You are a clever man, but you have a lot to learn about life. He took my virginity when I was still a child. I am only now beginning to understand that what he did to me was wrong. No-one in the village said anything. I remember pain, but my mother just let it happen. With no protection or advice, I just assumed life was like that. For some women in Hobbswood, it has always been so. Perhaps you can now understand why there is no feeling between my mother and me."

Inigo struggled to believe Hazel. Such things were totally alien to the protected life he had led at school and the seminary. How could any mother abandon her daughter to a creature like Lucas? This, even more than the black Mass and all the other perverted behaviour he had seen, proved to him that Hobbswood was rotten to the core. The sooner it was wiped off the map the better. But even now, he felt there would be a few more surprises in store for him before this night was spent. He tried to reassure Hazel.

"Let's just concentrate on getting through tonight. After that,

I'll take care of you."

He did not know what he meant by that, but it seemed to steady Hazel.

Suddenly, a voice called from outside. It was Seth Greenwood.

"Shapmire! Hear me, Shapmire!"

Michael called back, "What do you want?"

"We have no argument with you, Shapmire," said Seth, trying to sound reasonable. "You may keep the girl and the fat policeman, if you wish. Just give us Boscabel and we'll leave you in peace."

"I'm not fat!" shouted Teach from the bedroom. "And you can be sure, Seth Greenwood, that you and your accomplices out there will answer for your crimes. Give yourselves up now before things get worse for you all!"

"Leave this to me, Constable," said Michael. "Your warnings mean nothing to them in their current state of mind. They fear their dark master far more than you."

Raising his powerful voice, he spoke to Seth again, "Tell your master that he shall never have the blood of the innocent while I am here. Together we stand and together we shall die if we have to, but not before you and many of your friends bite the ground."

There was silence for a few seconds, then came the chilling reply, "Then die!"

Hazel held Inigo even tighter, but Michael spoke to his companions.

"My friends, be not discouraged. The odds against us are not as great as you might suppose. The villagers are driven more by the fear of their master than by hatred of us. Fear is a less formidable adversary than hatred because it can be turned upon

174

itself."

Inigo said, "But why won't Lucas just accept he has lost this time? Now that the solstice has passed, has not the chance for Hobbswood to be free of your yoke also passed?"

"I'm afraid not. The black Mass, once begun, must have its sacrifice. The ritual, which started on the solstice with you as the victim, is still incomplete. The villagers know that if they fail to complete it by sacrificing one of us, preferably you, their master will take one of them."

"But they will still be imprisoned here in Hobbswood?"

"True, Inigo. There is now only one way the Dark can spread beyond the confines of the village, and that is by breaking me."

"Is that possible?"

Michael replied reflectively, "It could happen, but no real challenge has been made until tonight. Even now, it seems the agent of the Dark prefers to use its minions rather than face me itself."

Constable Teach, who had been listening to the conversation with growing concern, said, "Never mind all this fanciful stuff about sacrifices and agents of darkness. I suggest we concentrate our attention on real threats, like the murderous rabble outside here. I would never have believed it. I've lived within a few miles of Hobbswood all my life. I admit, I have always thought of the villagers as a bit odd, rather like those strange sects who set off for America hundreds of years ago and still live in isolated villages somewhere in the prairies, but there's never been any suggestion of this sort of behaviour before."

"Not in your lifetime, at least," interjected Michael. "But your forefathers may not have agreed with you."

Teach continued, unruffled by Michael's interruption, "And I don't understand your part in all this, Mister Shapmire, but I shall require a full statement from you when all this is over."

Michael smiled as he tried to keep the amusement out of his voice, "Certainly, Constable. I shall write only the truth, but I rather doubt you will believe it."

"Listen!" whispered Hazel. "They're coming."

Inigo looked out of the kitchen window. In the moonlight, he saw seven or eight shadows approaching the back of the house. Four of them were carrying a pine log, which was doubtless to be used as a battering ram, but before he could decide what he should do, a shout from Teach in the bedroom warned that the front of the house was also under attack.

The first blow from the battering ram was comfortably absorbed by the thick, oak back door, but the sound of more breaking glass made Inigo run back to his post in the kitchen.

He shouted to Hazel, "Watch the back door and call me when it's about to break."

In the kitchen, one of the mob, axe in hand, had already wriggled half way through the broken window.

Inigo sprang forward and brought down his pick axe handle hard on the villager's shoulder. He could not yet bring himself to deliver a fatal blow by striking the head. It was not enough. The attacker howled in pain and anger but still managed to force his way in and despite another blow from Inigo, this time on the back, he struggled to his feet. He was a large, black-bearded man with a weathered face and a muscular frame, generated by years of hard agricultural labour.

Drawing back his heavy axe, he snarled through yellow teeth, "Bastard!"

Inigo's wooden handle was no match for the axe. He bitterly regretted not being more ruthless when he had the chance. He prepared to try and parry what looked like his death blow as the

176

villager delivered a mighty stroke that would have split him in two from head to pelvis. Mercifully, the axe head struck one of the low ceiling beams at the apex of its arc, bringing clouds of white plaster down onto both men as it stuck fast. The close brush with death released all inhibitions as, with a whoop of fear and anger, Inigo swung his pick axe handle in a horizontal arc, avoiding the low ceiling, and smashed it into the side of his adversary's head, felling him into a twitching, bloody wreck.

He raised his bludgeon again, this time to attack the next man who was trying to climb through the window, but when he saw what had just happened to his comrade, the villager beat a swift retreat. Inigo suddenly caught a glimpse of himself in the long kitchen mirror. He saw a howling, frenzied animal in a fight to the death. It was a picture of Mankind in his primeval, brutalised state, a flashback to how he might have looked in the days of darkness before he emerged from the swamp. How thin was the veneer of civilization, yet how vital!

Hazel cried out, "Inigo! The back door; it's breaking!"

He ran to the back door to find the lower bolt broken and the hinges about to give way. Only the top bolt still held the door in place.

He unceremoniously shoved Hazel into the bathroom with Wellington.

"Lock yourself in there with the dog. He'll protect you. I'll call you when I need you."

Looking across the living room at Michael, he could see that the huge man was fully occupied defending the front of the house against at least three villagers, one of whom was the powerful Ambrose Samphyre. The front door was hanging by a single hinge and only Michael's bulk stood between Lucas' minions and a bloody victory. Inigo was, for the moment at least, on his own.

Standing hard up against the back door of the cottage, he waited for the next thud of the battering ram. Within a few seconds, it duly came, rattling the door and splintering the lower hinge. He slipped back the top bolt and pulled at the broken door. It grated on the floor but opened far enough to let him through. The four men carrying the pine log were suddenly confronted by a wild-eyed maniac screaming obscenities and wielding a pick axe handle around his head like a fiend from Hell. But they had grounded their weapons in order to manhandle the battering ram, so they were temporarily defenceless. The only option was to flee. Dropping the log, they scattered to the far recesses of the back garden with Inigo in hot pursuit.

But in his blood-crazed madness, Inigo gave chase too far. Hazel shouted a warning from the bathroom, but when he stopped and turned round, he saw three more men, including Seth Greenwood, standing between him and the cottage. These three were armed and ready to fight. The fear, which had briefly been displaced by uncontrollable ferocity, came back and the fire that had rushed through his veins turned to ice. The all-conquering Boscabel now felt leaden-limbed and very weak, but he knew he must take on odds of three to one before the log bearers returned with their weapons to make it seven to one. He tightened his grip on the pick axe handle and walked steadily towards his enemy.

"Got you at last," sneered Seth, as he raised his bill hook to strike, but he had reckoned without the resilience of the Suffolk Constabulary.

William Teach, yelling unintelligible curses derived from his Anglo-Saxon heritage, burst through the still-open back door and felled Seth with a single sweep of his pick axe handle. It was only a glancing blow, a direct hit would have severed Seth's head from his shoulders, but the unexpected attack startled the other two villagers, who bolted, leaving Inigo able to return to the comparative safety of the cottage unchallenged.

"That'll give them something to think about," growled Teach as he helped Inigo wedge the door shut again. "Never liked old Greenwood much anyway. His eyes are too close together."

Inigo smiled at the constable's less than scientific method of character assessment and said, "I'm sorry I've caused you so much trouble, Constable, but at least now you know I wasn't spinning a yarn this afternoon."

"It is I who should be apologising to you, lad. I was too eager to get off duty."

The struggle had reached a temporary impasse; all was quiet again. Michael had driven off his opponents, and the attack on the back of the cottage seemed to have been suspended for the time being.

Teach whispered to Inigo, "That Michael Shapmire's a strange cove. How long have you known him?"

"Only a few days, but it seems much longer than that. I've never met anyone quite like him."

"He seems to think we're involved in some kind of religious crusade."

"Religious or not, it's still bloody dangerous, Constable. I don't know who he is any more than you, but he stands for right against wrong, just as you do; for Christ against the Antichrist."

Teach shook his head dismissively.

"All religion is nonsense to me and only seems to cause trouble. As far as I'm concerned, Jesus Christ was just a lad who gave up a good apprenticeship as a carpenter to become a social worker; that's all."

The bathroom door slowly opened, and a large, black, furry muzzle appeared, followed by Hazel. Both expected Inigo's undivided attention, but Wellington soon contented himself by leaning hard on his master's legs, a typical large dog's method of showing affection. At the same time, Hazel threw her arms around Inigo's neck and planted a long, lingering, affectionate kiss on his lips.

"I thought I had lost you," she whispered in his ear. "For a while it looked bad out there in the garden."

"It certainly was," agreed Inigo. "But the good constable saved the day."

Teach acknowledged the compliment with a curt nod and then asked no one in particular, "I wonder if they'll come back. I reckon I took two out of the contest."

"And two also for me," added Inigo. "One when we were running away from Hobbswood and the other who's still lying on the kitchen floor."

Michael said, "Then with my three that makes seven, which is about a third of them. That's a high casualty rate by any standard. They may have had enough, but I suspect they'll be back, driven on by their dark master. We must remain at our posts for the present. Try to stay awake."

III

Inigo lay slumped against the back door, trying not to doze off. Hazel was asleep in his arms, her head resting on his chest, while Constable Teach, who was accustomed to night duty, sat on the settee absentmindedly picking at the rough end of his pick axe handle. Michael had gone outside to try and find out what the villagers were up to.

Forty minutes had passed since the assault on the cottage, during which time the broken glass from the windows had been collected and stored safely, and the corpse in the kitchen had been dumped outside the back door. Inigo struggled with the fact that he felt no guilt for taking two human lives. All was quiet, but the fear and frantic violence of only a short while ago created a reaction in him that took the form of overwhelming tiredness. He dared not allow it to overcome him. As he considered the tumultuous events of the last few days, he began to realise that he still knew virtually nothing about Michael Shapmire. Apart from being a member of an obscure, highly secret religious sect, the large man remained a total mystery. True, Inigo had spent a considerable amount of time talking to him, yet somehow Michael managed to reveal remarkably little about himself, though he was certainly forthright about his views on life and philosophy. But whenever the conversation began to focus on Michael himself, something would happen to end it, or the subject would be gently deflected along a different path. Now, Inigo determined to be more single-minded next time the opportunity arose, but if the villagers came back again, there might not be a next time.

There was a knock on the remains of the front door. It was Michael. Inigo and Teach moved the chest of drawers that now held the splintered door in place to allow Michael to squeeze into the cottage. He looked worried.

"I was hoping the villagers might have had enough, but they're coming back for more. We'd better prepare ourselves."

Wellington's vast bulk, which lay stretched out in front of the fire, was disinclined to move, but after a minute's heaving and cajoling, the large, fawn rump disappeared back into the bathroom. It was just as well because, only seconds later, the first petrol bomb flew through the front window and landed exactly where the mastiff had been lying.

"Bloody hell!" gasped Teach. "Molotov cocktails! The bastards mean to burn us out!"

A second petrol bomb missed the window and exploded against the cottage wall.

Michael began stamping out the flames from the first bomb with his huge feet.

"There are two buckets by the sink in the kitchen," he shouted. "Fill them with water and bring them here!"

Hazel and Teach ran into the kitchen just as another petrol bomb struck Michael on the leg, sending a wall of flame up his back. Inigo ran to the bedroom, pulled a blanket off the bed, and smothered the fire on Michael's back.

Surprisingly, Michael was unscathed, apart from some scorch marks on his black coat, and when he turned round, Inigo was astonished to see he was smiling after having been within seconds of man's worst fear; death by burning.

"It's all right, Inigo, fire holds no fear for me. It's my

weapon, not theirs. You will be of greater service if you help Hazel and the constable stop the house from burning down. Soak everything, all the furniture, the carpets, even the walls, to prevent the flames from catching hold."

The next few bombs missed the windows and exploded dramatically but harmlessly against the cottage walls. The furniture and carpets were well soaked before another, more accurate bomb arrived, landing on the settee, but the flames were soon doused by a combination of water from the buckets and dampened blankets. Two more petrol bombs hit their mark, but each time, the defenders managed to quench the flames before they spread. They seemed to be getting the upper hand.

At last, the assault ceased and all went quiet once more. Hazel, Teach, and Inigo, all soaked, grimy, and panting from their arduous work, stared expressionlessly at each other, wondering if they had done enough.

Michael peered out of the shattered front window, scanning for the enemy. Then he turned to his comrades, for that was what they had become through the shared experience of battle; they were now more than mere companions.

"This time I think they will not come back, but we must remain watchful until dawn. We can allow ourselves some sleep if we are careful. Constable Teach and I will take the first one-hour watch. Hazel and Inigo, you can sleep until then."

Inigo did not argue. He went into the bedroom and collapsed onto the bed with Hazel beside him. They were both asleep in seconds.

It seemed to Inigo that he had only just closed his eyes when he was woken by Michael. The big man looked preoccupied, even frightened.

Inigo disentangled himself from Hazel, sat up, and whispered, "Is it time already? Has something happened?"

Michael simply beckoned him to follow and went back into the living room. Inigo looked at his watch; one fifteen. He had slept less than half his allocated hour. The same could not be said for Constable Teach who, despite his guard duty, was slumped beside the front door snoring quietly.

"It's all right, Inigo, our constable may continue his sleep. The villagers have had their fill of this particular fight."

"Then we've won!"

"I'm afraid not, at least not yet."

"I don't understand. Surely all we have to do now is to wait for the morning and then fetch the police? Teach will verify all that has happened, which is just as well because nobody would believe us otherwise."

Michael shook his head. His broad brow was deeply furrowed, and anxiety welled up in his azure eyes.

"The enemy has raised the stakes. He is calling me. He has laid down a direct challenge, a face-to-face confrontation between the two of us."

"Don't accept it; you don't need to."

"But it has a certain classical quality, do you not think? Rather like the challenges made between Greek and Trojan warriors in Homer's Iliad."

"Don't let that influence you, Michael. Even in those far off days, an offer to settle a conflict by a clash of champions was only ever made by the commander who feared he would lose a full-scale battle. Refuse the challenge!"

"You're probably right," agreed Michael. "But there's more to it than that. If I win, the evil in Hobbswood will be extinguished and my vigil will be over. If I'm satisfied with the

184

partial victory we have already gained, then the evil will be merely contained, and my vigil will continue."

"But what if Lucas, Sefton, or whoever the enemy is, wins?"

Michael lowered his eyes. "Then the Dark will be free to spread unhindered."

"Is it worth the risk?" asked Inigo, who was beginning to feel distinctly uncomfortable at the thought of losing Michael's towering support.

"We won't find out unless I try," came the unhelpful reply.

And now Inigo's heart sank. He felt the icy coldness of fear re-enter his veins. He had begun to hope the fight was over, but now it seemed that the desperate struggle they had endured was merely the preliminary skirmish which heralded the main battle, the battle that could see the end of all of them, including Michael Shapmire.

Even as he spoke, he knew he was wasting his breath, "Michael, can you not be satisfied with a partial victory?"

"No, I do not want to be tied down here any longer. I must take the opportunity to free myself from this vigil."

"But how do you know you can trust your enemy? How can you be sure he will not betray you by arriving with all the villagers to help him?"

"I do not know for sure but…" the large blue eyes looked at him. "You could help in that respect, if you choose to. I have no right to ask though."

Much as he would have liked to say 'no', Inigo could not refuse.

"What do you want me to do?"

The relief that showed on Michael's face disconcerted him. He could not imagine how his puny efforts could make any difference to this clash of Titans, nor could he draw any encouragement from the previously imperturbable Michael, who was now obviously very frightened. Whatever lay ahead was sure to be hideously dangerous.

Michael looked into the fire. Strangely, the flames seemed to be enhanced by their reflection in his eyes. He appeared to be deep in thought, perhaps thinking about faraway places and long forgotten times, and then, just for a few moments, the huge, black frame, which was leaning against the mantel piece above the fire, seemed distinctly vulnerable.

Then, as if he had somehow consolidated his inner strength for the coming fight, the old, confident Michael returned and smiled. "The Creator knows of your contribution to our struggle here. I am able to reveal to you some things you have a right to know before we set out for this final battle. In particular, you should know the true identity of our adversary."

Inigo enquired feebly, "Is it not Lucas Fairweather or Sefton Lightwell then?"

"Inigo, what I must tell you is what I believe to be the truth. You will decide whether or not you wish to share my faith, but it is my duty to speak more openly to you than I have done before. It will mean revealing more about the Order to which I belong, but I am now authorised to do this. But whatever you may think you have deduced about us, I would ask you to keep to yourself."

Inigo swallowed nervously. He was certain he was not going to like what he was about to hear. He wanted to sit down, but the floor and furniture were still soaking wet, so he contented himself with leaning against the wall by the splintered back door.

Michael looked at Teach, who was beginning to stir, and lowered his powerful voice, "You remember I told you that both Light and Dark are contained within the single, universal intellect of the Creator?"

Inigo nodded.

"Well," continued Michael, "they are not merely abstract concepts. Light and Dark operate through beings that exist to implement their needs."

"Like Adolf Hitler for the Dark and Mother Theresa of Calcutta for the Light?" suggested Inigo, trying to be helpful.

"At one level, yes, but there is another, superior level which, when it manifests itself, is far more formidable and terrifying. Regrettably, that is what faces us now. Your faith identifies these entities as demons or darker, even more horrifying creatures."

Inigo laughed nervously. "Come now, Michael, you cannot really be serious. No one believes in those sorts of things any more. They are the stuff of ancient myth and medieval superstition. Modern science and reason replaced them long ago."

"You seem very sure of yourself, Inigo. Do you not consider that some myths at least have a kernel of truth?"

"Well, yes, but not to the extent you're suggesting. Demons and monsters were simply one of the means by which primitive religions, including Christianity, kept their flocks in order. We don't need them any more. Times have changed."

"Indeed they have, and as you say, such beasts of the Dark have been replaced, in men's minds at least, by more modern concepts that discount the idea of evil being present anywhere except within the human mind. But denying the existence of the Dark will not make it go away."

Michael leaned forward and whispered, as if some nearby presence might overhear him.

"I tell you, Inigo, we ignore the creatures of the Dark at our peril. Refusing to face them gives them more strength. In Hobbswood there exists a rare, but very real, threat. A dark angel of the highest Order, who came here three centuries ago. Then he called himself 'Sefton Lightwell', now he is known as Lucas Fairweather."

"You intend to take on a dark angel! If what you say is true, then you have no chance! How did this creature get here anyway?"

"If there really was no chance, I wouldn't do it. When Sefton Lightwell came here, he had already been corrupted, but that was not so with Lucas Fairweather. Five years ago, when the doctor came to live in Hobbswood, he was an ordinary country general practitioner who settled in well. I saw him as no threat. But ever since Lightwell's human body expired, the dark angel has been looking for another carrier. In the mid 1650's, a witchfinder, the supporter of the Light against the Dark, was an ideal carrier. But now, in our more enlightened times, something else was needed. Imagine how this creature must have rejoiced when a doctor, a preserver of life, entered his domain."

"So what happened to the original Lucas?"

"He was subsumed into the entity we face now. He won't have noticed anything, but gradually his independent personality would have changed as the malignant force took over his mind and body. His behaviour remained unaltered because the dark creature would not have wanted to alert those around him, at least not until the time came to reveal itself, but inside the pleasant, easy-going outer shell, the original Lucas is gone, absorbed into the entity within him. Three hundred years ago, poor Thomas Messynger, brave though he was, never stood a chance against such a formidable adversary and to our never-ending regret, my Order failed to recognise what was happening until too late. Thomas' young blood gave the Dark its foothold here, and yours would have enabled it to break free of me. Had it not been for your courageous dog, we would have failed again because the creature of the Dark managed to shield itself from me like it did before. It was able to travel back and forth, passing under my nose into the Suffolk hinterland at will, while all the time my eyes were elsewhere because I believed it was bottled up in the village."

"You have still not named our enemy," said Inigo quietly.

"He has many names, none of which pass easily across my lips. You may know him as Belphegor, one of the seven high angels of the Dark."

Inigo had to steady himself for a moment. He could hardly believe what he was hearing, but there could be no doubting Michael's sincerity. Inigo thought back to his seminary research and recalled the names of the seven black angels of the Judeo-Christian pantheon: Lucifer, Belial, Asmodeus, Leviathan, Mammon, Beelzebub and Belphegor. He could not let himself share Michael's certainty, but if he was right, how could a mortal hope to overcome such powerful entities?

Michael could sense Inigo's concern and tried to reassure him.

"Belphegor can be beaten. I can tell you that he and all his vile companions have known defeat at one time or another."

"But how? A spirit cannot be killed."

"No, but its influence can be destroyed at certain times and in certain places. Belphegor has been forced to reveal himself, an act of desperation on his part. In doing so he has increased his power over the ignorant Hobbswood villagers, but at the same time he has opened himself up to an attack from me. It's true, I cannot destroy him, but I can dilute him, like pouring a tub of excrement into an ocean of water, so that his influence will be negated until, at a date well into the future, in some unfortunate place, he'll at last be able to consolidate himself again. Thus, it has always been."

"And this epic struggle is taking place within the universal intellect I used to call God, but you call the Creator?"

"Exactly, Inigo. Our universe is actually the Creator. The planets, the stars, and the galaxies all constitute the Creator. It is possible that there are many universes, millions of them perhaps, each with their own Creator."

"But where are they, then? Why can't we see them?"

"They are here, and we can already see the nearest ones to us."

"I really don't understand what you are talking about, Michael."

"Then consider this. You already know that, on a microscopic scale, all matter in our universe is composed of molecules, which are in turn composed of atoms. Each atom is made up of a nucleus with electrons orbiting around it. Now look at our universe. For molecules, see galaxies. For atomic nuclei, see suns. And for electrons, see planets. The laws of physics may not be the same as ours, but the analogy is persuasive."

"Are you saying there are forms of life within the atomic structure?"

"Why not? We shall never know because we can never see or communicate with it."

"Never is a long time; there's no telling what science can achieve."

"There is the problem of relative time. If the analogy holds true, then each orbit of an electron would be equivalent to one of earth's years. An electron orbits a nucleus hundreds of times a second, so the equivalent of an earth life would be finished in less than a blink of an eye in our world. If, somehow, a person from that atomic universe could visit us, all he would see would be rigid statues because of the difference in relative time. One of our seconds would be lifetimes to that person, but nevertheless we exist in the same space."

"I begin to see now, but would the atomic galaxy you speak of have its own Creator, its own powers of Light and Dark?"

"I don't know, but it would make sense, wouldn't it? And taking it further, the atomic universe we are speaking of may have an atomic universe of its own far beyond the reach of our observational equipment, and that subatomic universe may yet have another of its own, and so on *ad infinitum*. All in the same space, each with its own Creator."

"And is there a Creator of all these Creators?"

"Maybe, but I haven't finished yet. You can take the analogy equally far up the scale from our universe as well as down the scale. We may live on the electrons orbiting the atomic nuclei of the next dimension above us. If we were able to visit the people of that universe, all we would see would be static images because of the relative time. We would live and die in the blink of an eyelid in their time. Yet they may only be living on electrons orbiting the atomic nuclei of the next universe up the scale, and so on, but all in the same space."

"Michael, you're making my brain hurt."

"That should be no surprise because you have just glimpsed the edge of infinity."

Inigo sighed. "Well, what worries me at the moment is that I may see a lot more of infinity sooner than I would like after tonight if we don't beat Belphegor. What you've told me is all very logical, but I have to tell you that your image of God, who you call the Creator, seems disappointingly impersonal to me. You speak of Light and Dark, but nowhere have I heard the word 'love'. Ever since I was a child, I have been taught that God loves us and we should love God, but how can this universal intellect you call the Creator love such inconsequential creatures as us as individuals? Without love, what binds the Creator to us?"

"Love is a very human expression. You'll remember I told you that the Creator takes a particular interest in life on this world because of the way it's evolved. It reproduces by the combination of male and female, which results in the originality the Creator treasures. While I cannot use the word 'love' on the Creator's behalf, I am certain you are particularly valued as the unexpected result of a quirk of evolution that stimulates originality and pleases the Creator. Does that answer your question?"

"I suppose so. But being a quirk of evolution does not feel the same as love."

"Well, it should do. The Creator has revealed itself three times to this world, using its own creations as the means to do so because you are valued so highly. The first time was to Abraham, the father of the Israelites, then to Jesus Christ, and finally to Mohammed when it was clear that Christ's message was not being implemented as it should have been. Since then, Mohammed's message has also been distorted by the dark powers that exist in the universal intellect. I don't know if the Creator will try again, but if democracy succeeds, it may not need to."

"But why has the Creator failed to get its message through to us on three occasions? It seems incompetent to me."

"That's the proof of how much the Creator values you. The message is complex. It has to be given in the form of analogies and parables. You cannot expect a bronze age patriarch, or an iron age Messiah to understand the message I have just given to you. It must be couched in contemporary language. That is why the Creator allowed itself to be referred to as 'he'. Anything else would have been dismissed as ludicrous by the people of the time."

"And what about life after death?" enquired Inigo. "That's of particular interest to me now."

Michael laughed. "I've already told you. You've proven yourself. If the worst happens here, the Creator has already chosen you."

"Then let's get started. It would be bad form to keep your enemy waiting."

Chapter Nine

It was a little after two o'clock in the morning when Michael and Inigo left the cottage and headed towards Dunwich Heath, which was to be the trysting ground between the forces of the Light and the Dark. Constable Teach had been left in charge of Hazel and Wellington, ready to organise the defence of the cottage should the villagers unexpectedly renew the attack.

The moon, more than half full, was now in the western sky and lit up the open, heather-clad heathland in silver and grey. The two men followed the path Inigo had used on the morning of his first encounter with Michael four days earlier when, unlike his master, Wellington immediately recognised who stood for the cause of Light. So much had happened since then; it seemed more like four weeks than four days. They climbed steadily until they reached a clump of gorse bushes, which marked a local high point. From there, Inigo could see the lights of ships far out to sea, but of more immediate impact was the star-studded night sky, which stretched to all horizons like a huge, silver-speckled, black velvet blanket. He still struggled to believe Michael's concept that such an immense, beautiful vastness was no more than an atomic void in some greater universe of static giants. Surely nature must have a higher purpose than that.

Michael suddenly stopped at a junction between two footpaths.

"Well, Inigo, this is where we must part company. You are clear about what I need to know?"

"The means by which Belphegor intends to fight you."

"Exactly. He, like me, will employ weapons of nature forged out of this world. We will not be wrestling or shooting arrows at each other, but if you can find out what he intends to use, I will have a few precious minutes to prepare counter-measures."

"Will you remain here until I get back?" asked Inigo.

"Certainly. You understand that I cannot come with you without entering my enemy's domain and handing him the advantage. Dunwich Heath is neutral ground, which is why the confrontation must take place here. If you are unable to discover anything of use, do not start taking chances. Just come straight back here. If you were to be captured, I would be obliged to try and rescue you, which would mean fighting the Dark in its own back yard. Good luck."

Inigo set off on the footpath, which led towards Hobbswood, carrying his pick axe handle in his right hand and the carving knife he had already used to terrible effect that night in his belt. Michael had explained that this path would take him more or less to the centre of Hobbswood from the landward side, cutting through the forest in which he had sprained his ankle on that fateful day he had first set eyes on the village. He walked quickly down the sandy track, but just before he entered the forest, he paused briefly to look at the sea once more. Something was happening on the horizon; it seemed to be losing its clear-cut definition, and low in the eastern sky, the stars seemed to be going out as if a giant, unseen hand was slowly raising an impenetrable barrier out of the salty depths. It was a disquieting sight, but Inigo knew he was in an overwrought state of mind and resumed his mission. It was probably just a night-time sea mist.

Now he walked more slowly, taking care to avoid tripping over the roots and brambles that lay across the path, hidden in dark recesses created by the tree canopy, which reduced the moonlight to isolated pools of silver amongst a sea of shadows. He wished he had Wellington with him, but the mastiff had already made a major contribution to the struggle against the Dark in Hobbswood, and once again, stealth was needed, a quality not contained in Wellington's armoury. After a quarter of a mile, the trees began to thin out, but just as he caught sight of the lights of Hobbswood between gaps in the tall pine trunks, he began to smell the familiar odour of decaying rats again. This time the smell was stronger than ever, and he wrinkled his nose in disgust.

He abandoned the path just before it emerged from the forest and slowly worked his way through the undergrowth towards the first house — Seth Greenwood's. Halting behind the trunk of a mature Scots pine, Inigo waited for a while, concealed in the forest eaves, wondering what to do next. Lights were on in all but one of the houses, but no one was visible out of doors.

The whole village seemed to be holding its breath, waiting for something to happen. The only dwelling that remained unlit was Lucas'. Despite Michael's strongly held beliefs, Inigo still thought of the doctor as Lucas, not some mythical dark angel from the underworld. Now he was alone again, away from Michael's powerful personality, he felt able to think more clearly about things. Although he did not doubt Michael's sincerity, he found the big man's explanation about recent events fanciful to say the least. On the other hand, he felt a far stronger affinity with the down to earth views of Constable Teach, which did not seek for explanations for good and evil beyond what we all carry within ourselves.

It soon became clear that Inigo would learn nothing of value to Michael from his present position. He decided to move a little closer to the village, but just as he was about to leave his post beside the Scots pine, he heard footsteps approaching softly behind him. They were slow and measured and were coming down the path he had used only minutes earlier. Although not blessed with a sixth sense or sensitivity to atmosphere, he was nonetheless certain that the footsteps brought danger. He froze and remained utterly still, except for tightening his grip on the pick axe handle. Waiting in fearful silence, he somehow knew that the weapon would be of little use if he was discovered now.

At its nearest, where it swung to the right, the forest path was less than twenty yards from Inigo. There was almost no undergrowth here, so he could clearly see the path from where he stood. The footsteps came nearer and then began to slow down. Inigo held his breath, but his pounding heart seemed to be beating louder than the bass drum of the Brigade of Guards.

Along the path, a tall, black figure drifted into view from the left. It stopped. Once more, Inigo experienced terror in its purest form, terror of the same magnitude as on the night of his intended sacrifice. The ominous figure had its back to him, but he knew he was being stalked by a hunter for its prey, sought out by senses beyond his comprehension.

Ten long seconds passed. Suddenly, the figure span round and seemed to stare directly at him. In this one fleeting moment, all the doubts Inigo had felt about Michael's faith were extinguished by what confronted him now. The moon was low in the sky but still cast enough light to illuminate the terrible face scanning the forest for its victim. Lucas Fairweather's features were still just discernible in the sallow, spectral face, but now the dark angel was not attempting to conceal its true aspect; there was no longer the need. The cheeks had sunk, the cheekbones protruded, and the previously well-groomed hair hung in streaky grey, lank strings down to the shoulders. The broad brow was heavily lined, and the mouth was drawn back in a cadaverous snarl, revealing jagged, animal-like teeth. Most terrifying of all, shining either side of the thin beak of a nose, were fearsome eyes of hate. They seemed unnaturally bright, as if they might be channels for an internal fire which lit them with stale, putrid yellow light.

There was no longer any doubt in Inigo's mind. The fearsome predator hunting him was the black archangel, Belphegor.

Almost imperceptibly, the creature's head began to sway from side to side, like a cobra mesmerising its victim before it strikes. Inigo wanted to bolt and put as much distance as possible between himself and his dark enemy. All his instincts cried out, 'Run! Run!'. But he knew that would be fatal for, however fast he fled, Belphegor was sure to be faster. Yet the desire to flee was beginning to overwhelm him despite the logic that told him to stay still, and he could not prevent himself starting to edge backwards before this horror, whose formidable sensory powers might at any moment pinpoint his hiding place amongst the trees.

An unaccustomed flash of insight saved Inigo that night. The dark angel was obviously able to sense his presence but not his exact location, at least not without a time-consuming search. Instead, it was trying to use the power of its mind to encourage him to flee, to flush its prey out of cover with terror, like a beater at a pheasant shoot. Inigo quietly congratulated himself for his presence of mind and maintained his position in complete silence.

But he had only bought a little time. The dark figure left the path and started to walk slowly in his direction, sniffing the air as he approached. Inigo slowly raised his pick axe handle, ready to strike, determined if needs be, to sell his life dearly. Suddenly, the oppressive silence was shattered by a call from the seaward side of Hobbswood, somewhere near the clifftops that cut back here to less than a hundred yards from the village. The senses which had been seeking Inigo out were distracted; the imminent moment of discovery was delayed as the creature of hate turned round and returned to the forest path.

"It comes, Lord! It comes like a black veil blotting out the stars!"

The voice was Seth Greenwood's, who was running up the path from the direction of the village almost prancing with delight. Obviously, the blow he had received from Constable Teach outside Michael's cottage had not been too severe.

He stopped in front of Belphegor and said breathlessly, "Lord, your power is indeed wondrously great. You will surely triumph now."

His news seemed to be sufficiently important to suspend the search for Inigo. For the moment, the power of that terrible mind was directed elsewhere.

"What would you have me do now, Lord?" whimpered Seth, like a young schoolboy eager to please a bullying senior prefect.

His master replied in the same deep, carnal whisper that Inigo had heard during his first night at Lucas' house, when Hazel was being subjected to brutal, violent sex.

"Return to your house, shut the windows, and lock the doors. Tell the others to do the same. Then wait for me to come to you."

Seth ran back towards Hobbswood. The cold, yellow eyes looked once more in Inigo's direction, but the creature had lost interest in the hunt. Instead, it turned its back on the forest and slowly walked towards the cliffs. Inigo remained motionless until the hideous black shape had disappeared from view, but although he was anxious to get away as soon as possible, he had not yet discovered anything of value to help Michael. He was fairly sure that whatever it was that had excited Seth so much might be relevant to the coming struggle. So, fighting his desire to escape while he could, he decided to wait for a while.

In order to get a better view, he carefully picked his way between the trees until he reached the forest path. That all-pervading stench of death and decay became stronger as he arrived at the point where his evil adversary had been standing. Keeping well within the shadows of the overhanging boughs, he followed the path up a gentle gradient until he could see the rim of the clifftops, which, from his position on the landward side, blocked his view of the sea. The broom and gorse covered slope, which led up to the cliff tops, shone silver in the bright moonlight, contrasting sharply against the black, star-speckled eastern sky. Fifty yards away, at the very edge of the cliff, stood the menacing figure of Belphegor. He was looking out to sea with his back to Inigo, arms outstretched in the attitude of prayer. Inigo briefly flirted with the idea of creeping up behind him and pushing him over the edge, but within a few seconds he changed his mind.

Slowly, but at first barely noticeable, the sharp distinction between the silver-lit clifftop and the black, starlit sky started to become blurred. Something was happening, which made the rim of the cliff appear to move. Soon, this movement grew from gentle stirring into a more violent motion, as if the ground was bubbling and seething like boiling liquid. The dark figure ahead remained motionless, and as the ground appeared to rise around it, Inigo realised that some kind of sea mist or fog was flooding over the tops of the cliffs and enveloping the landscape in a thick, black, gaseous blanket. The mist began to roll down the reverse slope towards him, but it was unlike any sea mist he had ever seen. Although the moon still shone brightly, no moonlight penetrated the foggy cloud, which seemed to devour light as it advanced. It moved in wave-like, erratic pulses, similar to the rolling clouds of incandescent lava he had seen in dramatic television pictures of volcanic eruptions.

Even before the ominous sea mist reached him, Inigo was backing away. Belphegor had already been swallowed up by the inky blackness, which was doubtless an ally of his, but instinct warned that, whatever it might be, the mist was unnatural and unfriendly. The leading spur of the black cloud was about ten paces away when Inigo was assailed by a disgusting, throat gagging smell. His stomach heaved as he inhaled that familiar Hobbswood odour of sewers and putrefaction, but now so concentrated that it was impossible to bear; the vile stench of Belphegor. He turned and ran back up the path towards the forest.

Initially, Inigo made ground against the invading fog but the path swung to the left soon after it re-entered the forest and ran parallel to the cliffs for the next quarter of a mile or so before it turned right and began to climb towards Dunwich Heath. This meant that, for about four hundred yards, the fog would gain on him until he reached the point where the path turned inland again. So, the next sixty seconds could determine the outcome of the fight between the Dark and the Light as well as his own survival. He stretched his legs and ran faster than he had done for many years.

For the first two hundred yards all was well, but then the dreadful smell, which warned of the proximity of the dark cloud, returned. It was advancing through the forest on his left. Seconds later, it caught up with him. The charcoal grey of the night suddenly turned dense black, as if someone had thrown a blanket over him. The smell was so bad it forced him to slow down in order to throw up, but each time he gulped for breath, his stomach revolted as he drew the vile gas into his lungs. He staggered on, reeling like a drunkard, feeling rather than seeing his way forwards. But even more crippling than the smell was the icy cold that accompanied it.

Inigo's limbs and joints were quickly chilled to the bone, as if he was being freeze dried. He knew it could only be a matter of seconds before he collapsed and succumbed. He dropped his pick axe handle and wrapped his arms around his torso. Then, summoning his last reserves of strength, he forced his leaden legs forwards for a few more yards.

In the pitch black of the cloud, he could see no more than three paces ahead, but the sand-coloured path guided him forwards. On he went, each step taking more out of him than the last. He retched again and fell sprawling on the path. Had it not been for the loathsome smell, he would have stayed there and allowed the cold to lull him into the sleep of death, but the pain in his heaving stomach drove him on a little further. He staggered to his feet and tried to picture Wellington and Hazel waiting for him, hoping this would give him the extra strength to go on, but the images soon faded; he could only think of his own survival. His eyes watered, the tears on his cheeks froze, he was going down.

But at this moment of utter despair, he sensed he was beginning to climb; he must be heading inland at last. If only he could last just a little longer, he might be able to get above this lethal fog from Hell. The dense blackness seemed to become a little paler, the path a little clearer. He looked up and saw stars in the sky. He had won through!

As soon as he emerged from the fog, his body began to thaw

out, but he had to struggle another twenty-five yards to get clear of the worst of the stench. He sat down for a moment, but only for a moment, because the black cloud was still advancing implacably up the path towards him. Having experienced it already, he had no intention of allowing it to get near him again, so he resumed his flight towards Dunwich Heath.

The speed of his recovery surprised Inigo. Soon he was able to break into a steady trot and put a good distance between himself and Belphegor's cloud of death, which still followed him slowly, but inexorably, up the path to the heath. The pain had been severe, but now it all seemed worthwhile because he had personally experienced the weapon the black archangel intended to use against Michael in the coming battle.

II

"If the smell doesn't finish you, the cold certainly will," said Inigo, as he looked back down the path he had just used to escape from Hobbswood.

"How long do you think I have before the cloud reaches the heath?" asked Michael.

"Fifteen, perhaps twenty minutes, no more."

From the knoll where the two men were standing, Inigo could look down on Dunwich Heath, which stretched out as a moonlit plateau about thirty feet below them. The final act in the three-hundred-year-old saga was about to be played out. He frowned.

"I don't see how you can win this, Michael. You know how badly you feel the cold. It almost finished me, so what chance have you?"

Michael betrayed no sign of panic. The fear he had shown earlier that night now seemed to have left him.

"Inigo, you have won me time enough to prepare. That might make all the difference to the outcome."

"I don't see how."

"Have faith, my friend. Now I want you to go back to the cottage and be ready to help Constable Teach and Hazel if the villagers return."

"No!" objected Inigo. "I'm staying here to help you fight Belphegor."

Michael tried to be patient, but the effort was ill-disguised.

"Do not say his name. He is like a dog. He will come if he is called."

"Not all dogs come when they're called," said Inigo, ruefully thinking of the large, furry creature sitting in the bathroom back at the cottage.

Michael smiled. "He came when it mattered most. Now, you must understand that you can be of no use to me here. In fact, you will be a hindrance if I am obliged to consider your welfare while engaging the enemy. Please return to the cottage where your contribution will be effective if called upon."

"But I want to stay here. You owe me that at least after what I have done."

Michael drew himself up to his full height. "Go! You are wasting some of the precious time you gained for me by arguing."

"All right then, if you insist. God go with you; oh, I suppose I should say 'may the Creator protect you'."

They shook hands; the heat now radiating from Michael's glove made Inigo wince. When they parted, Inigo walked in the direction of the cottage. But not for long, because he had every intention of at least observing the grand finale so, after a couple of minutes, he turned round and doubled back to the knoll. Michael had gone, but Inigo had heard Seth being ordered to stay in his house to escape the effects of the black cloud, so he knew the villagers would be unable to attack Michael's cottage even if they could summon up the courage to do so.

The central plateau of Dunwich Heath is roughly one mile square. Inigo hoped that his vantage point on the knoll was high enough to remain clear of the advancing fog, like an island in an incoming tide, but behind him the land fell away into a shallow valley. He knew he would need to stay alert in case the fog threatened to cut off his escape route to the cottage. It was now almost three o'clock. Soon the first hint of dawn would begin to colour the eastern horizon. The south was already visible, thanks to the lights illuminating Sizewell power station further down the coast, but the moonlight that gave the heath its silvery luminescence was fading because the moon was now low in the west. Inigo looked at his watch again and waited.

Ten minutes passed, during which he twice nearly fell asleep. He countered this by pacing back and forth, like a sentinel on guard duty, but he could see no sign of Michael on the heath. He looked towards the sea and saw the eastern edge of the heath beginning to undulate as the fog began to spill over the plateau. Onward it came, devouring the natural silver beauty of the moonlit landscape like a formless, voracious creature from the depths of the earth. Inigo somehow sensed that, if it managed to devour the whole of Dunwich Heath, the battle would be lost, and the evil of the dark archangel would be released to wreak havoc inland. He could still taste the vile stench in his mouth and looked nervously behind him to check that no surreptitious, black wisps of fog were feeling their way past the back of his position on the knoll. Where was Belphegor? He wondered. Probably somewhere in the midst of the stinking, poisonous cloud, poised to strike, like a huge, vengeful spider lurking in the centre of its web.

The cloud transgressed across the plateau steadily, implacably. After a few minutes, it had covered half of it, yet Michael had still not made his presence felt. Inigo, already extremely frightened and regretting his foolhardy decision to ignore Michael's instructions, began to feel panic welling up inside him again. Had something happened to his comrade?

Perhaps the creature of the Dark had left its protective cover and surprised him. Maybe he was already dead!

More long, stomach-churning minutes passed. There was less than a third of the plateau still free of the dark cloud when, at last, Inigo's heart leaped as a bright orange light appeared about a hundred yards in front of the black tide. It was a small fire. Close beside it, another flared up, then another, followed by others in quick succession until a line of small bright fires, twenty or so yards apart, burned fiercely across the full width of the heath, barring the path of the advancing fog. The immense blackness seemed to accelerate towards the challenge; Inigo's misgiving returned. How could Michael hope to stem this evil with such meagre means as a line of small fires? He was not quite sure what he had been expecting from his huge friend, but if this was all he could come up with, then the battle would be over before it really started. Surely the freezing cloud of stench would quickly snuff out Michael's flames with ease?

Inigo's fears were speedily confirmed moments later when the fog overwhelmed the line of fires like a death shroud. There was not even a shudder or a check to its remorseless advance. The light from the fires disappeared within the all-consuming blackness, like matches snuffed out in a storm. Although Inigo's hopes sank, Michael was at least still alive and undaunted because no sooner had the fires been smothered, than another line of crackling flames sprang up close to the western edge of the heath, ahead of the approaching fog. This time the confrontation took place directly in front and below Inigo. Once more, the flames were overwhelmed by the inky blackness, but this time the oncoming shadow was briefly held before it resumed its inexorable progress inland. Clearly something must have happened, for the fog advanced more slowly than before. But even so, there was little comfort to be had because the heath was almost totally covered; the battle was all but lost.

Inigo wondered what he should do now. The great clash had been no more than the great anti-climax. It seemed that all the confidence he had placed in Michael was for nothing. But suddenly, a third line of fires sprang into life right on the western edge of the heath. Hardly daring to hope for anything, he turned away, not wanting to witness the demise of his friend and ally, but inevitably, his eyes were drawn back just in case. He felt compelled to watch, whatever the result might be. But just before the black cloud reached the last line of fires, Inigo noticed the putrid stench of decay again. Even as he turned to look behind him, he knew what had happened. His concern for the conflict taking place on the heath had driven everything else out of his mind. He had allowed himself to become isolated from Michael's cottage by the dark angel's terrible death cloud. He was marooned on the knoll, which would surely be swamped in the next few minutes by the rising black tide.

Now Inigo had to face the fact that he would not survive this battle. He stroked his ankle, which had begun to throb again, and considered his fate. During the night, he had been close to death on three occasions; during the pursuit from Teach's car when he had stabbed a villager, in the kitchen at Michael's cottage when a ceiling beam had saved him from being split in two, and half an hour ago when he almost perished in the freezing black cloud. But this was different. He was alone, watching a rising tide of poisonous gas, which would engulf him in a slow and painful death. He regretted having done so little in his life. Institutionalised, first at boarding school and then at the seminary, he had seen nothing of the world until he had staggered into Hobbswood. He regretted leaving his parents and

Wellington without saying good bye, but most of all, he regretted dying a virgin. He was, of course, frightened of death, especially the slow, agonising death that would be his when the cloud finally swamped him. But he still had the carving knife in his belt, and he hoped he would have the guts to use it on himself to speed the end when it came. He estimated he had about ten minutes left if the rise in the tide of Belphegor's fog continued at its present rate.

It seemed that Michael was beaten, but if that was really the case, and Thomas Messynger remained unavenged, then, apart from the physical pain, dying would not be such a bad thing. He had always believed that good would eventually triumph over evil; after all, that was the essence of Christianity. But if it was not to be so, then this world was not such a wonderful place to leave behind. The method of departure was, however, another matter. He had already experienced what the cloying, stinking, freezing cloud could do; he could smell it now as he watched the first few wisps embrace his feet, like black tentacles reaching up from some terrible, subterranean monster. He quickly retreated to the very highest point of the knoll. His estimate of another ten minutes now seemed optimistic; the rise in the black tide was accelerating.

The final, climactic clash took place, just as Inigo's island was being overwhelmed. He was already feeling nauseous again from the stench closing in around him; the fog was now above his knees. He shakily removed the knife from his belt and turned the point towards his stomach, but if he had time enough, he was determined to see the final confrontation between the leading edge of the cloud and Michael's last line of fires before ending his life.

But this time the blackness was held. Its progress was halted by the fires, but instead of retreating, it began to build upwards, as a large wave does when it approaches a shelving beach. At last, the wave broke over the fires like a massive Pacific roller, obliterating Michael's flames. The time had come to use the knife. His last thought was would it be quicker and less painful to cut his throat instead of burying the knife in his stomach? The delay in his decision was fortunate. The blackness of the fog, where the wave had broken over the fires, began to change into a dark grey. Then, a few moments later, spots of paler grey began to appear. He slipped the knife back into his belt and peered hard at the heath. He could see some of the flames again! They were blue rather than orange, but they were definitely flames. Perhaps, thought Inigo, the colour change was happening because of burning gases within the fog. More importantly, the cloud had definitely been halted and this time there was no wave build-up. He rubbed his tired eyes to make sure he was not mistaken. The embers of hope began to spark again; was it possible that the cloud itself was beginning to burn?

Soon the fires were growing rather than diminishing, as if they were starting to feed off the fog. Then, far to his left, a faint blue flame appeared inside the black cloud where the first line of fires had been. Within seconds, the second line revealed itself in a similar way. Far from being extinguished, Michael's fires had survived the all-consuming blackness, and after a short lull, were fighting back. The next few minutes saw the balance begin to shift. The flickering flames inside the fog began to spread, slowly at first, but then more quickly. Soon, large patches of glowing, blue fire radiated life out of Belphegor's black cloud of death.

Inigo looked down at his knees. The ominous, dark wisps of fog were ebbing away. Now he could see his feet again! The black tide had reached its zenith and was in full retreat. A flash of fire in front of him marked a new development. Here the flames had broken through the cloud, and having encountered the clean air above, recovered their orange hue. Soon, another dazzling orange plume flared upwards, then another. The cloud was starting to break up.

Inigo whispered to himself, "He's done it! He's bloody done it! I must find him."

Finding Michael was easier said than done. The retreating fog was still in possession of much of the battleground, so Inigo had to wait for a few minutes until his isolated knoll was reunited with the rest of the heath. Then he made his way through the dense heather until he reached the area at the western edge of the plateau, where Michael's last line of fires had been. He could only estimate the location, for although the fires here had died away, the dry heather had caught light, and the dense smoke made his eyes water and his throat choke. But at least he could see because the whole of the heath was now illuminated in a weird light of orange and blue flames.

The heat and smoke prevented him from carrying out a thorough search of the area, but after a while, an updraft caused by the heat began to generate a wind that blew the smoke back towards the sea. Now Inigo could see the footpath that formed the perimeter boundary of the plateau. He quickly made his way towards it, stumbling through burnt ground still hot from the fire. Each step he took created a cloud of soot and ash, which made breathing difficult, but as soon as he reached the footpath, where the air was clearer, he shouted.

"Michael! Michael!"

There was no response. All he could hear was the crackling sound of burning heather and gorse. The wind caused by the fire updraft was pleasantly cool, but he was desperately thirsty. There was no water on the heath; he would soon have to return to the cottage to get a drink, but he determined to search for Michael a little longer, even though there was every possibility he might have perished in his own flames.

A light to his right, in an unscathed area below the plateau and just to the west of the conflict zone, drew Inigo's attention. It was a single flame, about eight feet tall, presumably caused by a flying cinder or burning ash, but far brighter than anything he had seen so far. This flame was more gold than orange in colour, but there was something odd about it. Suddenly, he realised what was wrong; it was moving against the wind. Worse still, it was moving in the direction of Michael's cottage. Small though it was, it posed a far greater threat to Hazel, Wellington, and Constable Teach than the huge flames, which were even now consuming the black fog of the dark angel. But the rogue flame was still small enough to be beaten out by a determined effort, so Inigo suspended his search for Michael and ran towards it. In his haste, he forgot to take account of the myriad of rabbit holes that peppered the sandy heathland of East Suffolk. Before he was half way towards his target, he tripped and fell, briefly stunning himself when his head struck a large flint protruding from the thinly soiled ground.

Thankfully, his injured ankle was not aggravated by the fall, and he was able to get to his feet again, though he needed a few seconds to recover his balance.

But now the Boscabel in him was in full cry, desperate to save those who mattered most to him in the cottage. Wiping the warm blood from his wounded forehead, he tried to re-orientate himself, but try as he might, he could no longer see the flame that threatened Michael's home. Utterly bewildered, he methodically scanned the area once again, but the flame had disappeared. The danger to those in the cottage appeared to have gone, but Inigo knew only too well that the threat from Belphegor could not be discounted so easily. He sat down on the springy heather and scratched his head. So much had happened during this cataclysmic night that fact and fantasy were becoming inextricably mingled in his confused mind. What on earth should I do now? He wondered.

"Inigo, is that you?" Michael's warm, friendly voice came out from somewhere in the night.

"Yes!" answered a relieved and grateful Inigo. "Where the hell have you been? Are you all right?"

"I think so, but I'm very tired. What about you?"

"OK, I think."

Michael's huge, black figure loomed out of the darkness along the footpath where Inigo was sitting and sat down beside him.

"I thought I told you to go back to the cottage."

"I don't always do what I'm told."

"So I see, but I'm glad you're here."

Inigo remembered the rogue flame, which was still unaccounted for, and pointed towards Michael's cottage.

"I saw a tongue of golden fire, which was moving against the wind but in the direction of your house; now it seems to have disappeared."

"Er, yes," replied Michael hesitantly. "I saw it too, but it must have burned itself out."

"Could it have been Belphegor?"

"Maybe, but I don't think so. He is beaten. Let us return to the plateau and watch the disintegration of the angel of the Dark."

When the two men reached Inigo's knoll again, the eastern

sky was already a pale azure, presaging the imminent sunrise.

The black cloud had broken up into dozens of separate, incandescent, blue and orange patches, but the natural fire consuming the gorse and heather was also spreading rapidly.

Michael, who was so exhausted he could hardly stand, slowly sat down on the scorched ground and said quietly, "I was hoping to limit the collateral damage, but the ground is so dry it wasn't possible... to..."

He was suddenly interrupted by a long, deep, agonised groan, which came from somewhere within the main body of the burning cloud. It lasted for at least half a minute, then gradually descended into a rumbling growl as it faded away on the breeze.

To Inigo, the pain in that terrible sound seemed like the howl of a thousand tormented souls, the cry of utter despair.

"What on earth was that?" he gasped.

"The high angel of darkness has acknowledged defeat on this occasion," said Michael in a matter-of-fact sort of way. "His evil influence is being dispersed and destroyed before us. This time the Light has won."

Michael and Inigo watched together in silence as the dramatic scene unfolded. The breeze was strengthening and blowing seawards, which drove the flames towards the cliffs and helped to limit the destruction on the heath. The dawn light was now bright enough to show more detail, and Inigo could see large, scorched areas in the heather, which marked the passage of the fire, but when he turned to speak to Michael, his comrade's head was slumped forwards; he was fast asleep. Inigo decided to let the man, who had become a close friend, rest a little longer.

But the power that was Belphegor, the black scorpion of the Dark, still had a sting in its tail.

III

No sooner had Michael fallen asleep, than the wind changed. It might have been a co-incidence, but Inigo had seen too much to be convinced by that. The steady, offshore breeze, which until a few moments ago had seemed to be an ally, began to weaken and waver. There was a pause of stillness, then the breeze started up again, but this time it was haphazard and gusty. Inigo stood up and looked round. He sensed something had gone wrong, but from where he was standing, he could not see much. Glancing down at his exhausted, slumbering friend, he decided to investigate on his own and trotted towards the knoll he had used earlier to observe the great battle.

In less than ten minutes, he had reached the summit, and at first, all seemed well. Apart from the extreme eastern end, the end nearest the sea, Dunwich Heath was now clear of the black cloud. The heather was smouldering rather than burning, and Michael's fires did not seem to be spreading any further. But the burning cloud was not yet fully dissipated because, when Inigo looked out towards the east, dense plumes of grey smoke revealed that the forest around Hobbswood was now burning fiercely. Bright sparks and incandescent cinders were floating skywards from the pine forest, lifted like fireflies on the updraft. The Scots pine, which not so long ago had hidden him from the searching eyes of Belphegor, was probably now no more than a charred stump; Hobbswood itself must be close to incineration. If the villagers remained indoors, as their master had instructed, a horrible disaster was about to happen.

He looked south towards Sizewell, whose myriad lights were now visible again through the thinning smoke. Thoughts of Hobbswood's destruction were suddenly dwarfed by what was developing in the south. A large segment of burning fog had broken away from the main cloud and was drifting, or being driven, in the direction of the nuclear power station. Inigo had no idea what the fog might do to nuclear reactors, but another Chernobyl in East Anglia would be a final gesture of spite worthy of the enemy. A nuclear disaster in Suffolk would no doubt go a long way to assuage the defeated dark angel's frustration.

He abandoned the knoll. It was too late to stop the maverick cloud reaching Sizewell, but if the site staff had some warning, they might be able to take preventative measures, or even shut down the core if necessary. With luck, they might see the cloud approaching, but that could not be relied upon; the stakes were too high.

He returned to Michael, who was still in a deep sleep.

Shaking him none too gently, he shouted, "Michael! For God's sake, wake up!"

There was no response. Michael seemed more unconscious than asleep. No amount of nudging and prodding could waken him.

In desperation, he shouted in Michael's ear, "Michael, Lord Belphegor is calling you!"

The reaction was electrifying. Michael was on his feet almost before the words had left Inigo's mouth, his body alert and ready for action, but it was the eyes which were most startling.

They were wide open and seemed to glow, almost like the dark angel's, except that the light in Michael's eyes was a clean, pure white instead of a putrid yellow.

Inigo gasped. "Michael, what's happened to your eyes; they're on fire! Are you in pain?"

Michael closed his eyes, rubbed the eyelids, and opened them again.

"Is that better?"

"Back to normal, I think, but there's not enough daylight yet for me to see them properly."

"Do not misunderstand what you have just seen. It was only a reflection of the fire behind you. Look!"

Inigo turned and saw that the charred heather about fifty yards away had re-ignited as the strengthening breeze began to stir the embers into life again. Then a tone of irritation entered the big man's voice.

"Did you have to waken me like that?"

"It was the only way. I tried shouting, then shaking you, but you didn't respond. You seemed to be unconscious."

Michael relaxed again and yawned. "I expect you were right. I seldom require much sleep, but when I do, it's a deep sleep. Presumably you had a good reason to disturb me?"

"Certainly. We have a potential catastrophe on our hands."

Inigo described the threat he had seen approaching the power station and ended by asking, "Are you absolutely sure the Dark has been beaten?"

"Yes. You, yourself, heard the wail of despair. That alone should have convinced you. But in his bitterness, our enemy hopes to cause as much destruction as he can before he fades away, even if it means burning alive all his erstwhile followers; he has no need of them any more."

"But it's not only his followers who are at risk. We must alert the power station of the danger heading towards it."

"As you already know, Inigo, there is no telephone in my house," said Michael apologetically. "The nearest phone box is outside the Dunwich post office."

"But Constable Teach's car will have a radio link to Suffolk police headquarters. That should ensure Sizewell gets the earliest possible warning."

"Excellent!" said Michael. "Then you return to the constable while I head towards the power station. There might be something I can do to divert the threat."

"But you'll never get there before the cloud!"

"Not if I have to wait here debating with you. I can travel more quickly than you suppose."

"All right then but be careful. After I've contacted the police, I shall return to your cottage and wait for you there."

Michael, who had already started to walk across the scorched heather towards Sizewell with ground devouring strides, stopped and looked back at Inigo.

His face was blackened with smoke and grime, but he was smiling, and his bright blue eyes seemed to reflect the dawn light as he called back, "In case we do not meet again, I would like to say that, without your help, Inigo Boscabel, I should have been beaten this night. Remember our discourses and have faith in the Creator, even if it is not the god in whom you once believed."

"But my God loved us!"

"Did he really? Just read the Book of Joshua to see what he had planned for the Canaanites; ethnic cleansing that even Hitler would have been proud of! Remember, there is something beyond this life for those who really deserve it. You have already proven yourself, so keep up the good work. Good bye!"

That sounded remarkably like a final farewell speech to Inigo.

"Michael! Will you be coming back?"

But the tall, upright figure just waved, turned to the south, and strode purposefully towards the power station.

Inigo watched until Michael's huge frame was swallowed up by a fold in the terrain, then, heavy hearted, he trotted steadily along the footpath that led to the cottage. He knew he would not see Michael again. But there were still so many things he wanted to talk about, which would now have to remain unsaid, and so much he could have learned from the obscure, highly intelligent country man. And of all the strange things he had seen since he came to Hobbswood, he knew the last thing he would forget was that bright fire he saw in Michael's eyes when he awoke from his deep sleep after the battle with Belphegor. That had been the only moment his comrade's guard had been lowered, yet he still had no idea who Michael really was. Now he would never know.

But Michael's task had been accomplished; the evil of Belphegor was gone from Hobbswood forever. No doubt, new challenges lay ahead for him and his secret Order of guardians of the Light. Who were they? Were they all like Michael? The frustration of not knowing, but having been so close to finding out, was almost unbearable.

A lungful of poisonous fog quickly brought Inigo back to more immediate matters. Isolated patches of the dark cloud still lurked around the heath; he had just trotted through one. But the rapidly improving light caused by a new dawn enabled him to avoid the remaining outliers of the dark angel's malice.

Chapter Ten

When Inigo reached Michael's cottage, it was half past four and the sun's golden disc was just above the eastern horizon. Constable Teach and Hazel came out into the front garden to greet him.

While Hazel threw herself into his arms, Teach asked, "What's happening? Where is Mr Shapmire? When I woke up, you were both missing."

Inigo knew he would have to edit some of what he had seen on Dunwich Heath in order to retain credibility in the policeman's eyes, so he confined himself to saying, "Mister Shapmire and Doctor Fairweather have sorted out their differences up on the heath. You won't be seeing either of them again. I've come back to warn the staff at Sizewell power station that a cloud of burning, poisonous fog is heading their way."

Teach frowned, "I don't understand. What burning fog? Has there been a gas leak?"

"I mean precisely what I say," answered Inigo brusquely. "There's a cloud of gas of some sort, which is burning out of control and moving in the direction of the power station. It's already set the forest around Hobbswood alight, and the villagers are in serious danger of burning alive. Don't ask me where the gas cloud came from. I'll try and explain later, but now we must focus on warning Sizewell and saving the Hobbswood villagers, if it's not already too late. If we waste time talking here, we may be vaporised in an atomic explosion. There's no phone in this house, so we'll need to use your car radio to alert Sizewell if that's all right with you, Constable."

"Of course it is," said the confused policeman. "We'd better hurry."

Inigo and Teach left Hazel in the cottage with Wellington and ran down the track towards Hobbswood, but they had not gone far when it became apparent that reaching the officer's car was not going to be easy. The first inkling of trouble came when a gust of wind blew a flurry of fiery sparks over their heads. Seconds later, another, larger flurry flew past, scorching their clothes and singeing their hair.

They heard the fire before they saw it. The sound of crackling branches and splitting pine cones heralded the firestorm that met the two men as they rounded the last bend in the track just before the straight that led into Hobbswood village.

"Christ!" gasped Teach as they stopped, halted by the inferno. "The whole village has gone! No one could possibly survive in that!"

Inigo was surprised and a little ashamed of the grim pleasure he felt as he watched Hobbswood going up in flames. He decided he must have a vindictive streak, which had lain dormant until now, for there was no compassion in his heart for the terrible death that had befallen the villagers. He was especially pleased that Seth Greenwood had received his just deserts. It was a sort of rough justice that the fate that had destroyed the Hobbswood folk was much the same as what their ancestors had inflicted upon Thomas Messynger and his followers. The avenging of Thomas concluded the three-hundred-year-old saga in a most satisfying way.

"No time to stand and stare!" shouted Teach above the roar of the flames. "There's the car. We might just get to it before the fire does."

They ran the last few yards to the police car. The flames were rapidly working their way through the forest either side of them. A slight shift in the direction of the strengthening wind could easily cut them off from the escape route back to Michael's cottage. The heat was intense. Inigo folded his arms across his face as they ran, but he was not wearing gloves and the backs of his hands started to blister. Almost as bad was the acrid smoke, which seemed to scour the back of his nose and throat like concentrated acid. A few minutes ago, he thought he was going to survive this apocalyptic night, but now he was not so sure.

When they reached the police car, the nearest flames were less than fifty yards away and advancing rapidly. Inigo scorched his fingers when he touched the car's steel door handle, which was already hot, but Teach, whose gardener's hands were sufficiently calloused to grasp a boiling kettle without undue pain, opened the door for him. Both men jumped into the car to escape, if only briefly, the searing heat outside. Teach switched on the shortwave radio, but any hopes he may have had of delivering a short message then fleeing were soon dashed. Maybe it was the effect of the fire, or perhaps just the low-lying ground that caused the interference, but all he could hear were sporadic crackles and whines interspersed with the occasional faint sound of the Suffolk Police radio controller's voice asking him to repeat himself. Inigo swore quietly as he remembered Ambrose Samphyre hurling the car keys into the grass verge during Hazel's rescue. There was no way the car could be moved without them and there was certainly no time to look for them.

While the constable frantically tried to tune the radio to a better frequency, Inigo watched in horror as the flames raced towards them. The nearside wing mirror cracked, smoke began to enter through the air vents, and the dark blue paint on the bonnet started to blister. Still the radio would not respond properly and Inigo, who was sitting behind Teach, tapped him on the shoulder.

Trying to keep his voice calm, he said, "If we don't get out of here now, we'll be baked like a couple of spuds in an oven."

"You go," replied the exasperated policeman. "There's no need for you to stay here."

"But I can't just abandon you."

"Don't worry about that, I think I'm getting through at last. One short message and I'll be right behind you."

"Are you sure?"

"Just bugger off! Mr Boscabel."

When he opened the car door, the heat almost threw Inigo back inside again. He pushed himself out and began to run back up the track. Even as the choking fumes penetrated his nostrils and attacked the lining of his lungs, he could smell the unmistakeable smell of burning hair, his hair. But to stop now would be fatal, so he covered his head with his arms as best he could and ran until he reached the bend in the track where he and Teach had first set eyes on the burning forest. He stopped there, brushing his smouldering hair with his blistered hands, and looked back. The fire was already outflanking him, but worst of all, a curtain of flame had been blown across the track in his wake, obscuring the police car. Poor Teach was cut off.

Inigo dared not wait or he would be cut off himself. Michael's cottage was in the direct line of the all-consuming fire. Hazel and Wellington would soon be in danger. Michael's last words had made Inigo feel something of a hero, but his desertion of the policeman drove all notions of heroism out of his mind. He could only hope that the brave Suffolk constable had got the vital message through before the flames took him, and if determination was to be the deciding factor, Teach would surely have succeeded.

When Inigo reached the cottage, sparks blown from the burning tree tops were already starting small fires in the overgrown front garden.

Hazel, who was standing at the front gate awaiting his return, asked, "Where's Constable Teach?"

Inigo, whose conscience was already afflicted by guilt for abandoning the policeman, stared hard at his feet and said quietly, "I had to leave him."

"But is he all right?"

"I doubt it. The fire separated us. He was trapped. It all happened so quickly, there was nothing I could do."

"But how could that be?" she persisted. "Surely you must have stayed close together? You wouldn't have just left him behind."

Inigo felt wretched. True, the constable had told him to go, but he knew he should have stayed. But if he had done that, then Hazel and Wellington would probably have perished, too. This question would trouble him remorselessly in the future, but now, with the forest fire almost on the threshold of Michael's cottage, there was no time for inquests.

"He chose to stay in the car," he said coldly. "And if you stay here, you'll burn too. The fire's just behind me. This cottage will be ablaze in a few seconds from now. Start running up the track towards the Leiston road. I'll get Wellington and catch you up."

The heroic afterglow that had bathed Inigo in Hazel's eyes since her rescue from the village faded somewhat, but she obeyed him, and within a couple of minutes, he was beside her with

Wellington straining at the home-made lead Michael had made for him the day before. Soon they had left the forest and the fire behind and were able to slow to a walk. The early morning sun was obscured by a dense pall of smoke and there was no hint of the usual dawn chorus, but such considerations mattered not at all. They had survived!

II

It was just after five thirty in the morning when the crews from Southwold and Beccles fire stations came across two bedraggled figures, accompanied by a huge dog, sitting on the roadside at the junction where the track to Hobbswood left the Leiston road. The Southwold tender stopped and the officer in charge alighted.

"Are you two from Hobbswood?"

Inigo answered, "One of us is. The rest are probably burnt to cinders by now."

Seeing the state of Inigo's hands the officer asked, "Are you in pain?"

"Just a little."

"Stay here and I'll radio for help. We'll get you to a hospital in no time."

"What about my dog?"

"We'll find somewhere for him."

"Don't bother, he's staying with me. What happened at Sizewell? Is everything OK?"

"I believe so. The staff received a warning from the police before the fire got too near and had enough time to put the emergency procedure in place."

"Thank God for that," sighed Inigo.

He struggled to his feet and pointed down the track to Hobbswood.

"There's a very brave policeman down there, Constable Teach of the Southwold station. You'll probably find what's left of him in his burnt-out car. He was the officer who got the warning through to the power station. It cost him his life."

The fire officer looked at the flames leaping skywards from Hobbswood forest, knowing no-one could survive in that inferno. Then he examined Inigo's hands more closely.

"Listen Mr... er..."

"Boscabel."

"Your injuries don't look too severe. Would you like me to radio the Swan Hotel in Southwold? They take dogs in their annexe rooms, and we can get a doctor to treat your hands later today, but for now our first aider will fix you up with temporary dressings."

"That will be fine," replied Inigo gratefully, then looking sidelong at Hazel, he added. "Make it a double room please."

The hotel sent out a car, and in three quarters of an hour, Inigo, Hazel, and Wellington were settled in a comfortable suite in the Swan's annexe close to the town centre. While Hazel bathed, Inigo stared at himself in the full-length wardrobe mirror. He looked like something out of a horror film, hair wild and scorched, clothes ragged and torn, and a face as black as soot, but the bright blue eyes that looked back at him like two sapphire stars in a night time sky told a different story. Whereas five days ago he would have seen an overgrown schoolboy, pre-occupied with his own little world full of things that didn't really matter, now he saw a man quickly growing in self-confidence. One who had just faced and overcome a challenge that would have tested anyone to the utmost. It was very sad about Constable Teach, but the policeman had been right. There was no point in Inigo giving his life if it made no difference to the final result. That was reality, not romance, but the guilt still pressed down hard on him. He thought about Teach's wife and family. They would be in turmoil now. He would go and see them when things had quietened down a bit. But most important of all, Teach had managed to get the vital message through to Sizewell; there would be no Chernobyl in Suffolk.

Inigo looked down at his bandaged hands. The final step to manhood would have to wait a day or two. Anyway, all he wanted now was a bath and some sleep. But when a scrubbed and naked Hazel emerged from the bathroom, he began to have second thoughts. In any event, the decision was made for him because when he finally finished his bath and scrub-up, she was fast asleep. Meanwhile, Wellington snored thunderously in the corner of the room.

Inigo was woken by the telephone beside his bed. It was the doctor who had been contacted by the fire officer to attend to his hands. He sat up and looked at his watch; nearly six o'clock in the afternoon. Hazel was still sleeping soundly beside him, and Wellington lay contentedly in a sunbeam, grooming his huge paws. After all he had been through, Inigo was surprised he had not been tormented by more wild dreams of seventeenth century religious fanaticism, but thankfully, there had been nothing but oblivion.

The doctor was a dapper, fussy little man, who wore a spotted bow tie, but he expertly salved and bandaged Inigo's hands; the fireman's bandages had come off in the bath.

"I'm afraid you'll have to get your wife to feed you for a couple of days," he said, looking at Hazel's dark tresses spread wantonly over her pillow. "But there shouldn't be any scarring if you're careful."

Inigo looked at the doctor's neat handiwork. "Thank you, Doctor."

"I'll come back in the morning."

He dropped a newspaper on Inigo's bed and closed his bag.

"It's the evening edition; you'll find it interesting."

As soon as the doctor left, Inigo leaned back on his pillow and read the front-page headlines:

TRAGEDY AT DUNWICH — WHOLE VILLAGE DESTROYED IN BLAZE — MORE THAN THIRTY DEAD

But it was the sub-heading that really caught his eye:

Heroic Southwold policeman has lucky escape

The paper described how Constable Teach had remained too long at his post in getting the warning through to Sizewell, but a sudden change in wind direction saved him from incineration. He had escaped without a scratch! Inigo was bursting to tell Hazel the good news, but he forced himself to be patient and let her sleep a little longer. He turned the page with his thumb and the tip of his forefinger, which just peeped through the end of the bandage on his right hand, and read on.

Another column, written by an eminent consultant geologist, suggested that the burning cloud, which, as it turned out, just missed Sizewell, might have been caused by a deep fissure in the sea bed, allowing North Sea gas to bubble up through the salt water and float inland.

The expert did not, however, explain how the gas could have been ignited, nor what caused the deep fissure to close up again of its own accord. Still, it was not a bad effort at explaining things and certainly far more believable than the truth, thought Inigo wryly.

After reading more dramatic accounts of what was already

being dubbed 'The Great Fire of Hobbswood', he spent the next half hour going through the inner pages of local news and gossip until Hazel began to stir. He put down the paper and ruefully looked at his bandaged hands.

"Are you awake?"

Hazel acknowledged the question by rubbing her foot up and down his leg. He immediately felt himself hardening, but first he must break the good news.

"Constable Teach is safe and well."

Hazel sat up, now wide awake. "But that's wonderful! Are you sure?"

"It's all in here in the newspaper. He wasn't even injured."

She stretched across him to reach the paper and smiled as she felt his hardened manhood press against her waist. While she read the front page, he looked at her, at the long, raven-black hair framing her shoulders, the full lips moving slightly as she read, and at her full young breasts. He wanted her badly, even more than before, and to hell with scarring and bandages!

Soon she saw him looking at her, and dropping the paper on the floor, said, "I think the time has come, don't you?"

"My hands?"

She gently kissed his fingertips one by one, then looked up at him. "Don't worry, I think we can manage without them for the time being."

She threw back the duvet, untied his hotel dressing gown, and climbed on top of him; they made love at last. Yet even as this final piece of the complicated Boscabel jigsaw puzzle fell into place, he could not help wondering at the ease with which Hazel said nothing about her mother's fate. But it was only a fleeting thought as his virginity was consigned to history.

Even without the use of his hands, he made love to Hazel

well into the night. In truth, he was fortunate to have his first experience with her, for the delight they found in each other derived from her experience rather than his enthusiastic but unfocused energy. It was not until eleven o'clock that exhaustion, and a certain degree of soreness, finally brought a temporary halt to their passion, but unlike Hazel, Inigo could not simply roll over and go to sleep in the time-honoured male style. There was a third person to consider.

In order to avoid a repetition of what happened on the beach during the first meeting with Hazel, Wellington had been shut in the bathroom since the doctor's visit; his bladder was being tested almost beyond endurance. Putting on his dirty clothes was unpleasant, so as he got dressed, Inigo resolved to buy some more for himself and Hazel in the morning. He recalled seeing at least two clothes shops in the high street on the afternoon he had called in at the police station to report his near murder by the Hobbswood villagers. Thinking of the police station brought Constable Teach to mind again, and Inigo decided he would visit him as soon as he had purchased a decent shirt and some jeans to find out more details about the miraculous deliverance from the fire.

Wellington thought his walk was perfunctory, considering how long he had been confined, but despite a serious effort to steer his master further, Inigo was tired, and half dragging, half pushing the mastiff up the annexe steps, he eventually managed to return to his room.

Hazel was awake.

"Is everything all right? I was beginning to wonder what had happened to you."

"Everything is fine. I just had to see to Wellington."

He returned the grumpy dog to his bed of blankets in the

bathroom, threw off his clothes, and got into bed, but before turning out the light, he felt he needed to speak to Hazel about her mother.

"I hesitate to mention this, but you do realise your mother cannot have survived the fire?"

"Yes," replied Hazel in a neutral tone.

"Well, you don't seem very upset. I know how I would feel if that was my mother."

She looked at him in a way he had not seen before as a steely hardness edged her voice. "I told you before, there was no love between my mother and me. She would have let me burn instead of you. She made no effort to shield me after you escaped from the black Mass. I was a nuisance to her when I grew up because I replaced her as Fairweather's companion in bed. She was jealous, though I would far rather she'd continued with him instead of me, but it wasn't her choice. She was besotted with him."

"Your mother and Lucas were lovers!"

"Yes. She was not always as frumpy as she is now; or was until a few hours ago."

Inigo switched off the light, but as he waited for sleep, he felt disturbed that he still had so much to learn about Hazel. Her values were different to his. Would he ever really be able to understand her?

III

It took the whole morning to buy the new clothes. Hazel had never experienced shopping before without the formidable presence of her mother; the unaccustomed freedom had to be exploited to the full. In the end, she selected two dresses and a pair of lightweight shoes from Denny's, the high-class clothes shop opposite the Swan, while Inigo settled for a plain red shirt and black jeans. He felt a warm glow inside as he observed the pleasure his woman derived from the simple act of shopping and choosing for herself, which he had made possible for her, but Wellington, who had still not forgotten his truncated walk of the night before, made it a less than perfect morning by his determination to challenge every dog in Southwold.

After lunch, they parted company for a short while. Hazel, wearing one of her new dresses, preferred to enjoy her new freedom by exploring the town while Inigo went to see Constable Teach. He did not know where the constable lived, so his first stop was the police station, where he was brusquely informed that Teach was recuperating at home and not seeing any visitors. But when he explained who he was, the officer behind the desk became more attentive.

"Bill spoke of you with the greatest respect, Mr Boscabel. We'll want you to make a statement in due course; you're staying in Southwold?"

"Yes, at the Swan."

The officer looked nervously at Wellington. "Bill also mentioned your dog. I see he wasn't exaggerating."

"Do you think Constable Teach will see me? There are things we need to discuss."

"I'm sure he will. Do you have a car?"

"I'm afraid not; I'm on a walking holiday."

"Well, I'm sure I can arrange a lift for you," smiled the policeman. "So perhaps you would like to make your statement while you wait?"

Inigo's statement blandly related the bare facts regarding the fire, although he was obliged to tell a white lie concerning Hazel's presence at the cottage to explain why she had not been with the rest of the Hobbswood villagers when the fire started.

At this point, the officer gave him a knowing wink, but Inigo knew he would have to tell Bill Teach what he had said so that the constable could adjust his own statement accordingly when the time came. He made no mention of the terrible events that had preceded the fire. There was no need to, and no one except Teach would believe him anyway. The statement took longer to write than he had anticipated, and by the time he was dropped off at Teach's ivy-covered cottage just outside Southwold, it was nearly four o'clock.

"He's sitting in the garden, listening to the cricket match against Australia," said the cheerful, matronly woman who answered the door. "I'm sure he'll want to see you, Mr Boscabel."

"Thank you, Mrs Teach, I won't keep him too long."

The French windows at the back of the house were open and Inigo went through into the well-manicured garden, where he found Teach sitting in a deck chair, smoking a pipe, and enjoying listening to the Aussies getting a good clobbering for a change.

The garden was a riot of colour, with herbs, shrubs, and a superb array of roses, adding a delightful scent to the peaceful atmosphere. A green swathe of perfectly cut lawn, without a trace of moss or clover, set the whole scene of an English country garden off to perfection. Wellington released a single deep bark at a large black cat, which lay in the shade of a luxuriant euphorbia. It opened one eye, saw the dog was on a lead, and went back to sleep.

Teach put down his pipe and smiled. "Hello, Inigo. Cup of tea?"

"Yes, please."

"I'll get it," called Mrs Teach from the house.

Constable Teach looked very different out of uniform, more like a friendly uncle than an officer of the law. He pointed Inigo to the deck chair opposite him and Inigo sat down.

"Very glad you came to see me, Inigo because we need to talk" – he glanced back at the house – "alone."

"To get our stories straight?"

"Exactly." He picked up his pipe and took a long draw from it. "Have you made your statement yet?"

"Yes, just before I came here."

"Did you mention the fight with the villagers at all?"

"No, I saw no need to."

"How did you explain my presence at Mr Shapmire's cottage?"

"I said you were there when I got back from walking my dog, but I didn't know why."

"Good, best to keep it simple. I'll remember that for my own statement."

"I also said that Hazel was there because of me and let the officer at Southwold draw his own conclusions."

"Well done. So you said nothing about your disagreement with Doctor Fairweather?"

"No, nor about you giving me short shrift at the police station."

"Sorry about that," said Teach. "But you will admit, it was an unlikely story. I'm glad I didn't write anything down in the day book; otherwise, we'd have a lot more explaining to do now."

"Well, that was fortuitous, I suppose. Were there any survivors in the village?"

"No, everyone was burnt to a crisp, except Fairweather. The bodies were mostly unidentifiable but there was one body short of what there should have been. The firemen say they might have missed a heavily incinerated corpse in the debris and will look again tomorrow, but you and I know who's missing."

"What about Michael?"

"Also missing, but I have no doubt he escaped. You were the last person to see him."

Inigo raised an eyebrow in mock surprise. "Do I detect a change in your attitude to matters metaphysical, Constable Teach?"

"I think we know each other well enough now to call each other by our first names, Inigo. As far as meta whatever it is, I don't know what to think any more."

"If I were to tell you what happened on Dunwich Heath in the early hours of this morning, you'd be more confused than ever. I know I am, but I will if you want me to."

"No, thanks," said Bill emphatically. "How is young Hazel? Is she still with you?"

"Yes, we're staying together at the Swan. I intend to make our relationship more permanent. It's time I got married and settled down."

Teach's eyes widened. His own son had got married in the first flush of love. It did not last long. The experienced policeman replied to Inigo in a gentle, almost fatherly way.

"Now listen to me. You have led a sheltered life. I know that because Mr Shapmire told me so while you slept after the fight at the cottage. What you are now experiencing is young love. It can be very strong, though most people go through it in their teens, but you have only just woken up in that way. Hazel is an attractive young woman and you saved her from a gruesome death, but you may not find permanent happiness together. She is waking up in a different sense to you. The real world must seem exciting and full of promise to her. After a while, you may find you cannot give her the excitement and adventure she's looking for. Why not wait a while before committing yourself. I would not wish to see either of you disappointed."

This was not what Inigo wished to hear.

"But she's an orphan! Her mother has just died in the fire. Now she has nothing. Should I just cast her adrift in the street!"

"Of course not, Inigo, but there is no need to rush into a permanent commitment. Plenty of young people live together nowadays without getting married. Just give it a test period before the final act. I'm just cautioning you against too much haste."

"Perhaps," grunted Inigo, unconvinced.

"Tea's ready," called Mrs Teach, as she brought a tray into the garden.

Inigo noticed there were three cups on it and was ashamed by the irritation he felt at the intrusive presence of Bill's homely wife. From the clipped responses of her husband during the next ten minutes, he realised that the constable still had more to tell him. Unfortunately, Mrs Teach seemed disposed to remain with her guest, as a good hostess should, but Bill gained them the extra time they needed by requesting another pot of the excellent brew.

As soon as Mrs Teach disappeared into the house, Inigo asked, "How exactly did you escape from the fire in Hobbswood forest? When I ran away, the flames were within yards of your car. The newspaper said something about a lucky change in the wind direction."

"Lucky? It was a bloody miracle! If I were to tell anyone else what happened, they'd think I was round the bend! I'm already beginning to doubt my own memory, but if I describe to you exactly what happened while everything is still fresh in my mind, then at least you'll remember too."

Inigo said, "Don't worry. After all the things I've seen over the past few days, nothing could surprise me any more."

Bill took a long pull at his newly charged pipe and began his account.

"After you left the car, it took me another minute or so to get through to police headquarters. The bloody idiot on the switchboard made me repeat everything, and by the time I abandoned the car, the heat was melting the rubber round the window frames. I ran back towards Shapmire's cottage, but after only a few paces, I found my escape route was cut off. A wall of fire, blazing up from a fallen tree trunk, blocked the path and I was forced back."

Inigo drew in his breath. "I must have missed that by seconds."

"When I turned round, I thought the end had come," continued Bill. "All round me was a mass of flames. The forest either side of the track was ablaze; there was no escape through the trees. Through the smoke ahead, I could only see more flames, but not having the courage to throw myself into the fire and make a quick end of it, I ran back to the car to await my fate there."

"Just as well you weren't too brave, otherwise you wouldn't be here now," observed Inigo.

"True, the instinct for life is incredibly strong, even if only for a few extra seconds." Bill paused for a moment.

The next part of his story was going to be difficult to put into words. He glanced back at the house as if he did not want anyone, not even his own wife, to hear what he was going to say next.

"What I'm going to tell you, Inigo, is exactly what I saw, or thought I saw. You may call me a madman if you wish, but I will still feel better after I've told you everything."

"Well, Bill, if you're a madman then so am I."

Teach leaned forward and lowered his voice.

"The car was like an oven. The windscreen had been shattered by the heat, but it still provided some protection from the flames, so I got inside and shut the door. The seat stuck to my trousers and there was a strong smell of melting plastic. I shut my eyes and waited for the end, but something made me open them again, a morbid curiosity perhaps. I looked all round. An unbroken circle of flame surrounded the car and was closing in as it fed off the thick leaf mould that underlies the forest. I began to choke as the smoke found its way into my lungs. My eyes started to water. The shattered windscreen and my watery eyes blurred my vision of what happened next, so I may have misinterpreted what I saw, but I don't think so."

"Bill you can speak openly to me. I am the only person who will understand."

"The flames were only twenty yards away when, directly in front of the car, a tongue of fire began to push towards me in advance of the rest of the inferno, as if it was following a line of particularly inflammable material on the forest floor; an old, dried out log maybe. But then the unbelievable bit happened. The fire tongue detached itself from the background wall of flame behind it so that now, only thirty feet away, a separate column of fire stood between me and the rest of the forest blaze. For a few seconds, the column stayed still where it was but then, instead of coming closer, it began to spin, though only slowly at first. Soon the spinning started to accelerate, rotating on the same spot, like a whirlwind of fire. I must have been mesmerised because my fear left me; somehow, I knew I was not destined to die that night."

Inigo recalled the tongue of flame he had seen on Dunwich Heath, apparently moving against the wind and well outside the area of conflict with Belphegor's poisonous fog. Had Michael not said that fire was his weapon? But how could he have influenced the fate of a man cut off from all help by a forest fire? And the last time he had seen Michael, he was heading in the opposite direction, towards the power station. But he kept his thoughts to himself as Bill resumed his story.

"As I watched the spinning fire column, I noticed that the wall of flame surrounding my car also began to spin, as if in sympathy with it. It seemed as if the fire tongue was spinning so quickly, it was creating a sort of vortex that affected the rest of the blaze. But the important thing was the effect on me because the forest fire was no longer advancing on my car. It was like being in the calm eye of a hurricane while the storm rages all round you.

"Soon, the combustible material on the forest floor, which was feeding the fire, began to be used up. The flames weakened, except for the separate tongue of spinning fire, which continued to burn as fiercely as ever. By now I could hardly see a thing through my watering eyes, but as I peered through the smoke, I swear I saw the flame tongue detach itself from the forest floor and hover a couple of feet above the ground without losing its intensity, even though there was no longer any fuel to feed it."

"But how could that happen?" asked Inigo. "There must have been something feeding the fire."

"I told you it was a crazy story, but that is what I saw, or thought I saw. Like you, I found it difficult to believe at the time, so I rubbed my eyes and tried hard to clear them of tears, but when they began to focus again, the flame tongue had disappeared and where it had been, the ground was untouched by fire."

Bill sat back in his deck chair, emptied his pipe, and sighed, "Well, that's about it. The forest blaze passed me by, and I stayed with the car until the fire crew arrived."

"How did you explain your survival?"

"A sudden change of wind direction. It's the best I could come up with at the time."

"It's perfectly true, if you think about it," said Inigo.

A voice from behind them called, "Would you like some cakes with your tea, Mr Boscabel?"

Mrs Teach placed a tray on the garden table and sat down with them.

She put a plate of digestive biscuits on the ground in front of Wellington and asked, "Does your dog like biscuits, Mr Boscabel?"

But before Inigo could answer, the plate was empty.

Chapter Eleven

In due course, Bill Teach's misgivings about the stability of Inigo's relationship with Hazel proved to be correct. Inigo was true to his word and took Hazel home with him to London, where his surprised parents helped him with the finance he needed to set up home in a small, one bedroom flat in Kentish Town. Although highly educated in many academic subjects, he was not qualified in any practical sense, so he decided to take a course for a Bachelor of Education degree, which would qualify him for a career in teaching.

For Hazel, the excitement of city life palled as she gradually realised that her benefactor's income was insufficient to provide her with the attractive things that surrounded her. 'Wait till we can afford it' was a phrase that soon began to irritate her. While he was at college, she began to spend most of her time walking in Parliament Hill Fields or Hampstead Heath where she could at least enjoy nature, even if the thunder of London traffic was never far away. She began to wonder if she had done the right thing, leaving Suffolk so precipitously. The boredom was made even worse by Inigo's refusal to allow her to apply for what he considered to be menial work, even though she, like him, was unqualified for anything better. Eventually he relented and she quickly obtained a job as a waitress in a high-class restaurant in Tufnell Park, just one stop along the Northern line from Kentish Town, which meant that, apart from Sundays, she and Inigo hardly saw each other.

But in her new job, Hazel became the object of admiring glances from many young men of substance who frequented the restaurant for business lunches or in the evening after a hard day's work in the City of London. Soon the inevitable happened. A year almost to the day after the Great Fire of Hobbswood, Inigo came home bursting to tell her that he had passed his first-year exams with distinction and that his income was about to increase because he was to take up part time class teaching as a supplement to his studies. But when he entered the flat, he knew something was wrong. The flat was tidy and there was no evidence of Hazel's presence, no hair brush on the floor, no unwashed coffee mug beside the settee, and so on. Then he saw the envelope on the mantelpiece above the gas fire. His hand was shaking when he opened it.

The simple, child-like writing told him quite directly that she had found someone else, he would not see her again, and not to come looking for her. There was no attempt to sweeten the pill with sumptuous platitudes, but there was no malice either. That was Hazel.

Inigo was not really surprised. Hazel possessed a certain hardness, which did not really suit him, but he wished she could have been patient enough to stay on until he got real work.

Perhaps a decent salary instead of a student grant might have made all the difference. Now he would never know. Instead, he faced another year in the flat alone. The lease terms did not permit pets, so Wellington was now living with Inigo's parents again in Regents Park. He was tempted to return there and continue his studies from the parental home, but he knew that would be a retrograde step; fledglings, once flown, should not return to the nest.

So it was in September of the following year, just after his thirtieth birthday, that Inigo found himself back in Suffolk again. He had passed his final exams and secured a teaching job at Saint Benet's, the Roman Catholic primary school in Beccles. The rector, Father Aelward, who was also the town mayor that year, had found him a spacious flat in Ballygate overlooking the delightful Waveney valley. Best of all, Wellington was with him again. The mastiff was beginning to show signs of aging. His friendly muzzle was now more grey than black, but he still had a few good years left in him, and the future seemed bright.

Inigo took to teaching like a duck to water. He now understood that education of the young had been his true vocation all along, rather than the priesthood, and with his parents' encouragement, he threw himself into his new career with enthusiasm. Thoughts of the horror of Hobbswood, which had haunted him for much of the last two years, were finally beginning to fade, and as always happens, he started to question the accuracy of his memory concerning the more unlikely aspects of his ordeal. But although Michael's views on the nature of the Light and the Dark remained crystal clear in his mind, now more immediate, if more mundane matters, such as the preparation for classes, marking essays, coaching the school football team, and arranging school outings, took up most of his time.

Despite the loss of Hazel, Inigo had found contentment at last.

II

It was the last Sunday in November. The weather had suddenly turned cold, and a dusting of snow had given a white dressing to the red, pan-tiled rooftops of Beccles town centre.

Christmas lights already decorated the old market square, and illuminated trees lit up most of the shop windows. Inigo and Wellington returned to their flat after an early evening walk, and as usual, Inigo lost the race to secure prime position in front of the fire. He turned on the television, only to be confronted by holy programmes or appeals for worthy social causes, so he went to the kitchen to poach some eggs for a light supper. Before he reached the fridge there was a knock at the door. Wellington emitted a deep, sleepy bark but did not stir from the fire, and when he saw the visitor was Father Aelward, he did not even bother to get up; Aelward was a frequent visitor.

"Come in and sit down, Father," said Inigo to the old priest. "I was just going to poach some eggs. Would you like some?"

The short, stocky priest sat himself down in Inigo's favourite chair. His square head and close-cropped, grey hair always reminded Inigo of a German helmet with a piece of carpet stuck on top, but there was nothing Teutonic about Aelward's tastes.

His twinkling, brown eyes locked onto the whisky decanter like radar on a target as he sighed. "Alas, I'm not an egg man, my boy."

"Then what about some whisky? There's a good single malt in the decanter."

"Scotland's finest export! Just a small tot then, if you insist."

Aelward's small tots were triples by any other standards, so Inigo filled half a tumbler and handed it to the grizzled cleric.

"Is this just a social call, Father, or is there some other purpose to your visit?"

"A bit of both really," smiled Aelward, who seemed well settled by the fire, so Inigo abandoned his eggs and poured himself a whisky; this looked like being a long evening.

Father Aelward was now in semi-retirement. He had been the headmaster of the premier Benedictine school in England, which was probably, thought Inigo ruefully as he watched his whisky disappear, where he learned to drink so well.

The tumbler was quickly emptied, and as he handed it back for a refill, Aelward said, "Thought I'd pop round and see how you're getting on. I'm told by the headmaster that you're doing well at the school but living on your own can be a bit oppressive, especially for a youngster like you."

Inigo looked down at the large fawn creature blocking the heat from the fire and smiled. "I have Wellington."

"Of course you do, my boy, but no man can live on canine company alone."

"True, but Wellington and I have a special relationship. Without him, I would not be here tonight. To be honest, I'm always so tired after a full day's teaching that canine company is all I'm really fit for in the evenings."

"What about weekends?" asked Aelward.

Inigo thought of Hazel and said, "The weekends can sometimes be lonely."

"Aha!" exclaimed the priest knowingly. "I thought so. You need a wife. Our French teacher, Miss Williams, is a good Catholic girl and quite pretty, don't you think? I think she likes you."

Inigo frowned. "Father, you've not come here match-making I hope."

"No, just marking your card so to speak."

"Thank you, Father. You don't think I was wrong to give up the priesthood then?"

Aelward's eyes widened in mock horror. "And become a Jesuit! You had a lucky escape, my boy. On the other hand, if you'd wanted to become a Benedictine; well, that would have been another matter."

Cap badge rivalry between the various orders in the English Catholic Church was the subject of much light-hearted banter, especially between the Benedictines and the Jesuits, but the old priest's friendly chatter now took on a more serious tone.

"Truthfully, Inigo, I do not see you as material for Holy Orders, but did you ever consider returning to the seminary to give it one last try?"

"I might have, had it not been for something that happened two summers ago."

Inigo had intended to speak to no one about what happened in Hobbswood, but he knew his intelligent, eager listener would not be satisfied with half-truths and innuendos. Having started, he felt a sudden desire to unburden himself to someone whose wisdom and experience might make some sense of it all.

Aelward said, "Go on then. Was a woman involved?"

"Only peripherally. Have you time to listen to a long, incredible story that might shake your faith?"

The brown eyes twinkled again as Aelward held out his empty glass.

"Who could possibly resist such an invitation?"

Inigo spared no detail, and by the time he had finished,

almost three hours had passed. Aelward listened spellbound, and uncharacteristically, in silence. He even forgot to top up his glass.

"Well," said Inigo at the end of the story. "What do you think?"

Aelward's customary good humour was gone. The avuncular, worldly-wise priest that Inigo respected and looked up to seemed lost for words, out of his depth.

"I... er... don't know what to think. You have obviously gone through a terrible physical and spiritual ordeal which few men can have encountered before. I don't feel qualified to comment. Some of the things Michael Shapmire told you are indeed difficult to argue against, but that is where your faith can help you. Where doubt exists, hold tight to the teachings Jesus Christ handed down to us through his apostles."

Inigo was disappointed. He had expected more from Aelward than a simple recommendation to cling blindly to something without adequate reason. His tutor at the seminary had said much the same thing when he had first expressed his doubts. It made no more sense now than it did then.

"I suppose my patron saint ought to be doubting Thomas," he said. "I certainly feel a strong empathy with him."

"He lacked faith," snorted Aelward.

"That didn't stop them making him a saint."

The old priest's voice softened again. "It saddens me to hear one so young voice such cynicism. You will keep such thoughts to yourself so far as the school is concerned?"

"Of course, Father."

Aelward's good humour returned. "Enough theological debate! Tell me, what are you doing for Christmas? Going back to Regents Park?"

"No, not this year. My parents have been invited to New

Zealand by an uncle on my mother's side of the family, so I'll probably stay here."

"What do you call a sophisticated Australian?"

"I don't know."

"A New Zealander! They'll like that one! But seriously, I won't hear of you spending Christmas alone."

"I'll still have Wellington."

"I'm sure he can spare you for a couple of hours while you come and celebrate the birth of Christ at the presbytery with me. It's always full, on Christmas day, and Mrs Riches cooks a magnificent Christmas dinner."

"I'd love to come. Who is Mrs Riches?"

"My housekeeper. After dinner, I shall bore you with my collection of photographs of stained-glass windows in East Anglian churches. I've been working on it for twelve years. It must be the most complete record ever compiled since the Reformation. Some of the original windows have fallen to the elements or vandalism. I suspect my photographs might now be the only record of their existence."

"I shall look forward to it," replied Inigo as he refilled the outstretched tumbler once more.

III

Christmas soon arrived, though all hopes of a white Christmas were abandoned on the twenty-third of December when a wild, westerly storm drove back the cold, continental air and a penetrating drizzle established itself. This was to be Inigo's first Christmas alone. More than anything else, he missed buying presents for those dear to him; the pre-Christmas 'hype' only served to accentuate his isolation.

The Christmas before last had been the best ever, before Hazel's disillusionment set in. They had made love for most of the morning, gone for a brisk walk across Hampstead Heath, enjoyed a lunchtime drink at the Bull and Bush, and gorged themselves on a traditional Christmas dinner in the evening.

This Christmas, Inigo had attended midnight Mass and slept till half past nine. He would have slept longer had Wellington not decided it was time for his walk. At one o'clock, with a gift-wrapped whisky bottle in one hand, he knocked at the presbytery door with the other and was welcomed by Father Aelward to join an assorted throng of priests, nuns, and school children whose parents were working abroad. Inigo's inside pocket contained a plastic bag in which he hoped to salvage some Christmas dinner for Wellington and thus maintain at least one tradition. The mastiff always had a substantial chunk of turkey at Christmas.

The party atmosphere soon disposed of Inigo's morning gloom. Two of the priests were jovial Irishmen, full of good humour and jokes, and when he looked at his watch again, it was five o'clock. After a brief word with Mrs Riches, who happily filled Wellington's bag with a piece of gizzard, a wing, and a leg, he decided it was time to leave so the mastiff could have his Christmas treat while it was still warm. He found Father Aelward slouched in an armchair, enjoying a brief rest in preparation for the children's party games the Irish priests had planned.

"Thank you for inviting me to share your Christmas, Father," he said. "I never expected to enjoy myself so much."

"It's impossible to be miserable when Father Mulcahey and Father O'Brien are around, but you can't go yet, you haven't seen my church window photographs."

"I thought you'd forgotten," replied Inigo, a little wistfully.

Aelward led Inigo to his study where he pulled out three large photographic albums from a plan chest drawer and proudly opened the first one. The presentation was very professional and no doubt the collection was a valuable historical record, but stained glass was of little interest to Inigo.

The first album took half an hour to go through, but when Aelward reached over for the second one, Inigo said, "Don't you think you should return to your guests, Father?"

"They'll be all right for another twenty minutes. The party games don't start until six. We'll just go through this book and save the third for another time."

"OK then," agreed Inigo reluctantly, but when he saw the first photograph his body suddenly stiffened.

The old priest saw the change.

"Are you all right? Is this boring you?"

But Inigo did not answer, he seemed mesmerised by the photo.

"My boy, what's the matter? Have you drunk too much?"

Inigo answered without taking his eyes off the photo, "This

251

photograph; where did you take it?" It sounded more like a demand than a question.

Disconcerted, Aelward quickly looked on the reverse side of the print.

"At Barsham, just down the road from here. The church of the Holy Trinity. It's Anglican."

"Is it old, the stained glass I mean?"

"Not any more. It's a copy of a mid-seventeenth century window that was destroyed in a fire that burned down the church roof about ten years ago. But this photo is of the original. Is there something in particular that interests you?"

"There could well be. How accurate is the copy?"

"Very accurate. It was made by a master glazier, a local man, who reproduced the original in every last detail using a blow-up from the negative of this print."

"I would like to see it."

"Very well, I'll drive you down there tomorrow morning, after the competition's Saint Stephen's day service has finished. I know the vicar well. He's a good sort; we sometimes drink together at the White Horse in the old market square."

By the time Wellington got his Christmas turkey it was stone cold, but he did not seem to mind.

Boxing Day, 1997, dawned bright and sunny, quite a contrast to the previous few days. Inigo and Aelward opened the lychgate door and looked almost furtive as they walked towards the entrance to Barsham church, even though the vicar had already given permission to visit.

"I always feel I'm treading on foreign territory when I enter one of their churches," said Aelward.

"Well, it belonged to us until the Protestants stole it."

252

"Yes, yes, my boy, but I can't help it. You've not yet said a word about why you want to see this window so much?"

"Haven't I?" said Inigo, deliberately tantalising Aelred for a little longer.

As they pushed open the heavy oak door, he asked, "Where exactly did you take the photograph from?"

"It's a long time ago, but I seem to recall it was more or less in front of the altar. A few of the benches were lost in the fire; the rest have been moved around to cover more space, which has disorientated me a bit."

Inigo strode down the central aisle and stopped in front of the altar. He looked up at the window behind it. The morning sun shone through the stained glass, spreading a myriad of colour over the church floor and walls. To Aelward, who was standing a little to one side, Inigo's face seemed to light up as a sunbeam, filtered gold by a section of the coloured glass, landed upon it. The old priest recalled that this was how he used to imagine the warrior saints of old, when he was a young, idealistic scholastic. This would have been the way they must have appeared to their adoring followers. The essence of nobility and implacable determination.

Then he at last understood that there was something out of the ordinary about Inigo Boscabel, something that set him apart from other men. He had a kind of presence, no doubt born from his ordeal in Hobbswood two years ago. Clearly, it was the making of him. After all, could any man go through what he went through and remain unchanged? Inigo possessed a self-confidence, a certainty about the purpose of life, as if he knew while others could only hope and believe. Aelward prayed that Inigo's search would be successful; perhaps today he had found what he was looking for. He bowed his grizzled old head; he knew he could do no more.

"What's the matter, Father?"

"Nothing, my boy, nothing at all. Have you found what you are searching for?"

"I think so. Tell me, why are the archangels depicted with fire above them?"

Aelward looked up at the window. Below the trinity were five window panels. The centre three showed Raphael on the left, Gabriel on the right, and in the centre, Michael wearing armour and carrying a sword. Above them, floating like angry red clouds, were interwoven, stylised flames.

Aelward answered, "In Hebrew scripture, it's not really made clear what the true status of the archangels is, though some scholars, particularly in the Middle Ages, equated them with the Seraphim."

"Can you spell Seraphim for me? Is it with an 'f' or a 'ph'?"

"Spellings vary, but the most frequently used is S-e-r-a-p-h-i-m. That's the plural. The singular is just Seraph. I think it's in the book of Isaiah that the Seraphim are described as 'The Incandescent Ones'. Consequently, these warriors of God would sometimes be depicted amongst flames. Occasionally, they are even shown as being composed of flames. A physical distillation of fire, if you will."

"So fire would be their weapon?"

"I suppose so," agreed Aelward. "If you believe in that sort of thing."

"And what about their faces?" asked Inigo excitedly. "Who would have described to the original glazier how he should show the detail of the faces?"

"I expect he would have used a local person as a model. You are probably looking at the faces of seventeenth century peasants.

Why do you ask?"

"When I saw the photograph of this window in your collection, I thought I recognised one of the faces. Now I am sure, and I can tell you that the face of Michael was no peasant.

"Everything fits at last, thank God."

IV

But that same evening, fate had yet another twist in store for Inigo. The obligatory Boxing Day James Bond film had just finished, and Wellington was sleeping peacefully in front of the fire, when there was a knock on the front door. *I don't think I can stand another whisky session with Aelward,* thought Inigo as he struggled out of his chair, but Wellington was already up on his paws with unaccustomed alacrity.

The mastiff bounded to the door and began scratching at the paintwork amid whimpers of excitement. Even as he slipped the catch and turned the lock, Inigo somehow guessed the identity of his visitor. He opened the door and there, almost blocking out the houses opposite, was a huge, black-coated figure.

A deep booming voice rumbled, "Hello, Inigo, it's been a while, hasn't it? There's trouble brewing in the Middle East which you might be able to help me with."

Inigo looked up at the stars sprinkled across the night sky and thought, *Here we go again.*

"You'd better come in," he said.

The End